TOM CLANCY'S
NET FORCE®

GAMEPREY

CREATED BY

Tom Clancy and Steve Pieczenik

written by

Mel Odom

BERKLEY JAM BOOKS, NEW YORK

This is a work of fiction. Names, characters, places, and incidents are either the product of the author's imagination or are used fictitiously, and any resemblance to actual persons, living or dead, business establishments, events, or locales is entirely coincidental.

TOM CLANCY'S NET FORCE®:
GAMEPREY

A Jove Book / published by arrangement with
Netco Partners

PRINTING HISTORY
Berkley Jam edition / July 2000

All rights reserved.
Copyright © 2000 by Netco Partners.
NETFORCE is a registered trademark of Netco Partners,
a partnership of Big Entertainment, Inc., and CP Group.
The NETFORCE logo is a registered trademark of Netco Partners,
a partnership of Big Entertainment, Inc., and CP Group.
Cover illustration by John Blackford.
This book, or parts thereof, may not be reproduced
in any form without permission.
For information address: The Berkley Publishing Group,
a division of Penguin Putnam Inc.,
375 Hudson Street, New York, New York 10014.

The Penguin Putnam Inc. World Wide Web site address is
http://www.penguinputnam.com

ISBN: 0-425-17514-6

BERKLEY JAM BOOKS®
Berkley Jam Books are published by The Berkley Publishing Group,
a division of Penguin Putnam Inc.,
375 Hudson Street, New York, New York 10014.
BERKLEY JAM and its logo
are trademarks belonging to Penguin Putnam Inc.

PRINTED IN THE UNITED STATES OF AMERICA

10 9 8 7 6 5 4 3

MVFOL

VIRTUAL CRIME.
REAL PUNISHMENT.

TOM CLANCY'S NET FORCE®

*Don't miss any of these exciting adventures
starring the teens of the Net Force . . .*

VIRTUAL VANDALS

The Net Force Explorers go head-to-head with a group of
teenage pranksters on-line—and find out firsthand that virtual bullets can kill you!

THE DEADLIEST GAME

The virtual Dominion of Sarxos is the most popular war
game on the Net. But someone is taking the game too seriously . . .

ONE IS THE LONELIEST NUMBER

The Net Force Explorers have exiled Roddy—who sabo-
taged one program too many. But Roddy's created a new
"playroom" to blow them away . . .

THE ULTIMATE ESCAPE

Net Force Explorer pilot Julio Cortez and his family are
being held hostage. And if the proper authorities refuse to
help, it'll be the Net Force Explorers to the rescue!

THE GREAT RACE

A virtual space race against teams from other countries will
be a blast for the Net Force Explorers. But someone will go
to any extreme to sabotage the race—even murder . . .

END GAME

An exclusive resort is suffering Net thefts, and Net Force
Explorer Megan O'Malley is ready to take the thief down.
But the criminal has a plan to put her out of commission—
permanently . . .

(continued . . .)

CYBERSPY

A "wearable computer" permits a mysterious hacker access to a person's most private thoughts. It's up to Net Force Explorer David Gray to convince his friends of the danger—before secrets are revealed to unknown spies . . .

SHADOW OF HONOR

Was Net Force Explorer Andy Moore's deceased father a South African war hero or the perpetrator of a massacre? Andy's search for the truth puts evry one of his fellow students at risk . . .

PRIVATE LIVES

The Net Force Explorers must delve into the secrets of their commanders life—to prove him innocent of murder . . .

SAFE HOUSE

To save a prominent scientist and his son, the Net Force Explorers embark on a terrifying virtual hunt for their enemies—before it's too late . . .

GAMEPREY

A gamer's convention turns deadly when virtual reality monsters escape their confines—and start tracking down the Net Force Explorers!

DUEL IDENTITY

A member of a fencing group lures the Net Force Explorers to his historical simulation site—where his dream of ruling a virtual nation is about to come true, but only at the cost of their lives . . .

DEATHWORLD

When suicides are blamed on a punk/rock/morbo website, Net Force Explorer Charlie Davis goes onto the site undercover—and unaware of its real danger . . .

We'd like to thank the following people, without whom this book would not have been possible: Mel Odom, for help in rounding out the manuscript; Martin H. Greenberg, Larry Segriff, Denise Little, and John Helfers at Tekno Books; Mitchell Rubenstein and Laurie Silvers at Hollywood.com; Tom Colgan of Penguin Putnam Inc.; Robert Youdelman, Esquire; and Tom Mallon, Esquire; and Robert Gottlieb of the William Morris Agency, agent and friend. We much appreciated the help.

I

Strapped into her seat, settled comfortably in the cockpit of the sleek experimental jet, Madeline Green couldn't help smiling as she felt the jet perform. "What do you think, Matt?"

Matt Hunter occupied the rear seat of the two-man cockpit, serving as radio-equipment operator for the flight. Like her, he was dressed in a camouflage flight suit and full-face helmet. "This is a rush, Maj."

A grin spread across Maj's face until it was so tight she thought she was going to sprain something. "It took nearly three months of programming to get it right."

"This is what you're in Los Angeles to show?"

"Yep." At present Maj *was* in L.A., in an implant chair and connected to a computer in a downtown hotel room above the Exhibition Center she'd be attending tomorrow morning, Thursday. Matt was in Columbia, Maryland, where he lived, also logged on to the Net through his own computer. For the moment they were in her private veeyar in the flight simulator program that was her current pride and joy.

"Mind if I try it?" Matt asked.

Fliers always shared that enthusiasm, Maj knew, even if they had nothing else in common. "Sure. Say when."

"When."

"It's yours." Maj released the joystick.

"Man, it's got a lot of juice."

Matt guided the Striper from side to side, getting the feel of the big bird's movement and power. The V-shaped wings wobbled up and down over the Painted Desert scenery below. Maj loved flying out over the desert and generally ran that program even though she had dozens of other terrain sims written into the Striper's database.

"Ready?" Matt asked.

"Yeah." Maj breathed out and relaxed in the form-fit seat, watching as the Striper's nose lifted and the desert dropped away below. Almost between heartbeats, the view from the canopy switched to the blue sky, then deepened to the violet of the upper atmosphere. The mounting G-force shoved her deep into the cockpit seat. "Let me know if you pass out," she jibed.

"Right," Matt snorted. "That'll be me with the sudden sleepy sigh."

"Or if you fill your mask. That will be you with the big, bubbly gush."

"Not me. I was born to fly." And Matt proved his point by bursting through the loop-the-loop and immediately heeling into a series of right wingovers that dropped them furiously toward the desert deck below.

Maj glanced at the altimeter, watching as thousands of feet melted away to just hundreds. "Hard deck's coming up."

"The bird's doing fine."

"It's not the Striper I'm worried about," Maj said. "It's the nut behind the wheel."

Matt heeled over to the left and slotted the jet into a valley of stone. Sunlight glimmered briefly off the stream less than a hundred feet below. "Nice landscaping job."

"Thanks. Just make sure we don't end up as part of it."

"Going up." Matt cut power to the Striper's afterburners and rolled gracefully out of the canyon, returning to the hard deck. "I've got to hand it to you, Maj, this is one killer program. Probably the best I've ever seen you build."

Maj squinted against the sun through the polarized canopy and helmet faceplate, trying to figure out a polite way to ask for the joystick again. Still, it felt nice that Matt was having such a good time with the jet. Maybe others would, too.

Building flight-sims was a passionate hobby of hers, one that she'd put a lot of time into. She planned on showing the Striper flight-sim to game packagers, hoping that some of her time investment would pay off in either cash for college or a scholarship or sponsorship from a software corporation. She also liked a number of the computer games available online, which was another reason to take the trip to the gaming convention in L.A.

When she spotted the black dot against the too-bright sun, Maj at first thought she was just seeing spots because the polarization of the canopy and helmet weren't strong enough. However, what she saw was a spot, not spots, and that spot was continuing to get bigger. Matt held his heading, streaking toward the mass. "There's a bogie at twelve o'clock," she said.

Matt paused. "I don't read it on the instruments. I'll level off." The jet tilted, following his movements with the stick. "Do you know what it is?"

"No." And that was wrong. Maj had designed the aircraft and the environment; she *should* know everything in it.

The Striper leveled, turning slowly as it overcame the powerful thrust. For a moment it looked as if Matt was going to miss it.

Then the object dived, dropping down with a flap of huge, batlike wings, settling into a new glide path. In that instant Maj got a clear view of what the object was.

Huge and majestic, the dragon filled the air before the Striper's canopy. Mottled plum-colored scales covered the beast's back, slightly lighter in color on the huge bat wings that were wider across than the creature was long, even counting the long spiked tail that whipped restlessly back and forth. Underneath, the scales took on the hue of aged ivory, a deep buttery alabaster with occasional brown spots.

The dragon's rectangular head was at least twenty feet long at the end of a long serpentine neck. Horns spiraled up from its head, and thorny projections that looked like hoarfrost lined its huge eyes and crinkled mouth. Emerald eyes, intelligent and sensitive and nearly three feet in diameter, stood out on either side of the broad head.

Maj glanced at the dragon, somehow knowing if they slammed into it, the creature's thick hide would leave only broken splinters of the Striper. "Give me the stick." She closed her hand around the joystick.

"It's yours."

Maj banked the jet, kicking in the afterburners.

"No way!" Matt breathed hoarsely over the helmet radio. "Did you put that in the programming? It's beautiful."

Maj silently agreed that the dragon was beautiful, one of the most elegant creatures she'd ever seen. But there was a problem. "I've never designed anything like that."

The dragon's neck rolled in a serpentine motion, bringing the head around, revealing something on its back. The great wings spread and flapped, digging into the air as the right emerald eye fastened on the jet. The long jaws separated, revealing a mouthful of fangs.

Bumping the vid-cam controls with her gloved finger, Maj increased the magnification. She had only a moment to recognize the human shape seated on the dragon's back.

Then a roiling, smoking fireball spewed from the dragon's gullet and arced for the jet. The fireball's impact shivered through the Striper and wrapped it in flames.

Maj's helmet beat against the seat as the Striper blew through the swirling mass of the fireball. Blue sky filled the horizon again, but flames stubbornly clung to the Striper. She triggered the fire-suppression systems.

Pressurized jets released fire-retardant foam, creating a sudden snowstorm across the wings. A layer of frozen, dirty gray chemicals replaced the flames. Unfortunately, they also knocked out her left engine.

"Flameout," Maj warned, shutting down the other engine as they were yanked into a flat spin like the right wing had been nailed down. "I've got a dead stick."

"We can stay or go."

"Smart money says we bail." Maj watched the view through the canopy change as they rolled over, totally out of control. But where she expected desert landscape below, there was now a huge forest that stretched out in all directions.

"Feeling lucky?"

"No." Maj hooked a forefinger under the engine switches. "I'm feeling mad. If somebody hacked in here, I want to know why. Even if we logged back on after logging off, there's no guarantees that the dragon and the guy riding him would still be here."

"Guy riding the dragon?"

"Yeah. I saw him as we went over."

"I didn't see anyone."

"If I get these engines to reignite," Maj promised, "I'll give you a close-up of the geekoid." She gazed down at the forested lands below, close enough now to see the three large rivers that cut through them.

"If there is a guy on that dragon—"

"There is." Maj waited for the Striper to finish flipping one more time. "And he's crashing other people's programs. The last time I checked, that was definitely illegal. Especially in my veeyar. Although this might not exactly be my veeyar anymore."

"What?"

"That's forest below, not desert. We're not in Kansas anymore, Toto."

"I've been so busy searching for the dragon I missed that."

"Hang on." Maj tripped the ignition switches. The jets flared white contrails suddenly, then she was shoved back into the formfit seat again and the joystick became responsive. "Yes."

"I've got your dragon," Matt said. "Heading two-four-three."

Maj brought the Striper around to the right. She raked the sky with her gaze, noticing that it held different shadings. And two suns, one a red giant and the other a spot of blue slightly above it, were close to setting or rising to the south.

She surveyed the damage the dragon's fireball had done to the Striper. The silver paint was blistered and peeling, black in some areas. Tiny cracks threaded through Plexiglas windows that could take a direct hit from a 7.62mm rifle bullet. She didn't know if the jet could take another fireball.

She guided the Striper onto the dragon's backtrail, overtaking the creature swiftly as the huge wings belled once more and seized the air currents. With a gentle touch she inverted the Striper, going upside down over the dragon's broad back.

"I see him," Matt said.

Even though she knew she'd briefly spotted the guy on the dragon's back, Maj was relieved. And she was close enough now to see the surprised look that filled his face. *But why,* she wondered, *would* he *look surprised? Hadn't* he *crashed* her *system*?

"It didn't work. They're still there." Gaspar Latke studied the polished crystal ball in his huge three-fingered hand. The crystal ball showed the images of the great dragon and its rider, as well as the jet fighter.

"Try harder," Andrea Heavener ordered.

Latke's fear and frustration vibrated inside his chest. Even firmly entrenched into the veeyar, he could feel his heart hammering back in the implant chair back in the office Heavener had gotten for them. He had a hard time concentrating on anything while remembering how vulnerable his flesh-and-blood body was lying in that chair only a few feet from that woman.

Heavener was a special operative for D'Arnot Industries. She worked in the real world, though, and stayed out of the Net as much as possible.

"I'm coming out." Latke straightened, standing thirty feet tall inside the veeyar. He was basically man-shaped, but the differences between him and anything human were substantial.

Bright crimson skin stretched tight over a hard-muscled body that was nearly as wide as it was tall. The legs bent the wrong way, structured like a four-footed animal's so the knees bent backward. The feet only held three toes, but they were prehensile and had shiny black talons instead of nails. A loincloth girded his hips, holding a massive double-bitted war ax. His head was triangular in overall shape, possessing two curved horns and a gash of a mouth filled with serrated teeth. The white-feathered wings folded neatly across his back looked incongruous, too delicate for the misshapen body.

The proxy he'd chosen was native to the veeyar environment. He was a tera'lanth, one of the evil creatures in the realm who opposed the great dragon and its rider.

"Why are you coming out?" Heavener asked.

"I want to try to trace the two people inside Peter's veeyar." Gaspar strode to the center of Murof's Cavern, glancing up at the walls where nearly a hundred other tera'lanth clung to stalactites like bats. They watched him with predatory slitted yellow eyes. If they knew he was an impostor, he knew they'd try to rip him limb from limb.

"You can do it from inside there," Heavener said.

"No," Gaspar said calmly. *She's a killer,* he reminded himself. *She doesn't know that much about the Net or computer systems.* "Whatever I do inside here can be traced by Peter if he checks later. And with that jet suddenly appearing out of nowhere, you can bet he's going to check. This is his veeyar, not mine."

"I want this handled quickly." The cool, crisp voice didn't change audibly, but Gaspar recognized the threat in the words.

When he'd first met her, Gaspar had been with two friends in a small bar in Hamburg, Germany. Heavener had walked up out of the night, said, "Gaspar Latke," and he'd turned to her, grinning slightly because she was a pretty woman, and his two hacker buddies were immediately envious of the attention. Then she'd taken out a small pistol and shot them both. Her voice hadn't even changed when she stepped over the bodies and yanked him up from the floor by the collar. "Come with me," she'd said in perfect German. That had been eight months ago, when he'd been seventeen, yet it already seemed like a lifetime.

Inside the veeyar, Gaspar closed his eyes, concentrating till he could see the icons of his own veeyar appear before him. Disconnection from the Net felt different to different people. Gaspar felt the familiar chill breeze flow through his body, then he opened his eyes in the lineup chair.

He pushed his skinny frame from the implant chair and stood in the dark room. He experienced a moment of disorientation as gravity kicked in. He spent so much time online that his own body felt alien to him despite the isometric stimulation built into the implant chair. The feeling wasn't new, so he quickly adjusted and plodded toward the other implant chair in the room. The first implant chair was specially dedicated to Peter Griffen's systems, hidden so well that Peter had never known he was there.

"Hurry," Heavener commanded.

"I am."

Heavener stood in a corner, comfortably wreathed in shadows. She was slender and barely over five feet tall. Her platinum blond hair was cut short and spiky, colored with two distinct red and blue stripes that ran from her left temple to the bottom of her hairline. Silver earring strands glittered, catching the green light from the computer consoles. Her skin was pale, almost to the point of albinism. Contacts covered her eyes, giving them a crescent shape and an amber color that belonged on a hungry cat. She wore tight black leather pants and a black sleeveless top. Her black leather biker's jacket lay over the back of a nearby chair.

Gaspar made himself breathe. When he got really tense around Heavener, he forgot. He settled down in the implant chair, and the interior shrank around his slight form. He was maybe an inch or two taller than Heavener, still a couple inches shy of five and a half feet. His already sallow complexion had turned waxy over the last few months. He normally kept his dark hair razored short, but he hadn't taken care of it in weeks. Wispy beard stubble tracked his cheeks, only shadowing the acne pits.

He triggered the chair's implants. Then the programming seized his senses and pulled him into veeyar again.

He opened his eyes inside his personal veeyar. He'd modeled it on Ray Bradbury's office, borrowing several props the science fiction writer had kept around him for inspiration. He'd found the clutter relaxing, making him feel as if he was always in the middle of something rather than off by himself.

Gaspar sat at the antique desk and studied the Underwood typewriter before him. Instead of the alphabet, though, the typewriter keys had icons for the various software programs he had loaded.

He touched the triangular blue icon, and another gust of cold wind filled him, tightening his skin and prickling his scalp. He blinked and was on the Net proper.

Multicolored datastreams passed below him, flashing lights that carried information and encrypted data all over the world. Various symbols and shapes represented the online businesses, each linked to the other by the datastreams that flowed in both directions constantly.

Floating above the Netscape, Gaspar triggered the trace-back utility he'd built for Peter's Griffen's veeyar. Since it operated outside the veeyar and merely ferreted out connections, Griffen had never realized someone was spying on him. It helped that Gaspar had also been able to program blind spots into Peter's operating system when he'd had access to it.

Gaspar targeted the hotel where Peter was staying. On the

Net the hotel looked very much like it did in real life.

The Bessel Mid-Town stood thirty stories tall, topped by a helipad for corporate executives on the go. The fourteenth floor was open on three sides, providing a pavilion that included an Olympic-sized pool, a banquet area, and an open stage carefully sectioned off from each other by a plethora of plants and exhibit cases.

Gaspar dropped through the Net and automatically chose a nondescript proxy. By the time he landed on the carpet and stepped onto the canopy-covered area, he looked like a businessman.

A uniformed concierge braced him at the broad double doors. The proxy looked young, polite, and earnest. "May I help you, sir?"

"Just going up to my room," Gaspar replied. He flashed the faked hotel PIN card he'd mocked up.

The concierge glanced at the card, electronic pulses flashing in his eyes, then back up at Gaspar. "Of course. Thank you, sir." He reached back and opened the door, disarming some of the security measures that prevented uninvited visitors from gaining entrance to the hotel's online facilities.

Not all of the security measures were dismissed, Gaspar knew. The rooms each maintained unique safeguards. Getting the master override programming right had taken him some time because the Bessel Mid-Town had beefed up security for the software convention.

He accessed a pull-down menu in the hotel's veeyar with the master override. A window opened beside him, staying within sight as he crossed to the main desk. He touched the icon that brought up the list of employees currently working.

Ted Sheppard was the manager currently on duty.

Closing the window, Gaspar accessed the security programming protecting the building, got through with the crack he'd developed, and accessed employee files. When that menu appeared, he selected SHEPPARD, TED, then downloaded the information. The file included a picture and Sheppard's passcodes.

Not even breaking stride, Gaspar grafted the information into his proxy. The proxy shimmered, and he knew in the next second that the hotel computer's security systems wouldn't be able to tell him from SHEPPARD, TED. He continued toward the main desk.

An atrium filled the center of the huge, cavernous lobby, stretching all the way up to the fifteenth floor. The elevator drew the eye to the parade of plants and birds inside the atrium. Statues of ten-foot-tall Chinese dogs flanked either side of the main entrance.

Gaspar stood behind the desk, feeling better than he had in hours. Stealing into places where he didn't belong, that was what he did best, what he lived for.

He logged into the internal security systems through the icon-laden touchscreen built right into the hotel desk behind the countertop.

The icons cleared and the prompt printed, ID, PLEASE.

Gaspar laid his palm on the touchscreen, feeling a little giddy with excitement. He trusted the proxy and the programs he was using, but the uncertainty was always a thrill.

The touchscreen pulsed violet light in a bar that ran from top to bottom. WELCOME, SHEPPARD, TED. HOW MAY I HELP YOU? A new list of icons formed on the touchscreen.

Gaspar tapped the yellow telecommunications icon, bringing up another menu. He passed over the HoloNet and vidphone connections, choosing the icon representing Net access feeds. He entered Peter Griffen's room number.

GRIFFEN, PETER. STATUS: CURRENTLY LOGGED ON. COMMUNICATE?

Gaspar entered NO.

LEAVE MESSAGE?

NO.

TRACE OUTBOUND?

NO.

TRACE INBOUND?

YES.

The touchscreen blinked, then a name and computer access number floated to the top. HUNTER, MARISSA & GORDON.

Gaspar downloaded the information and closed out the security access on the touchscreen. Then he logged off.

"I've got a name." He gave it to her when he forced himself up from the implant chair.

"Get back into Griffen's veeyar," Heavener ordered, taking a foilpack from her hip pocket. She opened the ultra-thin silver-metal device and punched the power button and the vidphone configuration. The foilpack instantly reconfigured itself into a cell phone. "Find out if Griffen has communicated with those people. If he hasn't, prevent it."

2

The guy on the dragon's back wore silvery-gray ring mail armor that covered his torso as well as his arms and legs. The armored helm masked half his face but left his strong jawline visible. Long black hair trailed from the back of the helm. Gems studding the helmet and armor gleamed in the sun's light. A bright blue tabard covered the dragonrider's chest and bore the symbol of a red dragon in flight.

The dragon gaped its jaws, and Maj could see the roiling flames twisting up from inside the long throat. But the rider lifted a gloved hand and stilled the beast. In the next instant the dragon heeled over one hundred and eighty degrees.

"Did you see that?" Matt asked excitedly. "That was an aerial U-turn. Don't lose it."

"That's the general idea." Maj brought the Striper around in a tight turn.

The dragonrider hunched lower over his saddle and glanced back over his shoulder. With the magnification of the forward-looking vid cam, Maj could clearly see the confusion and irritation on the guy's face. His mouth was locked in a small smile, and behind the steel bandit's mask of the helm his eyes flashed.

Maj brought up the PA system and placed an outside hail. She spoke clearly into her voice mike. "Who are you?"

Reaching up, the dragonrider took off his helm. His black hair whipped back in the wind. He tried a smile.

"He can hear you," Matt said. "He just doesn't seem to understand you."

"That doesn't make sense." Online in the Net community was a universal translator program for—more or less—every known human language. Some dialects were still fuzzy, but basic concepts could be communicated easily. Encrypted code sometimes couldn't be broken, but that was by design. "My name is Maj Green. Who are you?"

The smile on the handsome face lost some of its electricity. He spoke again, but with the same incomprehensible result.

"Uh-oh," Matt said quietly. "That doesn't look good."

Maj swiveled her head forward, spotting the winged shapes fast approaching. They flew in formation like geese, but her intuition told her they were nowhere near as pleasant as geese following some migratory path.

In the next instant she recognized the flying figures as winged demonoids. Before she could draw another breath, they attacked.

"Matt Hunter is a Net Force Explorer."

Andrea Heavener's announcement brought a sudden rush of fear that flooded Gaspar Latke's system with adrenaline. His fear of Net Force was automatic and sprang from years of being an outlaw hacker on the Net.

"No one wants Net Force involved in this," Heavener declared.

"No," Gaspar repeated as he plunged through the veeyar to his target. For a moment, though, his mind flirted with the idea of intentionally letting Net Force get information on what they were doing. If Net Force caught him, he'd be arrested and maybe jailed for a time, but he'd be free of the terrors of the last few months.

"Why would Hunter contact Peter?" In the next moment Gaspar opened his eyes, back in the tera'lanth. He felt his wings beat, the huge muscles on his back rippling with effort as he sped through the sky. He searched the horizon ahead and spotted the dragon and the jet.

"He didn't," Heavener said flatly. "The connection you found in the hotel was a result of a bleed-over."

"Impossible," Gaspar said. "The game version Peter's testing shouldn't be capable of that. The effects of the bleed-over are very specific, very localized."

"People are tracing the outbound computer access line. Peter didn't make contact with Hunter's veeyar on purpose."

As the tera'lanth, Gaspar adjusted his flight and swooped down toward the dragon and the jet. Around him were a hundred other tera'lanth, all in full attack mode. The creatures in this veeyar were highly destructive. And they were all presently under his control because he'd accessed the programming he'd layered into the game's AI. He divided his forces. Part of them would be a sacrifice, a diversion for Peter Griffen. But the others would destroy the Net Force Explorers.

Maj tried to disengage from the demonoid attack by pulling the stick up and to the right. The jet's engines screamed as the thrusters kicked into renewed life, pressing them back into the seats.

The demonoids were faster than they looked, streaking through the sky and attacking from the left. Three of the nearest ones dived in at her with folded wings, halting twenty or thirty feet ahead and to the left of the jet in a perfect intercept course. Their wings unfolded, revealing long bone-white quills. Before Maj could adjust her course, the demonoids fired a salvo of quills from their wings.

The quills slammed into the Striper in a long row that stitched the side of the aircraft. Two of them speared through the Plexiglas canopy, imbedding six inches or so with another six inches behind them.

"They're playing hardball," Matt croaked.

"Hang on," Maj warned grimly as she worked the stick. The Striper grabbed air, shoved through the sky by the big engines. She looped and rolled expertly till the Striper's nose faced the cluster of demonoids again. She lifted the protective cover from the weapons activation switch, then toggled it up. The green READY light came on.

Maj depressed the launch button. Two air-to-air missiles sprang from the wings. The missiles achieved target locks on the creatures' mass at once, ripping across the distance to impact at the center of the demonoids.

The orange-and-black fireball knocked the creatures from the air, exploding a half-dozen of them.

Even as she completed her rollout, she got another target lock with the air-to-air missiles. She brushed the button and sent another pair streaking forward.

The explosion this time was much closer. With no way to avoid it, Maj flew through the flaming debris left behind. Burning chunks of demonoid bounced from the canopy with distant thuds, barely heard through the helmet. In the next moment she was free of the cloud of attackers.

She craned her head over to the side, glancing back at the attack scene. A group of demonoids had already taken up pursuit, letting her know at a glance that she couldn't outdistance them. But a second group surrounded the dragon and the dragonrider.

Maj brought the jet around, feeling it stutter in protest as it jammed across conflicting air currents. The target-lock peep sounded again, and she released another pair of missiles, finishing off her heavy payload and leaving her only two thousand rounds of machine gun bullets.

"That was the last of the missiles?" Matt asked with real concern.

"Not for long." Maj punched a quick selection of icons under the heading CHEAT MENU. "Now we're more heavily armored and have infinite ammo as well as infinite fuel." She worked the stick, diving toward the center of the demonoids. Her thumb moved restlessly across the missile launch button, releasing a salvo of missiles that hammered the winged creatures from the sky. Working the stick, she cut power and pulled into a barrel roll that brought her into a sharp approach path to the dragon.

"Look at that guy," Matt said, pointing.

Maj looked, following the line of her friend's arm. Incredibly, the dragonrider sat on one folded leg on the saddle, a bow pulled taut before him as he took deliberate aim. When he released, the arrow streaked forward and embedded in the chest of a nearby demonoid. Then it exploded.

"One monster," Matt said, "extra chunky."

Maj glanced up through the canopy and saw the phalanx of

winged demonoids approaching from the rear. "Is he the target, or are we?" she wondered out loud.

The dragon gaped its jaws and spat a huge fireball into the midst of the attacking demonoids. The flames fanned among the demonoids, blazing merrily as they ate the wings off the creatures' burning bodies. Wingless demonoids dropped from the air, turning into full-blown comets before they struck even the tops of the forest below.

More demonoids fired quills at the dragon and dragonrider. The quills shattered against the dragon's scaled hide, but Maj worried about the dragonrider. A sudden blue glow surrounded the dragonrider only an instant before the quills reached him. Unbelievably, the blue glow caught the quills. The dragonrider made another gesture, then the quills shot back at the demonoids.

"He's got a force field of some kind," Matt observed.

The dragonrider was already drawing back another arrow when Maj arrived.

She unleashed her arsenal, launching missile after missile as each target lock came up. She kept her field of fire away from the dragon. In seconds the demonoid horde was nearly decimated. The survivors flew away.

"They're coming down on top of us from behind," Matt declared.

The dragonrider's voice drew her attention. This time she drew a circle in the air, bringing up a record-audio function she'd designed in the programming to makes notes to herself.

The dragonrider kept speaking. His face showed concern that was mirrored in his words. He waved a hand, drawing her to him.

Maj juked the stick and swung toward the dragon. Despite her speed, the demonoids behind her closed the distance.

The dragon, urged by its rider, flew toward the approaching jet. The dragonrider waved Maj down.

Pushing the stick forward slightly, Maj dived under the dragon. For an instant the sky was reduced to the alabaster scales of the dragon's belly.

"Oh, yeah," Matt said. "And we were thinking we were the cavalry."

Twisting around in the seat once she had her course safely locked in, Maj watched a massive gout of fire splatter over the demonoid pack. There were few survivors, and they quickly turned tail.

Maj climbed again, cutting back on speed since the threat seemed to be gone. The dragon flapped its bat wings and dropped into the same heading she'd chosen. In seconds the dragonrider was at her side again.

Outside the canopy the dragonrider made a few gestures. A necklace of violet-red links appeared around his throat. He gazed at Maj and asked clearly, "Who are you?"

Excitement flooded through Maj. *Communication! There was nothing like communication!*

"Griffen has broken through the language inhibitor virus," Heavener said.

"I know." Gaspar reached back into his own veeyar and uploaded the power-ups he'd copied from the game. The power-ups were intended as bonuses and prizes for the other players as they worked through the quest levels in the game, but he'd written in additional programming that made them his anytime he wanted.

He reached into the game menu and accessed the enemy programming. At present the game was set on NORMAL play, allowing the destruction of the tera'lanth forces. He activated the AUTOMATIC RESPAWN feature and re-created his army. Instantly, the skies filled with the winged warriors again. Without mercy they descended on the dragon and the jet.

Quills rained destruction down on the jet. Black smoke trailed after the aircraft in clouds. The jet dived, taking advantage of rather than fighting gravity, descending like a striking predator.

Flapping his wings and taking advantage of his power-ups, Gaspar dived after them. He'd spent countless hours in the tera'lanth form, either watching Peter Griffen's activities and sometimes playing along, or in the version of the game he'd had to work with.

Gaspar followed the gleaming needle shape rocketing above the green sward. He folded his wings, diving into an interception course. He arrived less than a quarter mile directly in front of the jet.

He spread his wings, halting his downward momentum. With his heightened senses, he was aware of the two missiles leaping from the jet's wings as well as the fireball hurtling from the dragon's throat.

He unleashed his quill attack from his spread wings an instant before the two missiles slammed into him. The twin concussions hammered him, doubling him over, but the power-ups he'd used left him alive in the game.

Then the quills ripped into the jet. Less than a hundred yards out, silvery bits of metal and Plexiglas flew in all directions, followed by an explosion as the high-octane fuel blew.

"Game over." Gaspar grinned, but he didn't have long to enjoy his victory. The dragon's fireball hit him and burned him to a cinder.

Matt Hunter opened his eyes and instinctively lifted his head from the contact points on the implant chair. He could still feel the detonation that had destroyed the jet and triggered the Net's automatic log-off safeguard.

He scanned the walls and saw that he was in his own bedroom back in Columbia, Maryland. Questions filled his mind, but mostly he was worried about Maj.

He lay his head back on the implant chair and felt the buzz as contact was made. When he opened his eyes again, he was in his own veeyar.

He floated cross-legged beneath a star-filled sky that gave him a better view of space than most observatories. A comet streaked by overhead, leaving purple phosphorescence twinkling along behind it. In the next moment the comet hit the atmosphere and caught fire, creating a pyrotechnic delight as it burned.

Matt ignored the comet and reached out to the black marble slab in front of him. He punched the inch-high blue icon that opened the computer's vidphone function. A rectangular screen opened in front of him.

"You have messages," the computer voice announced.

"Save for later," Matt commanded. "Open phone database." He hadn't memorized the number of the Bessel Mid-Town Hotel where Maj was staying. *She's okay,* he told himself desperately.

The rectangle opened with a ripple. "Please state preference."

"Los Angeles, California. Bessel Mid-Town Hotel. Room five eighteen." Matt waited, listening to the vidphone ring the other end. His anxiety increased with every ring, but Maj didn't pick up the vidphone.

• • •

Breathing raggedly, Gaspar Latke opened his eyes in the darkness. His heart hammered inside his chest. *Too many hours online,* he knew, *and not nearly enough sleep.* A light film of perspiration covered him, chilling him in the air-conditioned room Heavener insisted on keeping just above the frost level.

"They're out of the veeyar?" the woman asked.

Gaspar held up a trembling hand, observing the quivering fingers with bright interest. The fireball had been so big and so real. He had to give Peter that. Gaspar hadn't been hit by a fireball in the game in months. Losing wasn't an experience he liked to repeat. "Yes."

"The veeyar overlap happened in the hotel," Heavener said.

"It had to," Gaspar said irritably. Everyone knew that the game's programming only affected local computer systems.

"We want you back online. We want her computer scrubbed."

"Scrub it if you want," Gaspar said, "but she'll still talk."

"No," Heavener said calmly, "she won't. We have people on-site there."

A chill even stronger than the air-conditioning filled Gaspar. He knew D'Arnot Industries had no qualms about killing, but he'd never been part of it himself.

"Find her," Heavener commanded, "and scrub any archived computer files she may have saved online."

Gaspar reluctantly pushed himself from the implant chair. As soon as he tried to stand, his knees buckled, refusing to take his weight. A fresh wave of perspiration covered him as he caught himself on his hands, just saving him from hitting the floor with his face.

Heavener cursed and crossed the room immediately. She grabbed him by the arm and yanked him to his feet. "Don't give up on me now, you little piece of feek."

Gaspar felt hot tears filling his eyes. He couldn't remember ever feeling so close to total exhaustion. The last few days he wasn't sure if he'd slept or not. D'Arnot Industries had wanted him pulling twenty-four-hour surveillance on Peter on the Net, and Peter worked incredible hours. But Peter Griffen was healthy and didn't have other assignments that D'Arnot Industries wanted from him.

Heavener dragged Gaspar to the other implant chair and unceremoniously threw him into it. "Get online. Find the girl and scrub her computer."

Gaspar's stomach rolled sickeningly. He retched, but only a thin, sour drool leaked down his beard-stubbled chin.

"Latke," Heavener barked, "now! We don't have time to waste!"

Raking the sour drool from his chin with the back of his arm, Gaspar lay back in the lineup chair. His implants touched the laser beam connectors. He felt the familiar buzz, started to enter his veeyar, but saw the cluttered room suddenly fade away before he could seat himself at the desk. He tried twice more, but each time the veeyar faded away.

Heavener stood at his side. "What's wrong?"

With a quivering hand, Gaspar pointed out the chair's vital signs readout. "My current level of anxiety, stress, and health are dangerous. The chair won't allow me on the Net until my vitals are within the tolerance limits."

"Then we'll beat the vital signs readout." Heavener took a slim case that Gaspar had never seen from her pocket. She opened it, revealing three slim hypodermics neatly held inside. She took one of them from the case, popped the protective sleeve covering the needle, then depressed the plunger to make sure there was no air inside.

"No!" Gaspar croaked.

Heavener popped him in the throat with her elbow, causing him to gag. "Lie down."

Hypnotized by the hypodermic, Gaspar grabbed the arm holding him down but wasn't able to leverage her off him. She forced him back into the implant chair and the automatic form-fit feature kicked in, shrinking the chair around him. The *pip-pip-pip* of the vital signs rejection echoed in the big room.

"No," he gasped. "Please."

Heavener's cold, amber cat's eyes shone as she looked into his. "You're alive only as long as you remain useful. You'd do well to remember that." Her hand flashed forward, and he felt the needle pierce the side of his neck.

A warm lassitude drifted through Gaspar's body. In seconds he felt removed from his body, even more distant than going online left him.

But inside he was still screaming.

The *pip-pip-pip* rejection from the implant chair slowed, then quit.

"Find the girl," Heavener commanded harshly over the audlink. "Find the girl or no one will ever find you."

"Sure," Gaspar replied. He didn't care. She didn't matter to him. Nothing did. He was on the Net, and for the moment he was as free as he ever got. Seated behind the desk in the cluttered room of his veeyar, he launched himself onto the Net and streaked for the Bessel Mid-Town Hotel.

3

Matt Hunter grew more frantic as the vidphone connection failed to complete.

"Attempt failed," the computer reported. "Would you like to retry or report failure to BellNet?"

"Run diagnostics," Matt said.

"Compliance. Diagnostics running." A menu screen popped into view inside the vidphone screen. "Systems parameters meet established criteria. Would you like to retry the number or report failure to BellNet?"

Matt didn't feel as if he had time to go through the automated services of the Net phone company. Even as fast as they were, he knew he could work faster. He punched Mark Gridley's number. Despite the fact that it was one o'clock in the morning in Maryland, the Squirt would be up and online somewhere.

"Attempt failed," the computer said. "Would you like to retry or report failure to BellNet?"

Matt's mind raced. If the vidphone system checked out but he still couldn't call out, that left only one option: Someone was shutting him out of the link. "Examine systems for virus."

"Diagnostics reveal newly installed programming," the computer reported. "It doesn't appear detrimental to this system."

Yeah, well, an effective virus won't appear detrimental to an ops system, Matt thought. "Open access."

"Compliance." The screen overlying the vidphone menu enlarged and the surface rippled.

Matt stood and placed a hand on the screen. The sensory input from the screen made it feel slightly chill and damp. When he drew his hand back, the surface tension clung to him. Taking a deep breath, he plunged through.

On the other side of the access panel, he spotted the configuration for the vidphone uplink. Thick cables covered a wall to his right, leaving the rest of the large cinderblock room undisturbed.

How long had it been since he'd been dumped out of the Net? Maj was on her own until he found a way to get help to her. Catie Murray was at the same hotel. Catie was another Net Force Explorer and Bradford Academy student and friend.

But the vidphone had to be operational before Matt could get word to her.

Accessing his operating-system tools, Matt stretched his hand out. Immediately a flashlight formed along his forearm, spurting out a wide-angled beam. He played it over the wall where the cables were. The shadows slithered away.

He stepped forward. The programming for the vidphone didn't actually look like the confusion of cables protruding from the wall, but that was how his computer operating system rendered them in veeyar.

Tiny green-shelled bugs moved among the cables, rerouting the interfaces so they constantly fed back into themselves. Receiving a signal from BellNet was no problem from this end, but getting out was impossible.

"Analyze," Matt ordered. Instantly the flashlight changed into a triangular device that fit comfortably in both his hands.

Slipping a virus along the BellNet lines was all but impossible. Whoever had tagged him with it knew a lot about Net systems. But who would try to shut him down? And why?

The triangular analyzer came up with a virus purge code in seconds. Mark Gridley had few equals in writing code. "Purge." The triangular analyzer reconfigured itself into a pump mister. He squeezed off a burst, and white powder drifted down over the virus.

As soon as the power touched them, the green-shelled bugs went into a frenzy, crawling along the various cables. Even as they were going on retreat, two cables suddenly snapped their moorings and shot at Matt.

He twisted and backed away, dodging the sudden strike. A brief image of a mechanical snake's head ghosted through his mind. He twisted and dodged again, completing a back flip that narrowly brought him out of range of the second mechanical snake as it plunged through the yellow octagon marking time.

Realization that the virus had come encoded with its own protection crystallized in Matt's thoughts. *Something as well put together as the virus was, I should have been expecting this,* he chided himself.

He started for the door only to see it slam shut. Dim shadows on the wall slithered and danced, closing in on his shadow. He leaped over another attack. Hard, cold metal rasped along his leg. In real time the impact would have broken his leg, but in veeyar it only knocked him from his feet.

He lifted his right wrist, aiming Mark's tools package at the closest mechanical snake. "Analyze."

The cable-snake waved from side to side as it rose to its full height. A liquid hiss squeezed from between the distended jaws. Saliva dripped from the snake's mouth, filled with bouncing electrical particles that sparked and spun.

Code strands spun on the triangular device's screen, then locked in as the cable-snake struck again. The open mouth flashed at Matt.

"Purge!" The analyzer morphed from the triangular device to a quicksilver glove that oozed over Matt's right arm. The wicked snout of a firearm protruded from his fist. He fired and a sea-green burst of laser light hit the cable-snake.

The light disintegrated the cable-snake's head in a white-hot explosion. The second attacker ripped through the shadows, moving too quickly for Matt to target. He rolled and came up firing. A cloud of sizzling sparks ignited around the cable-snake, and it vanished a heartbeat later.

Breathing heavily, Matt surveyed the room. Nothing moved except the tiny green-shelled bugs. He switched back to the first antivirus program and hosed them down. The tiny bugs dropped to the cinderblock floor with metallic *tinks*.

Matt stepped back through the access screen and into his veeyar again just as the comet slammed into the ground and left a crater nearly an eighth of a mile across. Returning to the black marble slab, he touched the vidphone and repeated his request for the number and room at the Bessel Mid-Town Hotel.

The phone rang and Matt waited tensely.

Gaspar Latke walked through the virtual doors of the Bessel Mid-Town Hotel and covered himself in the SHEPPARD, TED proxy. His head felt curiously full, but he didn't care.

He crossed the lobby and opened the computer interface at the desk. After bypassing the security, he brought up the Net access records, looking for the access port that had crossed over into Peter's veeyar.

The guest list scrolled under his finger as he touched the screen, complete with Net access records. Public housing kept excellent records. They had to so they wouldn't get implicated in any wrongdoing that took place under their roofs. They also held the right to block access to all records until handed a court order.

The guest record stopped moving when the search criteria were met.

Gaspar read the name out loud. "Green, Madeline. Fifth floor, room five eighteen." He closed the guest records and touched the vidphone link, punching in the room number.

The phone rang at the other end of the connection. When it was answered, Gaspar relaxed his virtual body's cohesiveness and flowed into the vidphone link.

The vidphone drew Maj's attention as she blinked her eyes open in the implant chair. She sat up and quickly checked her surroundings. The hotel room, complete with desk and chair, king-sized bed, chest of drawers, and computer, looked much more welcoming than when she'd first arrived that afternoon.

She punched the vidphone and brought the connection online. The taglines on the screen let her know the call was coming from inside the hotel. *I wouldn't be surprised if that bleed-over attracted the attention of the house detectives,* she thought. She grabbed her foilpack from the bed so she'd have her Net Force Explorer ID handy and turned to the vidphone.

The screen came up briefly, just a flicker that showed the mural behind the check-in desk downstairs. Then it closed.

"Weird," Maj said, disconnecting. "Though not the first weird thing I've seen tonight." She thought about Matt then, wondering if he'd gotten out of the veeyar in good shape.

The vidphone rang again.

"Yes."

"Are you all right?" Matt's voice would have sounded calm to most people, but Maj knew him well enough to hear the tension in his words.

"I'm fine. How are you?"

"I survived. Have you figured out what just happened?"

"Someone crashed my veeyar and invaded my system," Maj replied. "Unless you have any other ideas."

"No. Although I think the guy on the dragon wasn't the only person online."

"You're talking about the demonoid." Maj had already reached the same conclusion. "The question is, did the demonoid invade my system or the dragonrider's?"

"My vote is for the dragonrider. I find it interesting that the demonoid concentrated on us rather than the dragonrider. Maybe the demonoid was there to protect him."

Maj considered that, relying on the intuition that usually let her get to the bottom of problems. She'd been told her skills at recognizing the underlying conflicts in situations involving people and events were sometimes uncanny. "I didn't get that feeling." She glanced at the computer, watching as the files cycled through. "I'm going back in."

"I'll come with you."

"No." Maj climbed back into the implant chair. She felt anxious, ready to get off the vidphone and find out what was going on. She kept flashing on the confusion and concern that had filled the dragonrider's face. *He didn't know. He had no clue I was going to be there. Eyes that blue can't hide the truth.* She shook her head at herself. *And maybe you're getting too mushy.* "I'm sending two files your way. One of them is an audio file of our communication with the dragonrider. See if you can get it interpreted."

"Leif," Matt responded without hesitation.

"That's where I'd start," Maj agreed. Leif Anderson was

skilled in a number of languages. He'd definitely be able to get them down to a short list of possible dialects if he couldn't translate the transmission himself. "I'm also sending a copy of the Net address. I thought Mark could trace it."

"I'll get it over to him."

"I've got to go," Maj said.

"Don't keep me waiting," Matt said. "Get in *and* out quickly. And if Mark can find you, we may be along."

"I will." Maj lay back in the implant chair and felt the teeth-tightening buzz of connection. She let out a deep breath, then jumped into the Net.

She experienced a moment of freefall, saw the cerulean blue sky splash into place around her, then fell. The Striper formed around her, drawing together in a sparkling pattern that hardened into a ceramic and steel shell. The wind's battering force went away as the familiar feel of the jet's internal vibration filled her. She gripped the stick and kicked the thrusters in.

Since the instruments didn't acknowledge the dragon's presence, she whipped her head from side to side, hoping to spot the creature or its rider. Her optimism dropped immediately when she saw the craggy desert below instead of verdant forest.

Where had the dragonrider gone? Maj continued searching, knowing that wherever he was, he was definitely in some kind of trouble. She wondered if he knew it.

Nervous energy filled Gaspar as he looked down at the girl in the implant chair. He stood in Maj Green's room, dressed in a shimmering, blue leather bodysuit that symbolized the masking utility he used to evade the room's sensors. The room was equipped with holo projection equipment that would allow a Net visitor to virtually drop in on Maj, actually sit on the furniture like they were there.

The masking utility was one of his own programs and allowed him to enter the room and observe without being seen. The program also allowed him to interact with the room's holo projection programming to access the veeyar in operation in the room. He couldn't control the individual veeyar, but he could ride along.

He gazed down at the girl, thinking that she was pretty. Her brown hair was pulled back in a braid, and she was dressed in jean shorts and a red knit shirt. She went shoeless, relaxed in the room.

"Query status: finished," a computer voice whispered in his ear. Even though he was in the girl's room, he knew the masking utility would keep her from hearing the exchange.

"Report," Gaspar commanded.

"Green, Madeline, age seventeen," the computer said without inflection. "Brown hair, brown eyes." It continued with the particulars from the Virginia Department of Motor Vehicles, adding her address in Alexandria, Virginia.

She's younger than I am, Gaspar realized with a start.

"Her father, Martin Green, is a tenured political science professor at Georgetown University," the computer went on. "Her mother is Rosilyn Green, owner of a computer business. She has one older brother, Rick, and a younger sister, Adrienne. Madeline Green attends Bradford Academy, where she is an honors student pursuing studies in—"

"Enough," Gaspar said. He didn't need to know everything about her, and probably he already knew too much. So did Heavener.

He placed his hand on the lineup chair and sensed the data flowing through the connectors. At present the girl was accessing her own veeyar and the Net, but she was also open to the Bessel Mid-Town Hotel's programming through the telecommunications uplink she was using. With the mask utility in place and the parameters he'd adopted, Gaspar was part of that programming.

"Where are you?" Heavener demanded over the audlink.

"In her room."

"What is she doing?"

"She's back in her veeyar."

"Why?"

"I assume she's looking for Peter."

"She won't find him." Heavener's voice sounded uncertain.

"I don't think so." Gaspar wished he could leave the room, could leave the girl alone.

"Make certain she doesn't find him," Heavener ordered. "Scrub the files you can from inside the system. I've got a team en route to the room." She disconnected before Gaspar had time to reply.

He felt sorry for the girl then. He knew what Heavener's team would do when they arrived. Silently, knowing she was as doomed as he was, he closed his eyes and flowed into her veeyar.

4

"Hi. You've reached Mark Gridley. I'm not here at the moment. Ping me with your address, and I'll get back to you."

After leaving a message, Matt touched the IM icon for Leif Anderson next.

"Yeah?" Leif's voice sounded groggy.

"Matt. Catch you at a bad time?"

"I was asleep. A nocturnal thing a lot of mammals that aren't wired for the Net are prone to do. At one point, it was all the rage. What do you need?"

"There's been some trouble." Matt copied the audio file Maj had uploaded, then held out his hand and a tiny silver ear icon dropped into his palm. "Are you presentable?"

"By the time you get here, I'll have run my fingers through my hair and wiped the sleep drool from my face."

Matt followed the telecommunications link from Maryland to the New York City apartment where Leif lived with his parents. The apartment building was one of the tallest in the Manhattan area. Moonlight shimmered off the East River. The security programming showed as a tight-fitting silvery-blue bubble around the structure.

Matt stretched his hand forward and made contact with the security programming. Wintry chill raced along his arm. In the next instant he was sucked into the building, actually stumbling a bit when the holoprojector programming set up in Leif's room returned the sensation of gravity to him.

Leif's bedroom was huge. His father, Magnus Anderson, owned and ran one of the most prestigious financial investment firms on Wall Street. Leif's mom, Natalya, was a former New York City Ballet dancer and had founded her own studio.

Leif sat on the edge of the bed, far from sartorially perfect. His red hair stuck up rebelliously, and his eyes were bloodshot. His complexion was fair and freckled. He wore a well-worn dark green robe and furry slippers. He covered a yawn with one hand just a microsecond too late to be anywhere near elegant.

"Have a seat." Leif turned a hand over and offered the recliner across from the bed.

"No time," Matt said. "I've got an IM out for Mark, too."

Leif cocked an eyebrow in speculative interest. "What exactly have you run afoul of?"

Matt shook his head. "I have no idea, but I know that somebody slipped a virus into my system that shut down communication between Maj and me."

"Considering the Squirt designed a lot of the protective software in your system, that's impressive. Which brings me to the question of, what can I do?"

"Maj uploaded an auditory file she wanted you to take a look at." Matt tossed the silver ear icon across.

Leif caught it, pushed up from the bed, and walked toward the inline chair. "What am I looking for?"

"The language," Matt said. "We couldn't understand it."

Both Leif's eyebrows shot up. "On the Net?"

"Yeah. Something showed up in our world that wasn't supposed to be there—or maybe we showed up in its world. I don't know."

Leif lay down in the implant chair, making himself comfortable and pulling the robe over his body. He wiggled his toes. "You'll be on the Net?"

"Yes. Catie's my next contact."

Leif closed his eyes. "I'll be in touch if I find out anything."

Matt stepped back through the bedroom wall and hurled himself out over the cityscape below. He sailed along the grid crisscrossing Manhattan, took a bounce off a comm-sat, and arrived back in Maryland almost instantly.

Once more in his veeyar, he called up his address book again and looked for Catie Murray's room number in the Bessel Mid-Town Hotel. Before he found it, a window opened up to his right.

"Knock knock," Mark Gridley said.

Matt reached up and tapped the window with a forefinger, removing the protective programming. Mark Gridley appeared instantly in the rectangular opening. The Squirt was barely four-teen years old. His Thai-American heritage showed in his brown eyes, black hair, and olive complexion. He wore a red T-shirt depicting a popular Japanimation robot in battle stance with a sword that threw off green energy spikes.

Mark reached through the window and took Matt's hand, then allowed himself to be pulled through. "What's up?"

Briefly Matt sketched out the trip into the other veeyar.

"You don't know if the other veeyar is at the hotel?" Mark asked when Matt finished.

"No."

"Where's Maj?"

"Online. Looking for the veeyar."

"Let's see if we can contact her first," Mark said, accepting the compass-shaped icon Matt gave him that Maj had sent along.

Matt pulled up the Net address for Maj's room again, then punched the icon to connect.

"I'm sorry," the computer voice intoned. "That address is no longer valid. Would you like to try another?"

Cold dread filled Matt, but he punched in Catie Murray's hotel number.

Looking around, Gaspar saw that Madeline Green kept a really well-organized veeyar. He was deep in the veeyar's sysops, us-ing a masking utility that was barely holding its own with the security programming integrated into the system. At present, Madeline Green's system was reading his presence like he was a routine diagnostics check coming from the hotel's security system. If she'd been operating from home, without having to go through the hotel's systems for access, Gaspar didn't know if he could have gotten through so quickly.

The security programs were interpreted as an aquarium by his own veeyar's perception. If he'd been tied in with Madeline Green's systems, he'd have had the same perception of it as she did.

His own system currently modified him so that he perceived himself as a heavily cybered fish. His gills resembled grills and his fins were angled metal that would have looked at home on the experimental jet Madeline Green had piloted through Peter's world.

He glided through aquamarine water, scanning the various clumps of brain coral on the black and red aquarium rocks below that represented various folders where files were stored. He darted around a sunken tree stripped of leaves and bark by various scavengers.

Without warning, a section of the sunken tree exploded outward, swinging on hidden hinges. A ropy octopus arm erupted from the hollow space inside and wrapped around Gaspar's rear fins.

Automatically he squelched the impulse to run. He peered into the lavender translucent eyes in the wedge-shaped head inside the tree hollow. He accessed his hacking utilities, knowing he wasn't going to completely escape the tentacled arm holding him.

Smooth as a spider sliding down a web, he opened his fishy mouth and exploded through it in a smaller version of the fish body, leaving the husk behind him. As he swam off toward another clump of orange and turquoise brain coral, he glanced behind him.

Three other tentacled arms shot out of the hollow tree and wrapped around the husk he'd left. With all the programming carried inside his new body, it would take nearly a minute for the security program to process the husk and realize the veeyar's security had been breached.

He popped a timer into his peripheral vision and set it for forty-five seconds. Then he swam, going with the currents inside the aquarium when he could.

The brain coral in front of him set off a vibration that thrummed along the lateral line in his fish body. Just as in a real fish, the lateral line ran the length of his body and was particularly sensitive to pressure changes and movement in the water. Fish used their lateral lines for direction and also as a warning system announcing the arrival of threats.

Gaspar had set his own lateral line to detect the files relating to Peter's veeyar. The timer had dropped below thirty seconds.

Concentrating, he focused on the task ahead of him. Three-fingered hands attached to multijointed arms sprang out from the sides of his face. The appendages calmly searched the surface of the brain coral, ferreting out its secrets.

Seventeen seconds remained on the clock when Gaspar succeeded in cracking the brain coral file. The brain coral opened like wedges in an orange, exposing gleaming lines of data that circled inside.

Gaspar reached into the brain coral with his new hands. Their heavy talons raked the datastreams. One hand drew the existing datastreams in while his other pumped data back into the brain coral.

With four seconds left, Gaspar pulled out of Madeline Green's veeyar, popping back into the Net just outside the Bessel Mid-Town. He floated freely eight stories above the street.

Holding his hand out, he focused on the file he'd retrieved from the Net Force Explorer's veeyar. Immediately a miniature holo player appeared on his palm, the small case gleaming bright cobalt blue. He opened it and pressed the Play icon. Images of Madeline Green's encounter with Peter and his dragon flashed across the three-inch screen.

Gaspar closed the holo player and made it disappear. Accessing the feeds he'd kept open to the girl's room, he took a quick peek back inside. So far Heavener's ground unit hadn't arrived.

Suddenly a bright yellow sash snaked out in front of him, then wrapped around his right wrist. The sash had all the strength of cotton candy, but what it signified reminded him of how much he could lose.

Someone had found him with a trace-back utility, he realized as he yanked his hand through the yellow sash. Even if he logged off, the trace-back utility would locate his point of origin if the user was any good. And if that happened, he knew Heavener would kill him. The trace-back material parted easily. He turned, morphing from the hotel staff proxy into another proxy, one of a dozen he preferred on the Net. The suit dropped away, melting into the sigil-covered armor of his personal choice in proxies.

In the blink of an eye he was nearly seven feet tall and

broad-built. A large bearskin robe covered enchanted armor, wrapping his head in a peaked hood. He unsheathed the curved sword at his hip and took a two-handed stance as he turned around to face the trace-back.

The yellow sash wiggled in front of him, making tentative darts toward him without actually making contact. A slight figure approached from the other end of it.

It's just a kid, Gaspar thought as he studied the slim figure in the red T-shirt. Then he reconsidered that. He wasn't seven feet tall except through the proxy parameters. Maybe the kid *wasn't* a kid. Maybe he wasn't even alone. Whatever he was, though, he was good if he could make the trace-back tag.

The kid stopped less than ten feet away, hovering comfortably over the street. "Hi," he said in a calm voice as he crossed his arms over his chest. "I'm Mark Gridley, a Net Force Explorer." ID popped into existence over his left shoulder, legible even at the distance. "I thought maybe we needed to talk."

"Tell me Maj isn't in room five eighteen," Catie Murray whispered, glancing desperately around the hallway. No one was visible except the four men she'd spotted in the elevator on her way up to Maj's room after getting Matt's vidphone call. She wore her blond hair pulled back in a ponytail. She was dressed for suburban stealth in a warm-up suit and cross-trainers.

She opened the foilpack again, sliding aside a tiny compartment cover, and dropped an earpiece into her hand. She popped the earpiece into her ear, then plugged the micro-thin connector wire into the foilpack's aud jack.

"Can't," Matt said.

The men were young, average in height and appearance. They wouldn't stand out in a crowd. Curling wires at the back of their necks that led up to their ears advertised they were jacked into foilpacks or some kind of comm devices. All of them were grim-faced, moving in concert, as if they'd practiced. One pulled an electronic device from under his jacket and laid it over the door lock.

"They're breaking into her room." Catie turned and held the foilpack so the vid could pick up the men at Maj's door.

"Sit tight," Matt advised. "I've already called the L.A. Police Department."

Catie remembered the hallway she'd passed in the elevator

foyer. The rooftop facilities the Bessel Mid-Town Hotel offered included a swimming pool and banquet area. "Can you hack into the hotel computer system and set off the fire alarm?"

"You could do that."

"I'm going to be busy." Catie sprinted down the hallway, digging her feet into the carpet and pushing off. She used her arms to push off walls and make the turns back to the foyer. "And I need as much time as I can get."

"If I trigger the fire alarms," Matt pointed out, "the hotel doors automatically open as part of the safety features."

"I've got a plan," Catie replied as she reached the foyer, caught the handle of the door leading to the rooftop facilities. *Maybe not much of a plan, but it's all I've got.*

5

Maj guided the Striper through the blue sky high above the windswept desert. So far, she hadn't been able to find the dragon or its rider. Powering the jet down, she dropped toward the hard deck and unsnapped her facemask in frustration.

"Warning, Room Five Eighteen!" a shrill voice suddenly screamed. "Impending security breach."

A sudden chill ghosted through Maj. Her body was back in a hotel room, not safely tucked away at home. She forced herself to be calm. "Notify the security desk."

"The security desk no longer exists."

The statement caught Maj by surprise. "Check again."

The only way the security desk doesn't exist, Maj knew, *is if new programming has invaded the security system and redefined the parameters. The assault began on this room before someone started forcing the door.* "Bring up the door's external security vid scan."

A letterbox-shaped two-dee screen popped into the cockpit with her. Only gray fuzz showed on the screen.

"Where's the vid?" Maj asked.

"Scanning. Nothing exists outside the parameter of this room."

There was a sound like breaking glass, then the two-dee screen suddenly disappeared.

Near panic, Maj refastened the mask over her face, then slammed a gloved palm against the ejection button. The cockpit canopy blew free, swept away in the jetstream. The seats launched from the Striper a heartbeat later. Maj rode the seat high into the air. When she pulled her chute free, the drag yanked her up and back into the real world.

She opened her eyes in the implant chair in the hotel and watched as, across the room, the doorknob turned.

I have definitely had better ideas, Catie thought as she stared down the five-story drop to the street. Knowing time was working against her, she glanced around the rooftop facilities the Bessel Mid-Town Hotel offered.

A huge pool occupied an area just off-center, flanked by dozens of lounge chairs. Farther back to the left, the banquet area sat in quiet order, stripped of tablecloths and the flower arrangements Catie had seen earlier.

On the right was the low-roofed building that housed the gym. The third side of the rooftop opened up to the western skyline.

Maj is in trouble. As soon as the thought passed through Catie's mind, she was in motion. She oriented herself quickly, sprinting for the low-roofed exercise area. She played a lot of soccer when she got the chance, so she was in good shape and knew how to handle herself.

Small balconies stuck out from every room in the hotel, each equipped with a small plastic table and two lounge chairs.

Catie vaulted from the top of one of the huge pots on either side of the exercise room and grabbed the roof's edge. Wearing the foilpack strapped to her wrist, she hauled herself up onto the building. Dashing across the building, she found it wasn't as close to the nearest balcony as she'd hoped.

She halted at the edge and peered down through the darkness. Neon lights chased away a lot of the night's shadows, and it only made the view to the street below clearer.

Never look, she told herself as fear turned sour and cold inside her. *It's definitely not a good idea to look.* She took a deep breath and backed away from the edge.

"Catie!" Matt's voice burst from the foilpack earpiece.

"What?" *Forgot I still had the vid function on the foilpack.*

"What are you doing?"

"I'm going to get Maj." Catie counted the balconies. At least the balconies were closer together than the gym was to the first balcony on the fifth floor. And the jump would be more lateral without the vertical she faced now.

"You can't do that."

"Not with you yelling in my ear."

"Catie—"

"We don't have a lot of time here," Catie interrupted. "Those guys who are after Maj have to know she's a Net Force Explorer. That means they know what kind of trouble they're getting into. They won't want any witnesses."

"Wait," Matt urged. "I've contacted the LAPD. They're already en route. They can—"

Catie drove her feet hard against the roof of the exercise building, pushing away the numbing fear that made her arms and legs feel as if they'd been filled with lead. *I'm right, Matt, and we both know it. No time to argue. I just hope I can make this jump!*

Without hesitation, thinking of Maj's safety hanging in the balance, Catie threw herself from the building's edge, arching up high to reach the balcony above. The balcony railing thudded into her chest just below the level of her armpits. Her breath left her in a whoosh, but she hooked her elbows over the railing and pulled herself onto the balcony. She didn't waste time trying to make a great landing on the balcony, just dropping into a loose sprawl that tangled her briefly in the legs of one of the lounge chairs. Gingerly she tried the balcony door but found it locked.

"Matt," she whispered.

"Yeah. Just getting my breath back and trying to figure out how many ways there are to tell a friend how stupid she is."

Catie swallowed hard. The post-adrenaline shakes hadn't settled in yet. "Sound the fire alarm."

There was only a slight pause. "Done."

Alarms jangled inside Maj's room, echoed by the other alarms of the other rooms. Catie yanked on the balcony door and swept the heavy curtains away. Maj was rising from the implant chair, her attention on the turning doorknob.

"Maj."

Maj's head whipped around, her eyes widening in surprise. "How did you get up here?"

"Don't ask." Catie took Maj's hand and hustled her out to the balcony. "Worry about how we're going to get down."

Maj peered over the balcony. "Down doesn't look fun."

"We're not going that far." Catie levered her body over the railing, hung by her hands, then lowered herself down the bars till she was much closer to the balcony below. Her foot was only a couple feet short. Swinging forward, she forced her hands to release the railing. She fell.

Mark Gridley carefully watched the bearskin-clad warrior standing in the air outside Maj's room at the Bessel Mid-Town Hotel.

"No talk," the warrior roared in a deep voice. He moved the wickedly curved sword before him, catching glints from the neon lights around them.

"Who are you?" Mark demanded. Outwardly he remained calm, but he was angry that anyone would attack one of his friends.

The warrior didn't answer. But the sword came to a dead stop, pointed directly at Mark. A bright blue laser beam spat from the curved point directly for Mark's chest.

Mark lifted a hand, accessing one of the firewall security programs he had on file. A glowing green disk suddenly spread out from his palm till it was nearly two feet in diameter. The bright blue bolt impacted against the green shield, shattering it into myriad gleaming bits of programming the Net interpreted as energy patterns. They flamed out long before they hit the street below.

The warrior lashed out with the sword again, spinning off a bolo net made up of golden light.

This guy's good, Mark thought as he allowed himself to fall toward the street. The golden net sailed over his head, but he knew it would have caused a system crash if it had wrapped him up. He brought up his own menu again and armored up.

In an eyeblink he was clad in the space suit he habitually wore while attempting to break code in programs his mom brought home from Net Force. He added a streamlined MMU backpack to the suit. Only this manned maneuvering unit was capable of Mach speeds. He triggered the controls in his glove, blasting straight up into the air.

The bearskin-clad warrior slashed again, spinning out a jagged double-spike of ruby lightning.

Mark pressed a hand out, summoning up another shield. The lightning bolt smashed into the shield. Instead of destroying it this time, the air around him suddenly caught fire, wreathing him in flames.

The virus probed at the suit's weaknesses, finding none, but triggering one diagnostic check after another, effectively shutting Mark out of taking any active part in the Net. As soon as the automatic firewalls detected another tendril of the virus, they reacted, draining the suit's resources.

Rendered nearly inoperative and floating in a stasis, Mark accessed a purge program. He unleashed it in a blaze of silver that burst through the suit's seams. It also burned the virus out. In control of the suit again, sweating profusely as the on-board air-conditioning fought to make the environment livable again, he scanned the night sky.

The bearskin-clad warrior was gone.

Disgustedly, Mark pulled up his IM list and tagged Matt.

"Catie's not going to make it."

Matt gazed at the two-dee screen maintaining the vidphone link with Catie's foilpack. He didn't look at Megan O'Malley, who stood beside him in his veeyar. She'd been online with Catie when he'd gotten his call through. Megan was also en route to the game convention, but her plane had been delayed in Salt Lake City, so she'd used an inline chair at a cyber café in the airport. Megan was also a friend and an Explorer. She twirled a strand of her dark hair between her fingers—a nervous habit—and her brown eyes held worry.

"She'll make it," Matt said.

But they had no guarantee from the crazy view they had over the vidphone link. They caught occasional glimpses of the street below and the side of the Bessel Mid-Town Hotel as the foilpack swung on Catie's wrist.

"IM message from Mark," the computer voice announced. "Will you accept?"

"Yes." Matt watched as a two-dee screen dawned in an orange sunburst. Mark, dressed in his space suit, stood framed in the screen.

"Lost him," Mark said. "I'm going to stay here, see if I can pick up the trail."

Matt nodded. "Be careful. The LAPD cyber unit is going to be all over that area, as well as the fire marshal's office."

"Maybe they'll turn up this guy. I'm going to run some trace-backs on the address signatures Maj got."

"Keep me updated."

Mark broke the connection.

"I've got Captain Winters online," Megan said. Captain James Winters was a Net Force commander and the direct liaison between Net Force proper and the Net Force Explorers. He was a good friend and confidant.

"Go," Matt said. "Bring him up to speed on what we've got going on here."

"Gone," Megan said, fading from his veeyar and crossing the Net.

Matt watched the foilpack view, drawn by the feeling that only the worst could happen. Then Catie dropped, the two-dee image suddenly showing the street level rushing up.

"Parameters to hotel security systems have been breached," the computer voice announced.

Breaking loose from the dread that held him, wondering how long Catie had been falling, Matt shoved a hand into the crack-code datastream that allowed him access to the hotel's security system. It pulled him in at once, shooting him through a blinding tunnel of light.

He crashed through the flimsy defense the hotel security pro-gramming tried to erect after all the damage the hacker's viruses had done in shutting down access to Maj's room. A split nano-second later and he stood inside Maj's rented room, courtesy of the holoprojector entertainment center he'd been able to hack into.

Two of the four men inspected the inline chair while the other two raced for the balcony. Just beyond them, Maj leaned out and dropped over the balcony's railing. All four men carried silencer-equipped pistols.

Wanting to buy Catie and Maj more time if they'd made the drop to the fourth floor, Matt took a deep breath and said, "Hey!"

The four men turned and raised their weapons automatically. One of the men nearest the implant chair stepped forward, putting the muzzle of his pistol less than a foot from Matt's head. The man fired without hesitation, totally emotionless.

Who are these guys? Matt wondered just before the subsonic round entered his head.

"Where did he come from?" Heavener tapped the screen, indicating the dark-haired, dark-eyed young man standing in the doorway to the hotel room. He wore black windbreaker pants, tennis shoes, and a dark blue tank.

Gaspar took only a second to recognize the youth. On screen, the new arrival hollered, "Hey," drawing the attention of the four men in the room.

"That's Matt Hunter," Gaspar said. "Didn't you look at his file?"

Heavener pushed him back, almost causing him to fall. "I had other things to do." She turned her attention back to the screen. "I thought he was in Maryland."

"He is." Gaspar watched as one of the men approached Matt Hunter and shoved a pistol into his face. It was a grim reminder of what was in store for him if he failed any of the tasks D'Arnot Industries placed before him. "He's just there in holo. Tell them to get the Brainsucker set up. I wiped all the files in Madeline Green's veeyar. They have to take out the hardware there."

On the screen, the man fired pointblank into Matt Hunter's face, the slide snapping back on the pistol. Matt Hunter went down.

The fall from the fifth floor balcony was much easier than Catie thought it would be. She landed in a crouched position on the fourth-floor balcony, then pushed herself up immediately.

Peering up, she spotted Maj looking down at her. "Hang down. I'll help you." When Maj's feet came within reach, she snared them in an embrace. She took part of her friend's weight and guided her safely toward the balcony. The door in Maj's room banged against the wall, piercing the screeching fire alarms.

"There she is!" a man's voice roared. "On the balcony! She's getting away!"

"Matt," Catie called out over the foilpack vidphone as she scrambled to her feet.

"I'm here."

"We're on a fourth-floor balcony beneath Maj's room." Catie glanced up at the balcony over them as they pressed back against the glass doors. "I don't think it's a good idea for us to stay here."

Nothing happened.

"Matt," Catie implored, feeling a little more desperate. She glanced up at the balcony hanging over the area where they were.

"If we can make that jump, they can," Maj said.

"I know." Catie tried the foilpack again. "Matt!"

"Easy," Mark Gridley's calm voice called. "Matt's off-line. I've got you."

The next instant the alarm rang from inside the room the balcony was on.

Catie helped Maj to her feet, then grabbed the balcony door and shoved it open. She led the way across the room and through the door. When they reached the hallway, it was filled with people responding to the fire alarms on the fourth and fifth floor. Catie led the way down the hall, racing toward the elevators and the fire escape.

Catie glanced at Maj. "Where to?"

Maj held herself and shook her head. "Downstairs. Maybe we can find a computer we can borrow. But definitely not back up to my room. I've got a feeling only bad things are going to happen up there."

Matt's diving roll to the carpet was instinctive—and far too late. By the time he started going down, the 9mm round had already passed through his head and buried itself in the wall.

Without pause, the man with the pistol fired two more rounds, centering them both in Matt's chest. Both rounds penetrated Matt's hologram form without even ruffling his shirt.

"You're lucky, kid." The gunman lifted his weapon, a small, mirthless smile twisting his lips. He turned and took up a position beside the door.

The two men working on the implant chair hooked up a small device to the processing and memory modules. The other man came back in from the balcony. "The girls escaped."

"Pity," the man beside the door said. "May have to find them later. Could have saved us some trouble if they'd fallen."

"Who's the kid?"

The man beside the door smirked again. "Next best thing to a ghost."

Scared and embarrassed, Matt pulled himself together and stood. "Who are you?" He tried to make his voice as commanding as he could.

The gunman treated him to another cold smile. "Another ghost. I was never here."

"You won't get out of the hotel," Matt said.

"We'll see. We've gotten out of tougher jams than this."

The two men beside the implant chair stood. "Done here," one of them said. "Time to rock and roll."

Frustration and anxiety filled Matt as he watched the men move toward the door.

"You do this bit?" The gunman who'd shot him waggled his weapon toward the hallway where people were still evacuating.

Matt didn't say anything.

"Figure it must have been you," the gunman said. "Saving your little friend. Good plan. And it's going to work out for us, too." He motioned the three other men forward.

"One more thing," Matt said, accessing a piece of software from his utility menu.

The man looked at him.

"Smile," Matt said. He traced a square in the air and a camera popped out. He shot off a roll of "film" that was actually preprogrammed memory, storing image after image.

"Waste of time," the gunman promised. "You'll see." Then they were out in the hallway, mixing in with the crowd pouring out from the other rooms.

Instinctively Matt started forward, wanting desperately to keep them in sight. He yelled for Mark, hoping his friend was online and tuned in.

"Yeah?" Mark replied.

"Any luck?"

"No."

"I'm trailing the men who broke into Maj's room. Can you get a fix on them?"

"The hotel systems have shut down," Mark replied. "I got to the fire alarms on the fourth floor just before the access windows disappeared. I don't know if it was internal security or the people you're after."

Matt rushed out into the hallway and managed two steps before he went beyond the range of the room's holoprojectors. Suddenly he was a whirl of light, like sand trickling through an hourglass, and the hotel faded from view.

When his vision returned, he was back in his own veeyar. Megan was waiting on him.

"Captain Winters wants to meet with us," she said.

Matt nodded glumly, knowing Captain Winters might not be happy with the situation. But what else could they have done? "Maybe we'll get lucky," he said, "and hotel security or the LAPD will catch the guys responsible."

6

LAPD Detective Third Grade John Holmes walked through the door of the second-floor conference room the Bessel Mid-Town Hotel had lent Captain Winters for the debrief. The room was large and fully equipped with holoprojectors so even the Explorers who were in other places could attend in holoform.

Maj leaned against the window looking out over the hotel's entrance. So far the LAPD had kept everything low-key. Out in the street the last of the hook-and-ladder fire trucks that had responded to the fire alarm were clearing hoses while uniformed police officers kept the crowds on the other side of the red and white sawhorses.

John Holmes didn't look as if he'd seen thirty yet. He was earnest and neat looking in his charcoal gray suit. His badge gleamed as it hung out of his jacket pocket. He had an easy smile, but something had left a wicked pink and gray scar on his left cheekbone that stood out against his ebony skin.

Captain James Winters stood at military parade rest in the center of the room. He was a tall, lean man with sharp blue-gray eyes that glinted like a hunting bird's. His hair was neatly clipped in a Marine buzz cut. He wore a navy suit.

Holmes pulled out a chair at the table and sat, leaning forward and resting his forearms on his thighs. "The perps got away. Forensics is still going over the room. They've turned up a couple dozen fingerprints, and they've matched all but two through hotel records. At present we're not terribly enthusiastic about the odds of finding out who these guys are through fingerprints. We're running the images Matt took through NCIC and other crime databases. We'll have to wait and see."

"Did you get anything from my veeyar or the implant chair?" Maj asked.

"Whoever went through the veeyar and implant chair left it stripped of the whole encounter you've told us about. Your veeyar seems to be intact otherwise, but you'll know that better than us. However, all the Net record temp files archived since your arrival here at the hotel are gone."

"What about the dragonrider?" Maj asked.

"I've got uniforms canvassing the hotel now, but we're limited in what the management here will let us do. They don't want people to get the idea this isn't a safe place."

"You've got an attempted murder charge you can work with," Matt pointed out.

His words sent a chill through Maj. As Net Force Explorers, they'd been involved on the periphery of some Net Force operations, but being shot at really wasn't something she supposed people got used to.

Holmes nodded. "I think it's possible that those men knew you were in holoform and just pushed the performance. I don't think I'd have a problem getting a warrant from a judge based on the circumstances, but where would I go with it? The hotel's being as accommodating as they can be. They're even letting me post a few more uniforms at the convention than they'd like to have." He flashed a thin grin. "They think there's something about a uniformed police officer on the premises that will impede festivities."

"If people *believe* they are police officers," Mark put in. "Gaming conventions have a tendency to go totally bizarro. You'll find people in full costume from their favorite games, shouting, joking, all wrapped up in their own worlds. Covering the event isn't going to be easy."

"I know," Holmes said. "I've been here before. I game whenever I get the chance."

Maj was surprised.

"What about you?" Holmes asked Maj. "Are you working on something top secret that's going to turn the gaming world on its ear?"

"I've developed a flight-sim. It's nice, but it's nothing earth-shattering."

"Is there any reason anyone would be after your sim?" the detective asked.

"They weren't after the sim," Maj answered. "Those men came into my room because we bumped into the dragonrider."

"Why not go directly after him?"

"We don't know," Megan said. "We haven't come up with a good answer to that one."

"I'm beginning to think," Winters spoke up, "that we don't quite have all the right questions, either."

"I agree," Holmes said.

"What story is the hotel going to give the media?" Winters asked.

"HoloNet has a team covering some of the major designers and players who're going to be here for the weekend. So far, the hotel has told them that as yet unidentified parties pulled the fire alarms as a prank."

"But," Winters said, "any reporter worth his salt is going to notice the abundance of LAPD police officers responding to the call."

"I told them, off the record, that there were some reports of attempted corporate espionage we were looking into."

"That will also explain why you've got extra officers on the premises during the convention," Winters said.

"Yes. And not all of my officers are going to be in uniform. I'll have men circulating in plainclothes, too. The gaming convention is big business in LA. I didn't have any problems getting some overtime approved to run security for it, and no shortage of volunteers. There will even be some off-duty guys here." Holmes shrugged. "I negotiated some free passes from the hotel and a few other perks."

Winters smiled. "You've been busy."

"That I have." Holmes glanced up at the captain speculatively. "Personally, I think we're on a snipe hunt here. I think that the break-in last night was purely an advertising attempt by one of the gaming companies. They do this kind of thing. One year when I worked this convention, we picked up rumors of an assassination in the works. HoloNet picked it up, too. All of us were out here busting our humps to get the true skinny on it. Know what it turned out to be?"

"Last year?" Matt said. "Matt2Matt games killed off Zord, one of the benevolent lords in Crimson Steel."

"Right," Holmes replied. "Another year we thought we had a jumper off the building. Turned out to be a stunt rigged by X-treem Sportz who fuzzied the hotel's holoprojectors to make it look as if there was a skier shushing down to the street level. I could go on with the list. Some of it hit the media and some of it didn't."

"It's cheap advertising," Winters said.

"You bet. Even when we catch them, all they generally have to do is pay a fine. I'm going to look into this thing carefully, but I'm not going to overinvest. I assume Net Force is on the same wavelength?"

Winters nodded.

Someone knocked on the conference room door.

"Come on in," Holmes said.

"Detective Holmes," the heavyset uniformed police officer in the doorway told him, "forensics is ready for you up on the fifth floor."

"Good news?"

"Tarkington's not happy. They're not finding anything, and he's going to have to pull half his crew for a double one-eighty-seven that just happened."

Holmes nodded. "I'll be right there."

The uniformed police officer stepped back out the door.

"I'm going to have to go, but I do have one last question," Holmes said. "I play a lot of games, so I know about the restrictions and parameters of a personal veeyar. I know you can go online to a game like Sarxos, but that doesn't seem to be what happened here. How do you think this overlap between veeyars happened?"

"It's not supposed to," Maj answered. "Glitches do occur."

"Maybe," Holmes said. "But you might want to think about this one." He stepped through the door and was gone.

"What do you think he meant by that?" Megan asked.

"Just what he said." Captain Winters's expression was unreadable, but Maj felt he was thinking carefully. Winters wasn't someone who took an attack on one of his team lightly. "How many of you are going to be here this weekend?"

"Virtual or physical?" Mark asked. "I've arranged for a virtual pass."

"Physical," Winters replied.

Maj said she and Catie were already on-site. Megan added that her stranded flight would be leaving by morning and she'd be in Los Angeles by noon.

A doorbell sounded from the air above the conference table. "Permission to pipe aboard," Leif Anderson called out.

"Granted," Winters said. The conference room controls had been programmed to his voice. No virtual visitors could arrive without his invitation.

Leif Anderson materialized in a chair wearing slacks and a baggy sweater. He looked around the table. "Am I late?"

"Fashionably," Megan said.

Leif grinned. "Terrific. Just what I was aiming for. Did I miss anything?"

"The police interrogation," Matt said.

Leif's grin brightened. "Even better. Those tend to be an exercise in redundancy."

"Redundancy is one of the chief resources of an investigatory body," Winters said quietly.

"Yes, sir." Leif looked only a little chagrined, Maj thought. His naturally ebullient nature quickly reasserted itself. She wished she recovered from things so quickly. "I assume we know everything they know?"

"I think that's a safe assumption," Winters said.

"Fine," Leif said. "Then maybe someone could tell me what it is we know."

Winters recapped in clipped, succinct sentences. When he was finished, he said, "I was told you were searching for some information."

"Yes, sir. The audio file Maj saved and sent to me through Matt. I'm not sure why it wouldn't translate. It was in a variant of Kurdish, so I had to have a friend do the translation for me. There wasn't much. The guy was just asking what Maj and Matt were doing there."

Maj felt a little more disheartened. The night's events continued to escalate in confusion.

"Nothing else?" Winters asked.

"No, sir."

Silence filled the room for a moment.

"Back to your original questions about who was going to be here for the weekend," Matt said "Andy Moore and I are coming in tomorrow."

Leif leaned back in this chair. "I'll make myself available for the weekend as well."

"No other pressing engagements?" Megan asked.

Leif smiled. "None that I don't mind breaking." The other Net Force Explorers often teased him about being a playboy in the making.

"So what do you want us to do, Captain?" Maj asked.

"Keep your eyes and ears open," Winters replied. "I'm in agreement with Detective Holmes. I think when the local PD gets to the bottom of this, they'll find it was an advertising gimmick. Gaming companies spend billions of dollars every year in research and development and make billions more in sales around the world. A few fines for reckless endangerment barely touch their profit margins.

"But corporate espionage is a possibility. If someone was out to steal a game design before it hits the market and get out something similar before the game's release, they'd impact that corporation's bottom line in a big way."

"As well as making some serious cash for themselves," Mark added.

Winters shrugged. "Take a look around while you're here. You people know this industry. If you find something worthwhile, let me know." He looked sternly at Catie. "And no more diving off buildings."

"Yes, sir."

The meeting broke up with only a little more discussion. Maj didn't take an active part because her mind was reeling with everything that had happened. The hotel staff had moved her belongings into Catie's room. The police were busy ripping her old room apart, and all the other rooms had been booked. Maj felt better about not being left on her own for the evening.

Soon only she and Catie remained in the conference room.

"Are you okay?" Catie asked as they stepped out into the hallway and headed for the elevators.

"Me?" Maj acted surprised. "*You* were doing a trapeze act five floors up."

Catie shrugged. "I'm over it. I'll probably have a couple nightmares later on, but I tend to get past things. You seem locked in on this." She paused. "Not that I blame you. There's no telling what those men would have done if you'd been in the room when they got there."

Maj felt cold inside. *Actually, I think we know exactly what they would have done,* she thought. "It's the dragonrider. I can't get him out of my mind."

Catie smiled. "Cute?"

"Very."

"Then it won't be so bad thinking about him."

"No," Maj admitted, feeling some of her dark mood lift at her friend's good-natured teasing. "The problem is that I don't think he knows he's in trouble."

"If he's at the convention," Catie reassured her, "we'll find him."

"I know," Maj said, "but I don't think we're going to be the only ones looking."

7

"My dad would love this stuff," Megan O'Malley announced.

Still feeling the effects of sleep-deprivation due to a long bout of insomnia during the night, Maj glanced at her friend with a little irritation. Megan didn't get the hint, and Maj assumed that maybe it was because the morning sunlight streaming through the window made her squint and took some of the effect away. They sat in Catie's hotel room at the Bessel Mid-Town, Maj still in bed and Megan at the small desk. Catie was in the shower.

"I'm serious," Megan went on. "You've got mystery and danger against an interesting background. It's an adventure." Her dad was R. F. O'Malley, one of the hottest mystery writers in publishing.

"Sometimes," Maj croaked in a sleep-filled voice, "adventures are better in fiction instead of happening to real people."

"Like you would ever pass up the opportunity," Megan retorted. "I know you're planning on canvassing the convention downstairs as soon as you can." Megan was already prepared to meet the day. Her brown hair was pulled back the way she wore it for her martial arts meets, and her hazel eyes gleamed.

"Catie blabbed."

Megan shrugged. "We talked. You were asleep. And have I ever had the chance to tell you how cute you are when you sleep? Especially the whole open-mouthed snoring thing?"

"Don't even go there." Maj glanced at the time/date stamp on the holo playing high on the opposite wall. The cartoon channel was on, showing a popular Japanimation series Catie was currently hooked on. Her artistic interests were varied. It was 9:15 A.M. Maj figured she'd gotten maybe four hours of sleep. "The convention officially opens at ten."

"I know," Megan said. "I passed a number of people out in the halls downstairs who were setting up last-minute details to their booths. It's a madhouse."

Someone knocked on the door.

Apprehension instantly filled Maj, and she hated that it did. *How long is it going to be before I feel safe away from home again?*

Megan smiled. "I ordered room service, breakfast for three." She uncoiled from the seat behind the desk and slipped her Universal Credit Card from the small purse she carried. "On me. I wanted to splurge this morning."

"You could have warned me. I look as if I could be declared a federal disaster area."

"Then breakfast in bed wouldn't have been a surprise." Megan walked to the door. "Besides, it's probably a maid, and what's she going to care?" She opened the door and a handsome young man in an immaculate hotel uniform pushed a service cart into the room. He uncovered the breakfast buffet scattered on the various platters, swiped Megan's Universal Credit Card through the portable reader, and smiled at Maj.

Maj smiled back weakly, wishing she could turn invisible.

The handsome young man left.

"Or maybe it won't be a maid," Megan said. "There is an up side to this. He's going to think you were Catie."

"Who's going to think she was Catie?" Catie stood in the bathroom doorway, her hair turbaned in a white towel. She wore pink and charcoal striped pedal-pushers and a white sweater with the sleeves pushed up to mid-forearm.

"Room service," Megan declared, waving toward the service tray.

"Room service is going to think Maj was me?" Catie asked, glancing at her friend. "Should I care?"

"He was really cute," Megan answered.

Catie studied Maj more closely. "Is character assassination a crime in this state?"

"My dad makes a living at it," Megan said.

Maj mock-glared at them both. "When my sense of humor returns, you'll be the first to know." She scooted over to the edge of the bed and sat within reach of the service tray.

Megan handed her a plate with French toast on it. Catie sat on the bed beside her and started helping herself.

"Wow," Catie said, "this must have been expensive."

"It was," Megan admitted.

"We could have eaten at the buffet downstairs."

"I thought maybe we'd take a little time to ourselves this morning." Megan buttered a piece of toast and added peach jelly. "Besides, there was no telling who might be watching."

The statement was delivered with a light tone, but it seemed to chill the room temperature to Maj.

"Maybe I shouldn't have mentioned that," Megan said.

"I'll deal," Maj said.

Catie used the remote control and switched the holo display from the cartoon channel to HoloNet news. "Local channel," she explained. "They're supposed to be doing special coverage on the gaming convention. I figured we'd take a look."

Conversation dropped to a minimum of cursory courtesy as dishes and condiments were negotiated over and passed around. Maj found herself becoming totally immersed in the stories being unveiled on HoloNet. Evidently the media service hadn't spared any effort to totally cover the event. Stories slid by in three-dee, concentrating on games in development and about to be released, on creators, on designers, and on publishing houses old and new.

Gaming was big business, and the corporate sector was heavily invested in it.

"There was one hiccup in Bessel Mid-Town Hotel's accommodations for the gaming convention," a young blond reporter said.

She stood beside a display currently outside the main entrance to the convention hall. Holo images of games moved behind her. Garishly colored creatures culled from mythologies and imagination warred behind her. Other games featured high-tech hardware modeled on current military gunships and naval batteries. The series favorites were also represented, showing action sequences from best-selling shooters, adventure games, and role-playing games.

"Last night the fourth and fifth floors of the hotel were evacuated after someone activated the fire alarms," the reporter continued. "The police believe it's the work of a prankster, or one of the hotel guests burning off a little nervous energy before opening day."

"That's good," Catie said.

"Yeah," Megan said, "but it also covers the people who were responsible for the break-in."

"No one was hurt," the reporter went on, "but a number of people were inconvenienced. Detective John Holmes of the Los Angeles Police Department went on to say that while the convention may draw more than its share of fun-lovers, there will be no tolerance for anyone who breaks the law."

A quick newsbyte flashed on Detective Holmes from the previous night. He smiled easily for the camera. "I like games as much as the next guy, but there's a certain amount of courtesy that needs to be observed at events like this."

The scene cut back to the reporter, who wore a smile. "I talked to Detective Holmes myself, and he made a believer out of me. If anyone steps outside the lines at the convention, they'll probably find themselves—"

An image of a pig-snouted biker from a popular shooter series superimposed itself over the reporter along with the text: YOU'RE BUSTED, SNOWFLAKE!

"So plan on having a good time if you attend the convention," the reporter said, "but stop there or the LAPD will stop you . . . dead in your tracks."

The holo cut to commercial, introducing a new game by Prism Productions called Power Corps 4. It showed a man in a cape and mask battling alien invaders with power rays streaming from his eyes, promising larger worlds than ever before and more playing time for single-player games.

Maj recognized it as one of the games Andy Moore liked to play. More commercials in the form of news rolled, brief bytes of information designed to intrigue and entrance.

"In some circles," the blond reporter said when she returned,

"Peter Griffen needs no introduction. But until lately, those circles have been small and included predominantly producers, designers, and publishers of computer games and graphics. But after this convention, a lot of folks are betting Griffen is going to be a landmark name."

The holo changed, showing a file image of Griffen. It was a profile shot of him staring at a virtual tank where computer graphics were written for games without exposing them to the open Net. He was young and earnest, athletically trim. His dark hair was just long enough to hold the promise of wavy curls. He wore slacks and a shirt with the top buttons unfastened, his tie hanging around his neck.

"We tried to get an interview with Peter Griffen," the reporter continued. "However, we've met with no success. Griffen remains a mystery man." She flashed a million-dollar grin and lowered her voice. "And that's something reporters just hate, so be prepared to hear a lot about Peter Griffen if his product meets all the build-up Eisenhower Productions, his publisher, promises."

Her interest piqued, Maj abandoned her efforts on the waffle. She studied the still picture. *Why is Griffen so reluctant to seize the limelight if he has the chance?* Exposure translated quickly into profit. Even in profile, though, Griffen looked familiar, as if she'd seen him before. Her hand leaped out for the remote control Catie had laid aside. She punched the Copy mode.

The holo moved on, picking up more bytes from one of the new designers hoping to break into the market with a strat-sim based on the Civil War. The game featured a few twists, though, including the invention of the atomic bomb in 1830. Nuclear-ravaged zombies in Union blue and Confederate gray lurched across radioactive wastelands.

Across the service tray and the dwindling breakfast, Megan watched her keenly. "Did you see something we missed?"

"I'm not sure," Maj said, "but I know I want to get a better look at Peter Griffen."

"You think he's the dragonrider?" Catie asked.

Maj tapped the remote control, bringing up the copied still picture on the holo. Peter Griffen's image filled the holo field. "He could be."

"At any rate," Catie went on, "he's cute. Definitely worth meeting."

Maj made a face at her friend. She knew Catie was only teasing. But she couldn't shake the dread that filled her. *If Peter Griffen is the dragonrider, what does he know about last night's events? Is he guilty? Or is he in danger?*

Matt Hunter stood among the passengers boarding the one o'clock flight out of Dulles International Airport, trying desperately to hold back a yawn. He wore jeans and a red and black pullover under a light jacket. He held a carry-on in one hand and a backpack over his shoulder.

Passengers continued feeding into the jet.

"Hey."

Turning, Matt spotted Andy Moore trotting up. Andy's blond hair looked more rumpled than usual, but his blue eyes were alert. He wore jeans and a T-shirt featuring Captain Alpha, a hero from the popular superhero online game, Power Corps.

"I was beginning to think you weren't going to make it," Matt said.

"The autocab I got was on the blink." Andy shifted the backpack and the two suitcases he carried. "Something was wrong with the GPS system, and I ended up in an argument with the dispatcher over the amount."

"You?" Matt asked with wry humor. "In an argument? Say it isn't so." Andy had a reputation as class clown and as a bulldog for fighting for what he thought was right.

"Hey, it was a legitimate complaint. And I won."

The passengers continued filing through the gantry. Matt held his ticket out and stepped inside.

"Full flight," Andy commented.

"The airline overbooked the flight. A few minutes ago they were offering free tickets to anyone willing to reschedule."

"If they'd offered part of the ticket money back," Andy said, "I might have been interested. I had to ask my mom for a loan to cover this trip, and you know how I hate owing her money." His father had been killed during the South African Conflict in 2014, only a few months after Andy had been born. He'd been raised in a single-parent household, and things hadn't always been easy. His mom operated her own veterinary clinic in Alexandria, Virginia, and Andy worked there to make extra money.

"I know. This trip put a big dent in my savings. When it

comes time for a summer job this year, I'm not going to be able to be choosy about what it is. But with everything going on in L.A., I'd rather be there than here."

"Yeah. Me, too." Andy glanced around the crowd as they continued moving slowly forward.

Matt led the way onto the plane, nodding a brief hello to the young flight attendant.

"Where are we?" Andy asked.

Matt peered through the crowd ahead of them. Men and women filled the overhead compartments rapidly. "Row twenty-three, seats D and E."

Gradually the crowd thinned as people took their seats. Unfortunately, row 23, seats D and E were also occupied.

Matt looked at the two men in the seats, taking in the suits and the external Net hookups. Commercial class received links to the Net during the flight, but it was basically a mechanical access that allowed the users to handle phone calls, e-mail, and fact gathering from databases. Information was relayed over the laptop screens like flatfilm.

"Excuse me," Matt said politely.

The man on the outside edge looked up, then looked around. "Me?"

"Yes." Matt nodded. "I think there's been some mistake. I'm supposed to be in seat twenty-three D."

"The mistake's yours, kid," the businessman said. "This is my seat."

Andy nudged around Matt. "No. You've got *our* seats. The flight was overbooked."

The man looked away and shook his head. "That's not my problem."

Shooting the man a withering glare, Andy made a snort of disgust. "Look, my friend and I booked these seats weeks ago. Unless you can ante up and beat that, I suggest you look for another seat to steal."

"Stand down," Matt said quietly, in a tone Captain Winters might have used. "Let's see if we can get this figured out." He glanced back and caught the young flight attendant's eye. "We need some help."

The flight attendant made her way down the aisle. "How can I help you?"

Matt quickly explained about the ticket mix-up. "We've really got to make this flight."

"Tough break," the businessman. "But what you're doing can't be nearly as important as the merger I'm helping negotiate today."

Looking down at the man, Andy said, "I've got a HoloNet flash for you, buddy. If you don't get out of that seat, the only merger you're going to be negotiating today is my foot and your—"

Matt started to take a step toward Andy and separate him from the man. Andy didn't have much patience on a good day, and almost no fear at all of any physical confrontation. He went from class clown to bouncer in a nanosecond.

"Excuse me," a smooth voice interrupted. "Maybe I can help."

8

Glancing over his shoulder, Matt watched Leif Anderson stride down the aisle. Leif was dressed in a cream Armani suit that he somehow managed to bring off as casual wear.

"Who're you?" the businessman demanded.

"Just think of me as a guy helping you out of an unwanted merger." Leif smiled easily. "These two young men are trying to get into the wrong seats."

The man grinned in cold triumph and opened his mouth to speak.

"You see," Leif said, cutting him off, "they're actually supposed to be in first class. That's where the really important business goes on." He looked up at Matt and Andy, then made a sweeping gesture with one arm. "Mr. Hunter, Mr. Moore, if you would be so kind as to join me."

Matt wrapped a hand around Andy's upper arm and pulled him along. "First class?" Matt asked.

Leif nodded. "I upgraded your tickets this morning. Evidently you didn't get my message before you left your house."

"No. Why would you do that? We could have flown coach."

"True." Leif guided them to the first row of seats in the first-class section. "But I also upgraded my ticket. I was in the row behind you. Tactical planning on my part since Andy was involved. However, in light of last night's events I thought we'd be better served by flying first class."

At Leif's urging, Matt took the seat nearest the window. He considered, knowing Leif—despite his father's wealth—wasn't one to go around flashing money. "So why first class?"

Leif smiled. "Logistics, buddy. Physically we're miles and hours from Maj, Catie, and Megan, but we can be there virtually." He tapped the back of the chair. "In coach you get limited access to the Net, but up here the seats are outfitted with implant scanners. Once the plane lifts, we can go online and be at the convention when it opens at ten."

"I like the way you plan," Andy said, toasting Leif with his soda.

Matt nodded. "It makes sense, but I'm going to pay you for the first-class upgrade." *Maybe I can get a couple summer jobs.*

"No need." Leif put his seatbelt on and snugged it tight as the flight attendant took her place at the front of the first-class section with the oxygen mask demo. "My dad's picking up the tab. He's also going to reimburse you guys for your tickets."

"All right," Andy crowed enthusiastically.

"Why?" Matt asked.

"Because Anderson Investments Multinational has put together several portfolios for clients that include stocks in game design and development corporations. You just can't ignore the impact that industry has on the entertainment sector. If something's rotten there, Dad said he'd feel more comfortable knowing we were looking into it."

"He could hire a security team."

Leif nodded. "Sure, and he probably will. But where's he going to find a security team who knows as much as we do about games?"

Matt nodded. It made sense.

Leif went on. "He's going to comp Maj, Megan, and Catie as well. That way the team can concentrate on the mystery at hand, rather than money."

They sat quietly while the jet trundled out to the runway. In minutes they were airborne.

"Okay," Leif said, leaning the seat back and flipping up the covers over the implant contacts, "time to get virtual." He placed his head in the trough, closed his eyes, and let out a breath, gone in that very instant.

Andy followed suit immediately.

Matt hesitated. He'd never entered the Net while on a jet streaking through the air.

"Sir?"

Matt glanced up at the young flight attendant.

"Do you have any questions about the use of the on-board equipment?" she asked.

Matt gave her a grin. "So if the jet goes out of control—"

"You'll automatically be logged off the Net," the flight attendant replied. "Sensors from the jet are routed through the Net interfaces the airline provides. They're very sensitive. Sometimes turbulence will cause the connections to log-off. Some passengers think that gets frustrating."

Matt glanced around the first-class section and found that nearly everyone was logged on to the Net. He pushed his breath out and laid his head back. The brief, familiar sensation of logging on to the Net passed through him.

I don't know why I was thinking this would be easy. Maj stared out over the convention center.

Peter Griffen's booth was strategically placed at the heart of the cavernous convention room. Two information tables occupied each of the four sides, all of them by doors that led into the interior of the huge booth. At least, they would lead into the booth later. For now they were locked.

Advertising in the form of holoprojectors hovered in miniature over the walls, but none of them offered any information on Peter Griffen or what the new game might be. Fifteen minutes' worth of advertising about other games Eisenhower was doing spewed through the holovids, as well as some past advertising on games that had been major hits.

Even as large as the Eisenhower booth was, the convention center still dwarfed it. No other booth was as large, but most of them had holoprojectors set up to advertise games between the booths and the high ceiling. Gaming centers pushed into the four sides of the convention made do with two-dee screens that covered the walls from floor to ceiling.

Over forty thousand convention guests roamed the broad aisles, filling them to capacity. Voices created an undercurrent of noise that never stopped and was punctuated by bleeps, buzzes, sirens, and clangs from the different games. Excitement rattled through the air around Maj, turning her anxiety up a notch.

"Hey."

Startled, Maj took an involuntary step back, then she realized Catie had been talking to her. "Hi."

"Didn't mean to scare you," Catie said, dropping out of the flowing crowd to stand in front of her.

"I was thinking."

"Too hard," Catie agreed. "I can tell by the little squinkles around your eyes."

"Those are from lack of sleep."

Catie glanced back at the booth. "Has Peter Griffen shown up?"

Maj shook her head. "They have no idea when he's supposed to be here."

"You'd think this is the place he'd be."

"Unless he's somewhere giving an interview. Where's Megan?"

"With Mark. They got some time on Catspaw, so they're busy trying to get past the lethal defenses of a wrecked space station embedded in the side of an asteroid. They're supposed to collect the ship's journal and get clues about what really happened aboard the ship. It's one of those mystery-tech adventure games they enjoy."

Maj watched a guy in a wombat costume on Rollerblades weave through an applauding crowd that separated before him. The wombat waved a purple and yellow flag gleefully. *Normally that would make me laugh.*

Catie smiled. "I guess Wover's got a new game out."

"Yeah, and he seems to be pretty excited about it."

"I've got to go meet with an art guy," Catie said. "I'll check back on you later."

Maj nodded. "Good luck."

Holo displays crowded each other for space on top of the various booths. The holos moved and shifted in neon colors, replications of new heroes and creatures being marketed as well as updated versions and continuations of heroes that had helped create the computer gaming phenomenon. Two ninjas in futuristic energy armor battled each other with laser swords on top of the Fujihama exhibit. Sparks leaped outward when the blades met, but died within inches of the floor or the nearest person. The razored shriek of energy fields meeting boomed like thunder from the speaker systems.

Maj studied the crowd, searching for Peter Griffen, wondering how she was supposed to see anyone in the crowd.

"You are Soljarr," a nearby display squawked in a basso voice, "warrior-slave to the Tevvis colony. Your brain was removed from your body, then placed in an invulnerable drone so that you could help your captors fight against your own people. To disobey is to die. But there's a way out, and a way to save your people, if you're brave enough and clever enough to find it."

At least three dozen people stood in line between corridors of tape at the Soljarr booth. All of them talked eagerly, pointing at the holo over the structure. The holo showed a shimmering blue-steel exo-body that moved as fluidly as water. Virulent purple blasts erupted from Soljarr's fists, blasting through a line of squat, mechanical drones powering across an icy tundra, reducing them to flaming bits of metal and gears.

Maj kept moving, but then an uncomfortable feeling threaded down the back of her neck. She stepped from the crowd and looked behind her, studying the faces. Above them a holo displayed a giant panda with a long yellow scarf piloting a tiny biplane, zipping through the air and snagging metallic green coins resting on clouds.

Adults as well as kids and teens made up the crowd, all of them drifting by with the same sense of wonder on their faces. None of them appeared to be paying any special attention to Maj, but she couldn't escape the feeling that she was being watched.

Matt Hunter swung his sword and blocked the slash that would have taken his head off if it had connected. The shock traveled the length of his arm and knocked him slightly off-balance. He took a step backward to recover, then lost his footing completely as the uneven hillside gave way.

The Burgundian warrior facing him shouted in savage joy and leaped forward. Taking his swordhilt in both hands, he swung hard.

On his back and unable to get to his feet quickly, held down by the armor he wore, Matt raised an arm. *There won't be any pain. I'll just be logged off and have to listen to Andy's insults for a week or two.*

Suddenly another sword appeared, crossing under the Burgundian warrior's and knocking the attack aside. The Burgundian snarled a curse in his native language and turned to face the newcomer.

Matt didn't waste any time, but the fifteenth-century armor was heavy. Even with the special skills he'd uploaded from the computer program, it took time to get to his feet.

"Traitorous dog!" the Burgundian warrior shouted.

The new knight strode to face the man. His armor showed signs of prolonged battle, smudged with blood and mud, tiny green leaves from the brush stuck it. The shield he carried over one arm had a scarred *fleur-de-lis* on it.

"Hey," Leif Anderson protested in a mildly amused voice, "no name-calling." The sword seemed to come alive in his hands, sweeping forward time after time and driving the Burgundian warrior back.

Matt got to his feet, feeling the layer of perspiration covering his body under the heat of the armor. He took up his sword and set himself to meet the attack of another warrior bearing down on them.

The man was fierce and savage. His unkempt auburn beard showed under his helm and looked like a bird's nest. A four-foot-long battle-ax whirled in his hand.

Matt parried the weapon with his sword and wondered if the battle-ax was an anachronism. Maid of Orleans wasn't supposed to be historically accurate; it was supposed to be fun, an alternate reality of the Hundred Years' War between France and England.

The Burgundian warrior drew back at once, whirling the battle-ax again. He thrust the haft between Matt's legs in an attempt to trip him.

Stumbling, Matt barely kept his balance on the treacherous slope.

"You fall, you treacherous pup," the Burgundian warned with a big grin, "and I'm going to smash you open like a turtle, and that's a fact."

From the corner of his eye, Matt watched Leif hammer his foe to the ground, then lost sight of him as he stepped around the attacking warrior. Lifting his left arm, Matt caught the ax blow on his shield, then cut his own sword beneath the man's elbow.

The chain mail shirt the man wore prevented the sword from breaking skin, but the blunt trauma definitely broke some ribs. The Burgundian's face whitened, and he let out a pained howl. But he drew the battle-ax back and stabbed at Matt's legs again.

Anticipating the attack, Matt shifted and stomped a booted foot on the ax haft. The wood splintered with a sharp snap, taking off the lower third of the haft.

The Burgundian roared in rage and swung his weapon again. Computer-trained reflexes moved Matt into motion. His sword met the battle-ax in midstroke and broke the attack. He stepped forward and slammed his shield into the Burgundian warrior, barely able to move the larger warrior's bulk. Then he disengaged his sword and chopped at the man's neck.

The helmet and all it contained went spinning away in a spray of blood. The Burgundian's headless body dropped to its knees, then flopped forward.

Matt tried not to look at it. The Net's graphics were too real, and Maid of Orleans wasn't really his kind of game. Shooters where vanquished enemies went up in a puff of ash or flared and disappeared in a laser burst were okay, but the realism of this game was just too much.

"Now that was disgusting." Leif joined him, pushing up his visor to reveal a dirt-smudged face.

"Yeah." Matt stepped over the corpse and higher onto the hill. He stared down at the warriors battling across the uneven terrain. "We're losing."

"Simply a matter of numbers," Leif said. "There's more of them than there are of us."

"She shouldn't have brought them here." Matt felt bad for all the men who'd really died in the battle the game was based on.

"She felt she was doing what she'd been called to do," Leif said.

"No one should be asked to do this." Matt's heart felt heavy. Warriors on horseback battled with men on foot. Most of the time the men on horseback won. The defeated were run down and battered by the armored horses, then dispatched by the mounted warriors. But sometimes the men on foot succeeded in pulling the horsemen down. It was all savagely brutal.

"Lighten up," Leif suggested. "It's just a game."

"Maybe I'm just not in the mood for it." Matt shaded his eyes against the setting sun. The clouds around it were dissolving into bloodred, as if the sunset was picking up the color from the battlefield.

"The game's going to be a hit," Leif promised.

Matt studied the crimson drops running down the ferrules of the sword he held. "Not with me."

Leif flashed him a grin. "Well, I hear Wover's got a new game coming out."

"Defeating monsters in art deco dungeons and grabbing power coins, now there's a game I could get into right now." Matt shook his head. "This is too real."

"You've seen worse in history class."

Thundering hooves came up behind them.

Matt spun while Leif slammed his visor down again.

A rider pulling a small herd of unmounted battle steeds behind him spurred his horse up the steep incline, weaving through the fallen bodies of Burgundian warriors and the defenders of Compiègne. A handful of wounded survivors huddled in the bush.

The rider thundered to the top of the hill, then pulled back on the reins to make his horse rear dramatically. The riderless horses he was leading shied a bit, then stood quietly. Andy flipped his visor up to reveal a broad grin. "Hey, guys. Want to upgrade your transportation?"

"Having a good time, Andy?" Leif asked.

"Out of the three games we visited before this one?" Andy asked. "No comparison. This game is a blast." He stood in the stirrups. "Chaos and carnage, it just doesn't get any better than this." He paused. "Except zombies. They could have used a few zombies."

"Except we're looking for a dragon," Matt said. "This game appears to be historically accurate."

"Historically based," Leif said. "The game options also let you win the Hundred Years' War if you play correctly. The battle we're in now is the one where Joan got captured and imprisoned till she was burned at the stake as a heretic."

Matt surveyed the battlefield again, his attention drawn by the hoarse shouts of desperate men. Ragged pennants fluttered in the lackluster breeze, marking groups of survivors taking refuge in each other's defense.

Suddenly a new phalanx of Burgundian horsemen exploded from the woods to the left. The attackers swept through the irregular line of defenders with lances, breaking through the perimeter easily. Foot soldiers charged after the horsemen, and archers picked out targets.

"Man," Andy declared, "I can't just sit here and watch this, and I'm not logging off until I know those people are safe."

"They aren't safe," Leif said. "Back in May of 1429, they were routed and driven back toward Compiègne. Only the guy in charge of the city lifted the drawbridge before they could make it inside. Joan was one of the warriors caught outside. The Burgundians slaughtered and captured the rest."

"We have to watch that?" Andy griped. His horse stomped its feet impatiently, rocking from side to side and snorting. "What fun is that?"

Leif grinned and slapped his visor down. He took the reins for one of the horses Andy was leading and stepped into the stirrup. "None. So let's see if we can do something about it. Coming, Matt?"

Matt watched the tide of armed horsemen lunging across the battlefield. He wanted to log off and continue the search for the dragon, but the game held him captive. He couldn't sit by and do nothing.

"We've been good about searching through the other games," Leif reasoned. "It won't hurt if we take a few minutes out and enjoy this scenario. We're still hours from Los Angeles. They'll let us know if there's an emergency."

"You're right." Matt took the reins for the other horse and mounted.

"If we go out with a win here," Leif said, "maybe coming up empty in the other demos won't feel so bad."

Silently Matt didn't see how that was going to happen. Even after only the few minutes he'd been fighting in the demo, his arms felt like lead from carrying the heavy shield and sword. He spurred his horse and galloped down the hill after his two friends.

The strained sounds of a horn blowing retreat cut through the hoarse shouts of men. Pockets of activity erupted into sudden motion. Desperate men, fueled by fear and anger, surged toward each other and fought against the Burgundians.

Matt remained low over the saddle pommel, the sword trailing at his right side. A Burgundian warrior engaged a wounded man on foot a short distance ahead. Despite his reluctance about playing the game, Matt guided his horse on an intercept course.

Trained for battle, the warhorse didn't hesitate about smashing into the Burgundian and his mount. The other animal staggered and tried to regain its footing. The warrior yanked on the reins and spun in the saddle. "Hey," he said to Matt, "no fair attacking from behind like that." The words didn't carry a Burgundian accent.

Knowing the warrior was being played by someone else who'd joined the demo online, Matt felt a little better. He lashed out with his foot and unseated the Burgundian, who yelled frantically as he thudded painfully to the ground.

"My thanks," the rescued warrior said, standing on failing legs. Blood streaked his face, cutting into the lines of fatigue.

Matt offered a hand. "Mount up."

The man wrapped his hand around Matt's wrists and smiled his thanks. Together, they swung him up behind the saddle. The big warhorse took the extra weight without problem.

Matt turned the horse and spurred it toward Compiègne. The town had a stone wall around it, sealing it from the battlefield. Archers lined the ramparts and arrows filled the air as the retreating forces and their Burgundian pursuers raced toward it.

The man wrapped an arm around Matt's stomach and held tight. Then he started cheering. "Joan! Joan!"

Heart beating rapidly in spite of the fact that he could log off the game at any time, Matt glanced to the right and saw a large contingent of warriors sweeping into line with them.

Joan of Arc, the Maid of Orleans, rode at the head of the group. She wore a man's armor and carried a man's sword, but her head was bared, leaving her open to attack but immediately recognizable to her own warriors. Short cropped brown hair swirled around a beautiful face.

She leaned out and seized a standard from a nearby rider. "Here!" she roared to the warriors who halted uncertainly around her. She plunged the staff into the ground, leaving the flag fluttering near her face. "We make a stand here to break those Burgundian traitors and allow those on foot a chance to make the town!"

Hoarse shouts, not all of them in support of the move, filled the immediate vicinity.

Andy suddenly appeared beside the warrior maid, his blade bared and a crooked grin on his face. He lifted his sword. "For Joan!" he shouted. "For France!"

Matt shook his head, amazed at Andy's capacity for gaming.

"For France!" Joan yelled.

"Stop," the warrior behind Matt urged. "We must help."

Matt drew in his reins, feeling the horse gasping for air. He turned, looking back at the horde of Burgundian warriors riding hard for them.

"You ready for this?"

Matt glanced at Leif, who'd ridden up beside him. "Yeah."

"You don't have to do this," Leif said. "After last night, I'd understand."

Matt shook his head, speaking over the rising thunder of the approaching horses' hooves. "You know what's weird?"

"What?"

"I zipped into Maj's room in holoform, knowing I couldn't be hurt, and it was frustrating standing there without being able to do anything. But if I'd been there for real, I don't know what I'd have done."

"Yeah, you do," Leif said. "You'd have done what you could. That's what you're made of, Matt. Everything in you is bred for the heat of the moment. You're at your best when the pressure is on, when things are clearest for you." He grinned laconically. "Most of us are. But don't second-guess yourself about what you'd have done or not done."

"I keep thinking about it."

"That's natural. Bet you think a lot about flight-sims you've had trouble mastering, too. You'll get past it."

Matt looked at Andy, who was engaged in animated conversation with Joan of Arc as the skirmish line was set up. The warrior maid organized her warriors, taking advantage of the high ground. Men who still had spears lined up in the forefront.

Matt watched the retreating warriors running desperately before their attackers. "We're not going to win this battle, are we?"

"Nope." Leif grinned. "At least, not if the game is historically accurate. Joan gets taken here by the Burgundian soldiers after she gets locked out of Compiègne by Guillaume de Flavy, the guy commanding the town. The Burgundians sell her to the English, who keep her imprisoned for the next fourteen months, then burn her at the stake for being a heretic. But how often do you get the chance to fight alongside Joan of Arc?"

Matt took in a deep breath, then pushed it out.

"Andy's hooked on playing the hero," Leif said as they watched their friend riding up and down the skirmish line encouraging the troops. "Maybe it's because his dad never made it out of South Africa, and maybe it's because he got to spend that time in veeyar with that sim of his dad fighting in that war. And maybe guys like him are just born that way."

"So what is it for you?"

Leif laughed. "Me? I'm just here for a good time." The line of Burgundian warriors was less than a hundred yards away. The first of the warriors on foot reached the skirmish line, hurrying through it and heading for the town behind them.

The man behind Matt slid off the horse and unlimbered his crossbow, fitting a short, ugly quarrel into the groove.

"Attention!" Joan of Arc's voice rang out clearly across the battlefield. She lifted her sword, then dropped it to point forward. "Charge!" She rode her horse forward, leading the mounted spearmen.

Andy rode at her side, a spear held level.

Shedding his reluctance, Matt spurred his horse forward and readied himself to meet the attack. He hacked aside the spear that thrust at his chest, then managed a backhanded blow that caught his adversary in the head. Matt didn't think he'd injured the man, but he was successful in unseating him.

Dust clouded around him, obscuring the view. Matt pulled his horse around, gently enough that he didn't tear the animal's mouth. The horse trembled as its muscles bunched and it sought footing as clods tore free under its iron-shod hooves.

Matt breathed in deeply, smelling the stench of sweating horses and men, wet leather, and the dry dust that covered the battlefield. He lifted his sword and charged again.

9

By the time Maj reached the Eisenhower booth, the crowd was already a dozen deep.

Without fanfare, a young man in a crisp white suit, white turtleneck instead of a shirt and tie, stepped up onto the nearest table and faced the crowd. Immediately the holos around the Eisenhower booth altered, carrying the image of the young man.

He was clean-shaven and athletic looking, no more than twenty or twenty-one. His black hair was worn long enough to hold the hint of curls. A little-boy smile turned his lips, and he looked at the crowd as if amazed. "I didn't expect this." His amplified voice filled the nearby convention area. He looked up at the hidden speakers. "Or that."

The crowd laughed.

The young man gazed out at them, his sea-green eyes filled with obvious wonderment. "In fact, I didn't expect any of this." He cleared his throat. "My name is Peter Griffen, and I want to introduce you to my game."

Maj studied Peter, trying to imagine him on the back of a dragon. It wasn't hard at all.

• • •

Time passed in a whirling maelstrom of cleaving blades, hoarse shouts of pain, and thudding horses' hooves. Matt didn't know how much time actually passed, but it couldn't have been more than a handful of minutes. He felt winded, bone-tired, but the uploaded reflexes kept him in the game.

The Burgundian line broke, shattered into pockets.

Joan of Arc rode to the top of a nearby hill. "Sound the retreat," she ordered in a loud voice. The man at her side unlimbered a horn and blew the notes.

Immediately the defenders broke from the conflict, riding their flagging mounts toward the town.

Matt took a moment to watch, seeing the two groups disengage as the Burgundian commander tried to get control over his men. Then he put spurs to his horse and rode after the retreating warriors. Dust coated his lips and the inside of his mouth, making it hard to swallow. His teeth ground grit and his lungs burned.

The defenders wound through the trees and scrub brush, staying with the dirt road that led to Compiègne. The incline grew steeper as they neared the town.

Glancing over his shoulder, Matt saw that the Burgundians had recovered more quickly than he'd thought they would. Dozens of dead and wounded from both sides lay under dust clouds in their wake. The drawbridge was set into the high town wall. Even as he watched, another wave of arrows sped from the wall, looking like long, skinny birds with folded wings.

An instant later the arrows descended in a deadly rain. They rattled through the trees and plunged into the ground. Some of them hit the defenders in full retreat, pitching them from their horses.

Matt raised his shield over his head and heard two distinct impacts. He felt the horse stretch out its stride as they neared the town. Then, only precious seconds from the gate, the drawbridge started up. A sinking feeling filled Matt as he watched the heavy, ironbound edifice ratchet up in small jerks.

Howls of disbelief tore from the throats of the defenders, who suddenly realized they were being abandoned to their fate. Metal rang on metal as the armor pieces beat against each other.

Joan rode in the lead, flanked by Andy.

Then Leif stood up in his stirrups, bending his legs so he

could steady himself. He lifted a crossbow to his shoulder, paused, then fired.

The quarrel sped from the weapon and jammed into the chain winching the drawbridge up. Men rushed from the fortification and started trying to free the lodged arrow. Before they could do it, the defenders were upon them. They pulled the drawbridge back down, forcing the archers on the ramparts to defend their retreat.

The Burgundians withered under the concentrated arrow fire, but some of them rode forward. Warriors fought brief battles at the back of the group, then the drawbridge dropped to the ground. Joan of Arc led her troops inside the garrison, turning quickly and taking command of the manual effort to raise the drawbridge.

In seconds the Burgundians were locked outside Compiègne, kept outside arrow range. Matt dismounted his horse and followed Joan, Andy, and Leif up the narrow stone stairs to the ramparts.

"We did it!" Andy crowed. He shook a gauntleted fist at the Burgundians. A few arrows thudded against the stone wall beneath the ramparts where they stood in reply. "I love this game!" Impulsively he reached out to Joan and hugged her tight, then kissed her on the cheek.

"You know," Joan said, pushing her way out of Andy's embrace, "the real Joan of Arc would probably have had your head for that little display."

Andy stood back in shock.

Matt couldn't help himself; he laughed out loud. *Joan's not a character. She's another person playing online.*

Instead of being mad, though, Joan grinned. Then she said, "Hi, Leif."

"Hey, Kris," Leif greeted. "Looks like the game's really shaping up."

Joan blew a loose strand of hair from her face. "I think so. Another month or two of development and we should have it all. By that time your dad is going to know he made a good investment for himself and his clients."

Leif shook his head. "Dad already knew that or he wouldn't have gotten involved."

"I couldn't have done it without him." Kris looked around

and pointed at Andy, who was red-faced with embarrassment. "Do you know him?"

"Yeah. Andy Moore, this is Kris Emerson. She's the lead designer of Maid of Orleans."

"You could have told me," Andy grumbled. He focused on Kris. "Look, I'm sorry—"

"Don't be," Kris said. "I haven't been so flattered in years."

"And this is Matt Hunter," Leif said.

In years? Matt thought. That meant the Joan of Arc look was a proxy. Around him, the survivors settled down to the business of tending the wounded and getting the defense better organized.

Kris led the way around the ramparts. "So what brings you here? Checking on your father's investment?"

"No," Leif responded. "We're on our way to the gaming convention and thought we'd scope out a few of the demos available online."

"I'm glad you dropped in," Kris said. "If you hadn't, I'd have been spending the next few hours in chains, hoping someone had enough gumption to mount a rescue attempt. Maid of Orleans is based on the historical data of the period, but the story flows in a lot of different branches for the clever player. That was a nice shot with the crossbow, by the way. Not many people are going to figure that one out without being tipped."

Leif shrugged. "Seemed like the thing to do at the time. When I actually made the shot, I knew I was on to something."

"The game's set up that way," Kris said. "If a player attempts that shot, they'll make it ninety percent of the time." She halted and looked out over the battlefield. "So what were you looking for when you dropped in?"

"A dragon," Leif answered.

Kris shook her head. "You won't find any dragons here."

"I thought maybe you'd included one in a total fantasy mode for the game."

"No. I made the decision to do this game real. Except for the actual flow of events. There's a lot of gameplay involved there."

"Do you know anyone whose game has a dragon in it?" Matt asked.

"You haven't cruised through many demos yet, have you?" Kris asked. "Dragons are big in the games. You can hunt them, fight them, ride them, and—in some games—talk to them or even be them."

That isn't very hopeful. Matt considered the online brochure they'd gone through. At least four hundred games were coming out and on display at the convention. Some of them they'd been able to rule out immediately due to familiarity with the gaming product.

"I don't mean to be rude," Kris said, "but I've got to get back to the game. The people playing this demo are going to expect me to put on a show for a while. If I'd gotten captured, I could have relaxed in a Burgundian prison. Now I'm going to have to dip into my bag of tricks and stir up some more intrigue."

"Sorry," Leif said.

"Don't worry about it. I spent a lot of time imprisoned during the testing phase of the game. This will be stressful, but it'll be fun."

"Will you do me a favor?" Leif asked.

"If I can."

Leif opened his hand and swirling green lights coalesced into a coin. "This icon has my e-mail address. If you hear of any games that are really big on dragons, can you drop me a note?"

"I'd be happy to." Kris took the coin, then turned and marched away, bellowing orders to her troops while full dark settled over the town, demanding to see Guillaume de Flavy.

Andy fidgeted and paced restlessly. "Let's blaze. I'm done here."

Matt grinned at his friend's discomfort, but his mind stayed busy with how they were going to find the dragon and the dragonrider.

The gaming convention menu appeared ahead of Matt when he opened his eyes. The fatigue from the jaunt through Maid of Orleans quickly left him. Icons representing various games and gaming corporations spun against a backdrop of star-lit space.

Andy and Leif stood on the electric-blue sheet of crystal that oriented up from down. Andy swept the rows of icons with his eager gaze. "As I recall, it's my turn to choose."

Staring at all the selections, Matt felt totally lost.

"You look frustrated," Leif observed.

"I'm getting that way," Matt admitted. "There's no way we're going to be able to sample every game."

"We're not sampling every game," Leif said.

"Right," Andy added. "Only the cool ones. And I've got one here called Goblin King. It promises a fantasy setting and lots of combat action."

"We need a way of narrowing down the field," Matt said. "But I'm fresh out of ideas."

"Until you get one," Leif pointed out, "I'd rather stay busy. I don't think sitting and worrying—even in first class—is going to be beneficial."

Matt let out a long breath. "No. I just wish I knew for sure what Maj and I entered was a game."

Leif shook his head. "From the way you describe the environment, it couldn't be anything else."

"I know. But why did we get caught in the bleed-over interface?"

"I don't have an answer for you, buddy. I think we'll know that when we find the game we're looking for."

"If those guys in the black suits haven't found it first."

"That's a lot of negative energy to carry around." Leif smiled. "Remember, we're the guys who just saved Joan of Arc from the Burgundians."

"I'll try to keep that in mind."

"While you guys are flapping your lips," Andy pointed out, "we're burning daylight. Let's hit it." He touched a whirling red icon in the shape of a gargoyle, and red sparks spread over him, whirling him away in a sudden tornado.

Leif and Matt touched the icon and followed him.

Bitter cold soaked into Matt's body in the next moment. He blinked his eyes open and found his head encased in a round clear bubble. The air inside the helmet tasted stale.

He was also in orbit in a space suit around a slow-turning planet. He gazed up at the world, knowing that way was actually down. The planet was predominantly the blue-green of oceans with only sporadic splotches of red-brown earth. Scanning the curvature of the planet, he spotted three satellites, much closer than he would have figured possible with the gravity well that existed. Two of them were true green while the third was purple.

"Rhidher!"

Matt experienced a sharp, stabbing pain between his temples, then realized the voice came from inside his head. He twisted and spotted a huge shape bearing down on him. When he saw the bat wings that flared out on either side of the gigantic creature, he thought for a moment that they'd found the great dragon.

But the shape wasn't long and sleek like that of the dragon. Despite its enormous size, the creature's body was squat and man-shaped, possessing two arms and two legs. Blue-silver armor covered it, showing great hinged joints. Even the wings looked too stunted for its size.

"Rhidher! Sit!"

The great creature came to a stop in front of Matt with a flurry of bat wings despite the fact there was no atmosphere in space. The thing dwarfed him. A seat, built along the lines of a cockpit console, was strapped across the thick, broad neck. Long, tubular weapons occupied areas on either side of the seat.

"Rhidher!" The great beast looked at Matt imploringly with manhole-sized brown eyes that held glints of cyberwear. "You must sit! Enemy come!"

The voice inside Matt's head didn't hurt as much as it had. He reached out and caught the edge of the seat, pulling himself in. Belts automatically stretched across his chest and shoulders, locking him down.

Andy's face blurred into focus on the screen at the front of the console. "Welcome, Rhidher Matt." Like Matt, he wore the bubble helmet and bulky space suit.

"These aren't the dragons we're looking for," Matt said.

"We'll look around for a minute."

Before Matt could reply, a triangular-shaped aircraft attacked. Pink lasers strafed the darkness. The sizzle was even audible. The gargoyle beast he rode dodged automatically.

"Oh, yeah," Andy said. "Meet the enemy."

Maj peered up at Peter Griffen as the game designer held court on the table he'd climbed up on. In spite of the fact that he had a reputation for shying away from publicity, Peter seemed at home in front of the convention crowd.

HoloNet reporters stood in the forefront of the crowd with their equipment trained on him. "Why was there so much secrecy involved in this game?" one of them asked. Maj didn't know the man's name, but she'd seen him reporting on the upcoming gaming convention over the last few days.

Peter smiled shyly. "To get you to ask questions like that."

The crowd laughed.

Well, he has a sense of humor, Maj thought.

"Seriously," Peter said. "There were a lot of reasons not to talk about the game until now. How many times have we heard about a game's release date pushing out a month or three? Or even a year?"

The response from the crowd was a grudging acknowledgment of the industry's primary pitfall. Even with all the technology available on the Net, designers fell behind on delivery dates.

"I look around today," Peter went on, "and I can name six different games I can point to from here that were supposed to release six months and more ago."

"If you've found a way to fix that," one of the reporters commented, "you're going to make a mint."

Peter shook his head. "I haven't fixed that for anybody but me." He paced on the table, showing nervous energy instead of a planned attack to get more attention. "I've been in this business for four years. Luckily, I've gotten the chance to work on a number of well-received games."

"It wasn't luck," someone in the crowd said. "The guy has a real gift for picking the right property."

"I've written code, game designs, worked with art, done finished as well as concept treatments, written dialogue, and everything else it takes to make a really good game," Peter said.

Maj remembered reading that from the text files available over the Net. Peter Griffen had been a true Renaissance man in the gaming industry. There hadn't been any aspect of computer-based gaming that he hadn't touched.

Some of the articles Maj had read that were taken from top game review magazines had lamented at the loss of the crown prince of the game scene. But that had been then, eighteen months ago, right after the launch of the Promethean Directive, a game based on politics and economics that had rocketed up the sales figures in the gaming industry.

"Eighteen months ago," Peter went on, "I quit my position with my last software developer. I had an idea for a world, and for gameplay that would be so cutting edge that no man, woman, or child could resist picking it up. Ladies and gentle-men, I give you Realms of the Bright Waters." He waved his hand and the holoprojectors behind him filled with dazzling color that took the crowd's breath away.

10

"How are you doing, Montoya?"

Facing the security guard, Gaspar accessed a file on the man. The flatfilm pictures flashed by in the corner of his virtual vision, flipping through images. He found the one he was looking for. Leon Tatum was a day guard. According to the records Heavener's people had turned up, Montoya—the personality proxy Gaspar currently wore—and Tatum worked together only occasionally.

"Fine, Tatum," Gaspar replied. "Sleepy, I guess."

Tatum nodded. "You worked all the excitement last night?"

"Yeah. What's going on out there?"

Tatum shrugged. "Some whiz kid unveiling the goods. Getting quite a draw." He hooked a thumb over his shoulder. "You can get a free cuppa caffeine back there. Help you stay awake."

"I think I'll go see what's going on."

"Whiz-kid stuff," Tatum said. "Me, I'll take holo and a good ball game any day."

Gaspar walked to the outer fringe of the crowd and peered up at Griffen. Jealousy stirred restlessly within him, taking first place over the fear. Peter Griffen had it all—talent, skill, and the breaks to help him make the most of them, and Gaspar had nothing. For just a moment it felt good that he was helping take it away from Griffen.

Leaving his holo active, Gaspar accessed the deeper programs inside the virtual version of the hotel. Although the convention center stayed in place around him, Gaspar seemed to step outside himself, cloning his presence as he slipped into the security code protecting the veeyar that had been set up to run the Eisenhower Productions booth.

A freestanding doorway formed in front of Gaspar. He put his hand on the door and pressed. The metal felt cool to the touch. It also felt impenetrable.

Gaspar rubbed the door slowly, then more vigorously, using crack programs he'd developed, found, and traded for. Gradually the door's surface peeled away, leaving only the cycling orbit of atoms standing in his way. He kicked in another part of the crack program and turned his second virtual self into two-dee.

Moving carefully, he flowed through the orbiting atoms, sliding inside the veeyar controlling Griffen's presentation.

"The Realm of Bright Waters is bigger than anything out there," Peter Griffen said. "It's almost half again as large as Sarxos."

Maj watched the images on the holo, as mesmerized by the sheer beauty of the world as the rest of the audience. *This has to be the same place.*

"It's gonna *replace* Sarxos, dude!" someone shouted from the audience.

The viewpoint suddenly climbed, rising above the thickly bunched trees. For the first time the crowd saw how tall the trees were. Near the canopy, the branches and leaves thinned out enough that diffused green sunlight punched occasional holes through. Maj spotted the red sun above, and she didn't doubt that the blue one would be long in coming.

"Look!" someone shouted.

There, just for a wisp of a second, was a glimpse of a civilization built in the treetops. Materials stripped from the trees created fantastically shaped huts suspended in the branches of the huge trees. Narrow bridges connected them, some of them built with steps that led up or down. Small humanoid figures dressed in leaves and bark, colors added from fruits or vegetables, clambered through the bridges and branches. They drew back bows, and arrows whizzed too close for comfort, reaching out into the audience using the holoprojector set up in the room.

"Elves!" someone cried.

"The world," Peter went on, "is filled with dozens of races, all of them equipped with their own history, their own economic and environmental needs. There are physical talents, skills, and magic you can learn. You can be a warrior, a bard, a historian, or a mage. And all of those races and abilities are as evenly weighted as I can make them."

The viewpoint sailed above the trees, cutting through the green sky. The red and the blue suns shined. A diamond-bright river wound through the heart of the forest.

"The water is the key to everything in the realm," Peter said. "So many people's lives depend on the rivers, streams, and oceans that are in this world. Water is a thing of mysticism and power."

The viewpoint scanned down to a fishing village, then to an old man dressed in animal skins sitting cross-legged on the bank of the river. A dozen small children sat around him, their faces obviously enraptured. The old man stuck his hand into the water and drew it back. A shiny tendril of river water followed the hand out, twisting inquisitively. Then the tendril rolled into a ball that floated between the old man's hands. Images formed in the watery depths.

"You can explore and interact with small villages," Peter went on, "or you can journey to vast civilized areas."

The viewpoint hurtled across the sky again, then focused on a towering city carved from the side of a mountain. Roads twisted and ran through the buildings. Horsemen rode down the thoroughfares amid strangely shaped buggies pulled by large, wingless birds and huge lizards.

"You'll be called on to help kings," Peter said, "or you can aid those not so fortunate."

The viewpoint locked on a ragged beggar seated in the mouth of an alley filled with slithering shadows and hungry red eyes.

"You can live a totally alien experience." Peter smiled. "At least, as alien as I've been able to make it."

Images of creatures seemingly made of mud slithered through dank riverbanks under the water. Long millipedes the color of rainbows suddenly attacked the mud creatures, coring through them or tearing them to bits. Other mud creatures battled the millipedes, using iridescent pieces of shell that shot out white-hot beams.

"You can protect, or you can pillage," Peter said.

The sea blurred by, then a wooden submarine came into focus. It floated at the top of the waterline, obviously stalking the merchant ship racing the wind ahead. Suddenly a hatch opened, revealing a being with black chitinous hide. Its eyes sat on stalks, and its face was totally inhuman.

Peter paced, smiling proudly, his own eyes drawn to the holos. "You can build—"

Men and women struggled in an arctic wilderness, using hatchets, hammers, and chisels to punch holes into mountains of ice. Others fed campfires and turned spits of meat, all of them struggling to stay warm and alive. Suddenly the ice beneath them split and a huge whalelike creature surged high into the air.

"—or you can search abandoned cities."

Torch-lit shadows shifted across the interior of a collapsed building. The dulled sheen of beaten gold drew the eye, holding the promise of treasures yet to come.

Abruptly the holo images faded, leaving a ghost in the air for a moment. Then it was gone, too. And Maj knew there wasn't a person in the room who wasn't wanting to see more.

"It's a whole world," Peter promised. "A place of huge potential for gamers who love the wonderment of exploration, the thrill of battle, and detailed civilization. It's a game that I created, and one that I still enjoy adventuring in."

Conversation broke into dozens of pockets as the audience started talking excitedly.

"When is the game going on sale?" one of the reporters asked.

Peter waved to the booth. "Sign-up packages will be available as soon as we open the doors."

"What about sales over the Net?"

"Those will be available, too."

Lines started to form at the two doors Maj could see. She couldn't blame them. The view she'd gotten of the world the night before had only been the tip of the iceberg.

"You play this game?" the reporter asked.

Peter grinned bashfully. "Every day. I don't know if I'm admitting to gluttony or pride here, but anything that feels this good has got to be some kind of sin."

Another wave of laughter went through the crowd.

"When do we get a chance to play?" a girl in the front row asked.

"Actually, Eisenhower Productions was a little reluctant about letting anyone online until it was completely finished," Peter said.

"Why?" Dunn asked sarcastically. "Do they think it may impact the sales potential by showing that the world interaction isn't quite as good as you make it sound?"

"Actually," Peter said, "no. Even at this point players can join up on the game and run through a small adventure."

"Good," Dunn said. "Then maybe we can find out exactly how *limited* this game is before anyone starts paying for it."

Peter shook his head and looked at the reporter. "It's too late for that. Pre-orders for Realm of the Bright Water have already set new records."

The crowd cheered, then started chanting, demanding access to the game.

Peter returned to the middle of the stage. "What we're going to do now is give you a slight peek into this world."

The small group of businessmen who'd walked in with Peter started forward. Maj tried to read their expressions, but all she saw was concern, and no reason at all for it to be there. *What's going on?*

Peter stretched his right hand high into the air. Silver glitter splashed all around him, so thick it became a mist. Steel hardened in his fist, becoming a broadsword that splintered the light. In the next instant, silver armor covered him from head to toe.

It is *him!* Maj thought. As politely as she could, she started pushing her way through the crowd.

"Shut him down!"

Coiled up deep in Peter Griffen's veeyar, Gaspar barely heard Heavener's cold voice. He gazed around the veeyar, trying to orient himself. Griffen's private veeyar was huge, the biggest that Gaspar had ever been in. Even this one was larger than most personal systems.

"I'm working on it," Gaspar replied, taking long strides down the corridor. The veeyar was built like a huge warehouse, filled with long glass tubes wrapped by red and yellow electricity.

Gaspar accessed his search utility menu and made his selections. He opened his left hand and stabbed two fingers of his right hand into his palm. He pulled his fingers back out, trailing three crimson wires out of his arm that were yards long. He whipped the wires forward, and they assumed a life of their own.

Animated, oozing like they were made of oil, the wires slid through the warehouse, seeking out the databases Gaspar had programmed them to look for. He ran after them to keep up.

The three wires stabbed into different tubes. The connections flared as they were made. He grabbed the three wires and stabbed them into his left eye, linking up with the connections.

Images exploded into his mind. Bits of coding drifted in and out of his vision as scenes from the convention center overlapped vidclips from the Realm of the Bright Waters. The pain was incredible, and the difficulty in sorting out the coding he needed to allow him to shut the game down was almost impossible.

He built datastrings in his mind, kicking them into the stream that flowed through his vision. Tiny golden bugs formed on the datastrings, quickly chewing through the additions and striving to protect the primary coding. They were part of the antivirus program Griffen had installed on his system. Gaspar hadn't quite figured out how to get rid of the antivirus, but gaps appeared in the coding.

In the convention center he watched as Peter Griffen's armor encased him. Gaspar concentrated on writing code, trying to increase the size of the gaps and trigger a system failure.

"Hey, watch it!"

Maj planted an elbow in the guy's back ahead of her and used his movement to turn around at her to glide by him. She was still six people from reaching the table where Peter Griffen was. The holos remained fixed on the fantasy landscape, looking down on the forest from high above.

"Peter!" she called. "I need to talk to you!"

But there was no way Peter could hear her over the excited roar of the crowd. The guy she'd elbowed turned around angrily. "Come back here and try that again."

Maj kept moving, feeling equally torn between guilt over her aggressive behavior and the need to talk to Peter. The need exceeded the guilt and she kept moving, using her speed and her agility to navigate the crowd.

She was only two people deep from the tables when Peter raised his sword again and shouted, "Sahfrell!"

Blue lightning flicked down from the ceiling and exploded against the sword. Thunder filled the convention center, and several people in the crowd cowered back, including the men in business suits.

"Oh, man, this is totally cool!"

"I gotta get that game!"

Taking advantage of the surge back from the table, Maj broke through the crowd, sprinting to her goal. She was dimly aware of Nate at her heels.

Another thunderflash crashed through the convention center. This time the lights dimmed, dimmed again, then went out. Security alarms crashed through the darkness as backup lights flared to life.

The immense plum-colored dragon appeared against the ceiling of the convention center. The warm butter color of its stomach picked up the gleam of the security lights, and bright spots shone on the hoarfrost on its face.

More electronic-based detonations erupted from the other booths. The holos rippled, then comets crossed the areas contained within them.

Maj paused, stunned. She didn't know what had happened, but she felt certain it wasn't good.

Matt rode the flying goblin as it winged through space. The triangular ships pursued him, seemingly inexhaustible. He guided the goblin hard right, then brought the two cannon online. Triggering a dual attack, he watched the lead ship disintegrate, the pieces somehow flaming in airless space.

Goblin King definitely isn't going to win any prizes for technical accuracy, Matt told himself, *but it's going to make a lot of shooters happy.*

He still hadn't caught sight of Leif or Andy, but they'd maintained radio contact. His radar screen registered another approaching object. He jockeyed the goblin around.

"Rhidher!" the goblin cried.

Matt looked back toward the right, looking for the attacking vehicle. Instead of another triangular ship blazing in at him, he saw an event horizon dawn. A tidal wave of azure energy slammed into Matt.

When he opened his eyes again, he was standing in an old Roman chariot. The horse pulled the chariot at a fast canter, and the rough ride jarred Matt from his heels to his toes. He glanced down at the Roman armor and leather kilt he wore. A short sword hung in a sheath at his side.

Then an arrow slammed against the heavy bronze breastplate he wore. He glanced up and stared out at the battlefield before him.

Two chariot lines sped at each other from opposite ends of a desert. The two wheels of the chariot spun through the loose sand. A hot breeze whipped across the plain, lifting small spinning dust devils from the sand behind the chariots.

I got knocked from one demo game to another, Matt thought. It was the only possible answer even though he had no idea how. Even if the demo games were coming from the same programming, the programming was supposed to be distinct enough that crossovers like this didn't happen. But what had happened to Maj and him last night hadn't been supposed to happen, either.

He looked around, listening to the whir of the wheels along the greased axles as the horse closed the distance to the attacking line. He drew his short sword and got ready to try to survive the first onslaught.

Less than fifty feet away another chariot driver drove at him, a short throwing spear held in one hand. Matt picked up the heavy rectangular shield from the chariot moorings and slipped it over his arm. He held the reins loosely in his hand because the horse knew what it was supposed to do. He braced himself for the coming impact.

Without warning, a bloodcurdling scream rent the sky overhead.

Matt looked up, spotting the familiar plum-colored dragon almost filling the sky directly above the battle. The huge creature flapped its bat wings, moving swiftly. The massive jaws gaped and a fireball sizzled from the dragon's throat. There was just enough time for Matt to realize the creature was riderless, then the fireball smashed into the sandy plains between the two attacking groups.

The fireball hammered out a crater in the sand, fusing parts of the immediate area to glass. Heat washed over Matt and made him believe he was about to get parboiled in his bronze armor.

The horse pulling his chariot reared in fear, struggling to get away from the clumps of liquid fire that splattered all the nearby horses, chariots, and warriors. Matt tried to retain his footing, but the chariot overturned, spilling him directly into the path of the oncoming warrior and vehicle. The other chariot driver steered straight for him, intending to run him down with the horse and cut him in two with the bronze-plated chariot wheels.

Dozens of dragon images filled the holes above the other game booths. Maj stared at the booths without comprehending as she walked to the table where Peter Griffen stood.

"No."

Maj looked up, uncertain if Peter had actually spoken aloud or if it had been someone else. Strong arms seized her from behind unexpectedly.

"Hotel security," a stern male voice warned her. "Back away from the table. You can look, but you can't touch."

The crowd reacted to the dragon's presence by screaming out in fear and yelling out encouragement. Some of them still dived for cover.

Above, the dragon yawned suddenly and spat a fireball at the Eisenhower Productions booth. Heat—created by the holoprojectors—slammed into the nearest convention attendees, setting off a fresh wave of reactions that still appeared to be equally divided between shrill fear and enthusiastic support.

The person holding Maj took a step back, loosening the grip he had on her.

Maj bumped back against him, throwing him even further off-balance. The come-along grip the man had managed was effective, but only if he maintained it. She slid her wrists free of his hand and stepped forward.

"No."

This time she was certain Peter said that because she watched him. "Peter."

Horror stained the handsome face behind the helmet's visor.

The holographic flames burned along the Eisenhower Productions booth and created three-foot tall letters that read: GRIF-FEN GAMES! ONLINE AND ON TARGET.

"Peter!" Maj called, spotting the security guard moving in behind her again.

Peter glanced down at her. For the first time she realized how tired he looked. His eyes were bloodshot and held a haunted look. All the confidence he'd exuded before in facing down hostile reporters seemed eroded.

"Do you remember me?" Maj asked desperately, knowing the security guard was going to pull her back in just a moment. Another man she figured was a security team member approached from the left. "I was in the jet last night."

Peter held up the sword for attention. "No," he told the security men. "Leave her alone. I want to talk to her."

Above them the dragon circled through the air restlessly. The throb of the powerfully muscled bat wings rolled throughout the darkened convention center. The enthusiastic shouts intermingled with flagrant name-calling as well. Evidently there were more than a few people who didn't appreciate Peter's suspected grandstanding.

The two security men backed away reluctantly, suddenly busy with the other screaming fans who chose that opportunity to rush the Eisenhower Productions booth. Automatically Peter reached a gauntleted hand down for Maj.

Maj reached for the hand, but her fingertips plunged right through it with a cold sensation.

"I'm sorry," Peter apologized. "I forgot."

"It's okay. I just wanted to talk to you."

"I wanted to talk to you, too." Peter gazed in wonder at all the confusion sweeping through the convention center. "This wasn't supposed to happen."

"What?" Maj asked.

Before he could answer, a cold blue light suddenly dawned in the center of his stomach. It ate through his holo image like a flame charring through paper. In the next instant Peter was gone as if he'd never existed.

■■

Maj stared at the space where Peter Griffen had been standing, wondering if his disappearance had been planned, or if this was another circumstance that had been completely out of his control.

She whirled to face the middle-aged man standing behind her. "Are you the security guard who grabbed me?"

The man held his open hands up. "I was just doing my job."

"I know," Maj said. "But I think you need to find Peter Griffen."

"How?" the man asked. "As far as I know, he wasn't even here."

"Then I suggest you start asking people," Maj replied. "Wherever he is, I think he's in trouble."

The dragon continued flying above them, squalling out its impatience as if it, too, realized its master was missing.

Maj reached into her jeans pocket and took out her foilpack. She reconfigured it into a vidphone and punched in Catie's number. An automated message answered, offering to take a message. *She's probably still in a game,* Maj realized. She punched in Megan's number next.

"Hello," Megan answered.

"Tell me you saw what happened."

"I saw," Megan replied. "I just don't know what to make of it."

Maj pushed her way through the crowd, not even bothering with being polite. Something way too weird was going on, and the clock was ticking. "I don't think he did it on purpose."

Flashlights joined the security lights in opening holes in the darkness.

"If it was just for effect, it seems to have had the desired effect."

"Peter wasn't planning this." Maj put her free hand in front of her, testing the people in the crowd to find out how many were real and how many were holos. When she found someone who was holo, she pushed on through him or her.

"What makes you so sure?" Megan asked.

"I talked to him right before he disappeared. He was as confused by this as everyone else was."

"I don't think everyone was confused," Megan observed. "Some of these people think this was the greatest stunt ever."

A crowd gathered at the nearby gate leading into the Eisenhower Productions booth. They pounded on the gate and demanded entrance.

"Trust me," Maj said. "Get hold of the others. Especially Mark. Maybe he can access some of the security vid systems and find Peter."

"He was online in holo," Megan reminded. "He could have been anywhere."

"I've got a feeling he's here," Maj replied.

"If he is, we'll find him."

Maj folded the foilpack and held it in her hand. She looked down at the guy sitting at the Eisenhower table. "Where's Peter Griffen?"

The guy nervously shook his head. "I don't know. I thought he was here till he disappeared like that."

Maj glanced at the crowd pounding on the booth's gate, feeling the pressure of seconds ticking by. "Can you open those doors?"

"Not me. But maybe one of those guys can." He pointed at a group of men in business suits. "They're part of Eisenhower Productions."

Maj walked toward the men, opened the foilpack, and pressed one of the speed-dial numbers she'd programmed in last night.

"Los Angeles Police Department," the automated emergency voice answered. The voice was male, crisp, and efficient. The LAPD symbol filled the foilpack's small vidscreen.

"I need to speak with Detective John Holmes," Maj said. "He's currently on assignment at the Bessel Mid-Town Hotel. This is an emergency. My name is Madeline Green. Detective Holmes will know me."

"Thank you," the automated voice said. "I'll connect you momentarily."

Maj stepped in front of the men in business suits, stopping almost ten feet away because other men who were obviously bodyguards stepped forward.

"Please stay back, miss," a granite-jawed man said with thin politeness.

"In case you hadn't noticed," Maj told them, "you're about to have a full-scale riot on your hands. If you don't produce Peter or open those gates, you're going to get covered in some majorly bad press."

"The girl's right," one of the men said to a guy in round-lensed glasses and a thin mustache. "This wasn't supposed to happen."

Maj seized on that bit of information immediately. *What wasn't supposed to happen?*

"Peter knew better than this," the man with glasses said. "He didn't stick to the game plan."

"It's too late to worry about that now," the other man replied.

The man with glasses looked up at the big security guard next to him. "I want men inside the booth. I don't want anything dismantled."

"Yes, sir." The man spoke into a wristcom, too low for Maj to overhear. She studied their faces, hoping she would be able to identify the men later if she had to.

An excited shout rang out behind her. She turned and watched as the gates to the Eisenhower Productions booth opened and the crowd swarmed in. She hurried to join the crowd flowing into the huge booth. She glanced up at the dragon twisting restlessly above the convention center, wishing it could somehow lead her to its master. But the dragon looked as lost as she felt.

• • •

The wires in Gaspar Latke's eye started to burn horribly. He dropped to his knees in Griffen's veeyar, forcing himself not to pull the wires free. He screamed with pain, knowing Heavener was monitoring every sound he made. But he couldn't help himself.

The antivirus program stepped up the pace, filling the data-streams with bugs that worked furiously to repair the damage he was doing. Overlapping images from the convention center filled his vision, letting him know the whole area had gone ballistic.

"The program is bleeding over," Heavener complained in the distance.

"I can't stop it," Gaspar gritted out.

"Then stop what you can," Heavener advised. "I've got a team who will pick Griffen up."

Unable to control himself, Gaspar curled a fist around the three crimson wires shoved deep into his eye socket. But he didn't yank them out. Failing Heavener wasn't an option.

He cried out in pain again, but he held on to the wires and curled up into a fetal ball, trying to keep his mind clear.

Catie Murray started at the blue-white marble cistern in the center of the reception area. It was elegant, beautifully made. The water arced from a pot carried by a large brown bear reaching for a beehive hanging from a tree branch high overhead. In the physical world, and at the time of King Arthur and Camelot, tapping the artesian well in such a fashion would have been the work of a master. But in the Legend of the Lake game demo, it was gracefully rendered.

She stuck her fingers into the water, finding it cool to the touch. Impulsively she brought her fingers to her lips. The water was ambrosia, almost honey-sweet.

"They say," a pleasantly cultured voice said from behind her, "you're never supposed to drink the water from faery lands because you'll be forever trapped there."

Embarrassed, Catie turned to face the speaker.

Like the artesian well, he was beautiful, a blond-haired angel dressed in polished silver armor. A broadsword with a prominent crosspiece hung from his hip. He carried his helm in on arm, his gauntlets in one hand. His china blue eyes regarded her with interest.

"Lady," he said softly, "my humble apologies for startling you."

"That's quite all right." Catie found herself tumbling easily into the flowery speech patterns of the game. "I didn't mean to offend. There were no signs."

The man smiled. "As if that many people in these times could read."

"They say King Arthur expects much from his knights."

"From his knights, yes, but there are many common people here this day, too."

Catie followed the knight's gaze around the large room. A winding staircase made of the same darkly veined brown stone as the castle looked like a wide river moving sedately up to the second floor.

A chandelier covered over with a thousand or more burning tapers hung from the center of the ceiling above, augmenting the natural light that came in through the large windows. Banquet tables set up with meats, breads, and fruits looked as if they should have bowed under the immense weight. The stone floor was immaculate, made of huge flagstones carefully fitted together. Hundreds of guests stood around, talking in groups and sampling the fare from the tables.

"It's all so beautiful," Catie said.

"Of course it is," the knight said with a small smile. "It is Camelot. How could it be anything else?"

"I don't know." Catie shook her head in wonder. Legend of the Lake was an Arthurian fantasy, but now she felt guilty for having given the game description only cursory inspection.

"And on the day when the king officially chooses his queen," the knight said, "this room had best be filled with gaiety and laughter."

"Or else?" Catie couldn't help asking, then realized the comment was anachronistic to the time frame of the game.

The knight glanced at her briefly. "Or else," he agreed.

Catie laughed, taken with the moment, forgetting all the weirdness that had happened last night. "You're not from around here."

The knight grinned and shook his head. "No. And neither are you."

"I'm Catie." And in keeping with the game's design, she curtsied. She loved the way the long dress she wore fit her. The gossamer green material felt like silk and was artfully beaded with rubies and yellow amethysts.

"Roger," the knight replied, "and I'll be your Lancelot for your stay." He bowed effortlessly despite the armor.

"Lancelot is a big role," Catie commented.

"I like big roles. I like girls, too."

Catie laughed. *Uh-oh, I'll bet he's all of eleven or twelve.* "That's good to know."

"Do you want to go talk somewhere? A private chatroom in Hotel Camelot, maybe?" The little boy's leer on the angelic face looked totally out of place.

"Sorry, that wasn't on my tour itinerary."

"Hey," Roger said, "I'm Lancelot."

"Maybe on the outside." Catie turned and walked around the huge cistern to put room between her and the amorous knight.

Roger followed. "I've got a big part in this game. The Lady in the Lake gets attacked, and Arthur and I have to go save her."

"I'm sure there's plenty of adventure to go around," Catie told him.

"Yeah, if you're into subplots instead of the main event," Roger said. "I've kind of always been a main-event kind of guy."

"As I recall," Catie said, still on the move, "Lancelot wasn't a lech."

"You have something against bloodsucking invertebrates?"

"That's a leech." Catie considered. "Although I guess the line between the two does blur a little. I can see how you'd be confused."

Roger scowled, twisting the handsome Lancelot proxy's face into a distortion. "Hey, I got the cheats for this game from a place I know on the Net. This demo normally only runs a general audiences loop, but I can access the adult programming. Wanna play?"

Gross! Catie spun on Roger, bringing him up short even though he towered a full head over her. He rocked on his steel-clad tiptoes as she punched him in the chest with a forefinger. "Are you listening to me, you tin-plated little creep?"

"Anybody ever tell you that you are pretty when you are angry?" Roger tried another Lancelot grin.

"Have you ever heard of Morgan Le Fey?" Catie demanded.

"She was a witch trained by Merlin," Roger answered. "If

you know your King Arthur stuff, you know about her."

"Well, I'm her," Catie said, "and unless you want to spend the rest of the demo as an armored toad clunking around on your tiny tin rump all covered in wart pimples, I'd stay away from me if I were you."

"You wouldn't do that," Roger said, but he didn't sound so sure. "I've got a big part to play. I'm a hero. Without me, the evil sea hag menacing the Lady in the Lake won't get killed."

"I think we'd manage."

Roger narrowed Lancelot's china blue eyes. "You're bluffing."

"Ribbit," Catie croaked tauntingly.

"I'm too important to the game," Roger went on, gathering his courage. "I'm the hero. I'm going to save—"

"A dragon!" someone yelled.

Catie spun and glanced out the nearest window, following the line of people that suddenly formed there. She peered through the glass and spotted the dragon. It was impossible to miss. From the description Matt and Maj had given she felt certain that she'd found their missing dragon. She ran forward, trying to get a closer look.

The dragon flew straight for the castle, quickly passing overhead and out of sight.

"There aren't supposed to be any dragons in this game," Roger said at her side.

"You'd think there'd be a law against creeps, too." Catie looked across the great hall, trying to spot another window that would allow her a view of the dragon as it passed over.

"I'm not a creep," Roger protested. "I'm the greatest hero in all of Camelot. My bravery is renowned, a legend throughout the whole—"

"Trolls!" someone shouted. "We're under attack by giant armored trolls!"

Before Catie could do more than start to turn, the wall exploded and the sound of an incoming round filled the great hall in the next moment. The concussion knocked her to the ground and sent man-sized blocks spinning from the wall. Several of them crushed the banquet tables as well as the guests seated around them.

"To arms!" a regal voice bellowed. "To arms, my knights!"

Glancing up, Catie spotted King Arthur standing at the

second-story railing, peering down over the wreckage that had once been the palace's great hall. His flowing red hair reached his shoulders and his beard curled out imperiously. Two pages helped him pull his armor together, and he raised the mighty sword Excaliber.

Clanking noises sounded as the first of the armored trolls arrived.

Instead of some medieval giant in hammered plate, the troll appeared to be a forty-foot-tall futuristic robot equipped with lasers and rockets. It strode into the room through the hole left by the explosions. A machine gun mounted on its shoulder fired a steady stream of blistering death across the great hall.

"For Arthur!" a knight cried, charging at the new arrival with his sword raised high. "For Camelot!"

The machine gun swept across him, stitching him with heavy rounds that knocked him from his feet. The knight flew backward and disappeared, logged off in mid-flight.

"Forget it!" Roger yelled, pushing himself to his feet and hurling himself out of the line of fire.

Some hero, Catie thought sarcastically as she got to her feet. She stared through the swirling dust left by the explosions, noticing other shadows that trailed the robot.

A long, thin man with a white beard and a conical hat with stars and moons on it charged out to meet the first robot. His cape swirled around his shoulders as he gestured and cried out words Catie didn't understand. He threw his hand out, and a wall of force rocked the robot backward.

The metal creature stumbled backward and rammed an elbow through part of the stone wall left standing. Even as more debris tumbled down and banged against it, the robot righted itself, then lifted a foot and brought it crashing down on the old mage.

A young male voice pealed out with the electronic thunder of amplified speakers. "Permanent press, guys! Boo-yeahhhh!" He launched a rocket from the shoulder-mounted weapon that wiped out the second floor landing where King Arthur stood.

Mark Gridley suddenly appeared beside Catie. He looked at her in concern. "You might want to consider logging off."

Catie didn't question how Mark had known she was in Legend of the Lake. He'd walked her there before pursuing his own interests. "What's going on?" she asked.

"There's trouble all through the convention center," Mark replied. "The hotel security programs are getting fried with systematic failures, and Pete's dragon has shown up in most of the games."

"If I log off, I may lose the chance of figuring out what's going on here." Catie sneezed as the swirling dust triggered the reaction. Conversation was barely possible over the mechanized sounds of the giant robots and the screams of the banquet guests. "I'm part of this programming. Maybe I can isolate the dragon's signature here and track it back."

Before she could move, the giant robot turned faster than she'd expected, catching her up in one huge, three-fingered hand that curled around her like a steel prison.

"Hey, now," the thunderous boy's voice bellowed over the speakers, "you're a cute one!"

12

Unable to bear the pain anymore and knowing he was fighting a losing battle against the antivirus programming Peter Griffen had coded into the veeyar, Gaspar Latke ripped the three crimson wires from his eye. He was afraid to look at the wires, terrified that the eye had come with it.

He forced himself up on shaking legs, panting like a bellows as the familiar gut-wrenching ache of a panic attack filled him. "I'm logging off," he told Heavener. "It's over here."

"Then knock out the security programming in the hotel," Heavener directed. "We have to get Griffen off the premises."

"Who are you?" a sharp voice demanded.

Gaspar wheeled around, spotting Peter Griffen at the far end of the room.

"What did you do?" Griffen ran at Gaspar, drawing back a hand that suddenly filled with neon gases.

Working hurriedly, dropping back into the hacker's survival frame of mind, Gaspar made himself two-dee again and wound through the security programming protecting the veeyar.

Peter threw the spinning, gaseous ball.

Gaspar knew the ball contained a trace utility. Cold fear

stabbed deep within him. He had no doubts about Peter's ability to develop a trace utility that would be next to impossible to beat. He oozed through the security programming just before the trace utility splattered against the coding.

Then he was back in the convention center, watching from his holo self as the gaming crowd raced into the Eisenhower Productions booth.

"Hotel security!" a man yelled, pushing past Leif and heading for the besieged booth.

"Los Angeles Police Department!" a uniformed officer bellowed, hot on the security guard's heels.

Gaspar gazed around at the utter pandemonium that filled the convention center and felt guilty. He'd been to the convention a couple times in the past. He'd never gone legally, of course, always on identities he'd "borrowed" from corporate databases he'd managed to crack. Attending the convention those times had often been highlights of the year.

Now he was responsible for ruining this year's event.

"Latke," Heavener called.

"I'm working," Gaspar said. He took the specially built icon from his pocket, one of the best from his bag of tricks, and fed it directly into the hotel's computer systems through the reciprocal programming that maintained the holofeeds. He checked the progress of his program against the wristcom connecting him to the hotel security.

In seconds the program became part of the security system and every cam in the hotel went offline. "It's down," he told Heavener.

Matt stared at the ironbound chariot wheel swamping through the grainy yellow sand straight at his head. He tried to get up, but the sand kept slipping out from under him. The chariot wheel caught him dead center as the driver yelled out in savage glee.

Pain filled Matt's body, twisting him up, but it wasn't anything more than what he'd programmed on the feedback allowed from the Net. He was automatically logged off.

Matt opened his eyes and inhaled sharply, trying to get his bearings.

"Are you all right, sir?"

Matt blinked at the flight attendant, trying to remember where he was for just a moment. Then he felt the familiar sensation of flying. "Yes, thank you. I was playing online. It didn't turn out so well."

The flight attendant nodded sympathetically.

"So how'd you get it?" Leif asked. "Find out you had a really slow goblin?"

"It looked liked a Roman war chariot," Matt answered, "but I couldn't swear to it. I got shoved into another game from Goblin King. I also saw the dragon there."

"The one you and Maj saw?"

"Yeah." Matt glanced at Andy, who lay motionless in the seat beside him. "I don't think it belonged there, either. How's Andy?"

"Still playing," Leif replied. "Why didn't you think the dragon belonged there?"

"This demo felt like a straight strat game, and the dragon was just there, not really interacting at all. Where did you get shunted to?"

"Here. I got taken out by one of those little ships and was logged completely off the Net. I tried to get back into the demo veeyar, but it's off-line."

Matt looked at Andy and started to get worried.

"Then where's Andy?"

Andy studied the heads-up display available to him in the cockpit, recognizing the control configuration immediately. The Space Marines series of games were a personal favorite of his, and he had high scores on a half-dozen Net sites that ran the games.

Cyber-augmented gloves and boots encased his hands and feet and controlled the forty-foot battlesuit. Automatically he ran through the systems displays and weapons checklist. The arms and legs were all in good working order.

The helmet that fit over his head contained the HUD. Pull-down menus kept track of his heading and armament. A long, letter-box-shaped screen fit over his eyes like a visor, giving him a full 360-degree view around the battlesuit as well as overhead.

"Alternative vidscreen," Andy commanded. "Reduce field of view to one hundred eighty degrees with rearviews on the sides."

Immediately the viewscreen blurred out of focus, changing from the panoramic spread to an eyes-forward view. Two round sections on either side gave him the view behind him. The radar screen above it pinged targets, then the identify-friend-or-foe function kicked in, reading the signature of the other four cavalry units within the half-klick sweep.

Andy only thought about the sudden change from the Goblin King game to the Space Marines for a moment. It really didn't matter to him. Gameplay was gameplay. All he wanted to do was roll up a score. *I wouldn't have been able to talk Leif and Matt into this. There aren't any dragons in Space Marines.*

He flexed his hands and feet, moving the seventy-ton war machine into a distance-eating stride. The cockpit swung only slightly, helping create the illusion that he actually was the big battlesuit.

"Open comm," Andy said.

The comm opened with a crackle of static, and voices immediately filled the void. "Blue Niner, this is Blue Leader, do you copy?" a young male voice demanded.

"Blue Niner copies," another voice answered. "Have you identified the new guy?"

New guy? That must be me. "Blue Leader," Andy said. "I need a designation."

"Affirmative. Blue Leader reads you. Not all of our company made the jump from Space Station Zebra. Evidently we uncovered some anomaly in the targeted space station that transported us here."

"Understood." Andy swung the big battlesuit around, falling in behind the four units. "Kind of went through that myself."

"You weren't with us at the space station?" Blue Leader asked.

"That's negative, Blue Leader. Ended up here by accident myself." Andy easily moved the battlesuit up to a jog.

"Seems you've got a lot of experience in the suit."

"I've fought my share of battles," Andy agreed. Sweeping the terrain around him, he was only slightly surprised to spot the castle under attack ahead.

Space Marines traveled everywhere and fought anyone. As space-bred mercenaries living and dying on huge torus wheels spinning through known and unknown galaxies, they never knew where the next battleground was going to be. One of the Space Marine companies Andy battled with on a regular basis had been in existence for more than two years. He'd encountered futuristic worlds as well as medieval ones.

"Your designation is Blue Thirteen," Blue Leader said.

"My lucky number," Andy replied laconically. "What's the target?"

"Don't know," Blue Leader answered. "We were on a pure hit-and-git-shoot-to-kill mission when we ended up here. The way we figure it, everything here is fair game."

"Magnify vision," Andy said. His field of view slid forward, zooming in on the castle. One of the Space Marine units stepped through a hole blasted in the side of the castle. The machine gun blazed, driving back a group of men that had stepped forward to challenge the intruder.

Andy took in the banquet area and noted the medieval weapons the guards used. The combat was too one-sided for his taste. "You're looking at a massacre here, Blue Leader."

"You say massacre," Blue Leader responded, "and I say easy points."

A feeling of wrongness dampened Andy's mood. It was one thing to play Space Marines when challenging an adequate enemy force, but executions were another matter entirely.

The group Andy gamed with in the Space Marines comprised mercenaries with a conscience. They sold their skills honorably and stood by the contracts they undertook. In fact, Andy and his friends had, on more than one occasion, invaded solar systems in the game where outlaw Space Marines had holed up and killed any new gamers wanting to play in those areas.

The Space Marines walking through the huge hole blown in the side of the castle paused. The machine gun on the battlesuit's shoulder quivered and spent brass twinkled through the air.

Inside his cockpit, Andy cringed and turned cold inside. It was one thing to jump into a game to blow your friends up for fun, but this wasn't anything like that. The medieval castle couldn't even protect itself.

The Space Marine battlesuit in the palace bent down and plucked something up from the ground.

"Magnify," Andy ordered.

The viewscreen performed immediately, zooming in on the figure trapped in the battlesuit's three-fingered hand. Andy recognized her at once.

"Hey, Blue Leader, look at the prize I just took." The guy in the battlesuit swiveled, leaving his lower half locked down as he turned his upper torso.

Andy's hands flexed inside the cybered gloves. He watched the weapons systems flare to life within the HUD, and he marked the placement of the other three Space Marines. They were all enemies by his personal definition at that point.

He readied the anchor attachment that fit inside the battlesuit's left arm. Normally the anchor was only used in space battles to link back up with a friendly ship when a battlesuit had been blown free of a transport ship's hull. He knew he wouldn't have much time to act before the other three Space Marines turned on him.

"Target," he ordered. Crosshairs appeared on the viewscreen and glowed when lock was achieved.

"Warning," a soft, feminine voice said. "The target you have selected has registered on IFF as—"

"Override previous identification," Andy barked. "IFF is tainted. All controls over to ship's personnel."

"Confirmed," the computer voice said. "Safeguards are down. All systems available."

Andy closed his left fist and fired the anchor. A full meter of hardened steel flashed from the hollow groove of the battlesuit's left arm. It caught the battlesuit on the right side of the torso not quite halfway up. The sabot charge fired off on impact and sent the pronged head through the battlesuit, punching out the main servos that operated the suit's on-board motion computer.

"What the—" the guy in the paralyzed battlesuit shouted.

By then Andy was a blur of movement. He fired a salvo of smoker rounds into the ground immediately around him. A cloud of white smoke roiled up, filled with positively and negatively charged ions as well as burning cinders that would throw off the thermal and radar sensors of the other suits.

He jogged to the right, taking advantage of a copse of trees and the downgrade of the hill there. *Hang on, Catie, I'm coming.* Normally he wouldn't have been worried about Catie's welfare. If she received any serious injuries during gameplay, she'd have been logged off the Net. But he still didn't know how he'd gotten into the Space Marines game, so he wasn't certain if a normal log-off was possible.

He crouched down, taking advantage of the short grade of the hill. Machine-gun rounds whipped through the air above him as the other guys in the battlesuits responded to his attack. None of them had him in their sights yet.

"Release the hatch." Andy slipped his hands and feet out of the control boots and gloves. Pushing himself from the cockpit console seat, he grabbed the emergency jetpack from the space under the seat and buckled it around his upper body. He slipped on a pair of aviator sunglasses from his jacket pocket.

The front of the battlesuit's head folded open as the hatch released with a hiss of compressed air. He pulled the jetpack's control glove onto his right hand and pressed the ignition. The resulting explosion from the combustible engine fired him from the open maw of the battlesuit's head like a rocket.

Andy kept both hands stretched before him, his legs spread to avoid the jetpack's fiery contrail and to help him control his flight. He maxed out his speed, hurtling toward the paralyzed battlesuit that stood still as a statue. Machine-gun tracer rounds burned the air above and ahead of him, but he was through the area before the shooter ever got the range.

While playing the game with his friends, Andy had also spent time repairing and beefing his battlesuit up. If the game was played correctly without cheats, a battlesuit warrior spent nearly ten hours working on his vehicle to every one he or she spent operating it. As a result, he knew intimately where all the battlesuits' weak points were.

He also knew the battlesuit's secondary systems were struggling to come online and restore mobile capability to the stricken suit.

Andy powered down at the last minute, twisting in the air so he almost stalled out when he reached the battlesuit. He grabbed the clenched fist that held Catie captive.

"Traitor!" the guy inside the paralyzed suit screamed. "I'm going to get you!"

"Andy?" Catie stared at him in disbelief.

"Me," Andy said with a smile as he took in the frilly dress. "Going to a ball somewhere, Princess?"

"You'd think so," she replied, only sounding a little tense. "I met a real toad."

Andy drew the laser pistol from the cavalry holster on his right hip. "Step back." He fired from pointblank range. The laser cut through the thinner plates inside the finger joint where they had to slide over each other. In seconds the tension cables beneath were bared. Another two bursts and the cable parted with high-pitched squeals.

Holstering his sidearm, Andy stood and grabbed the finger that was taller than and just as broad as he was. It took everything he had to move the finger, but when it opened, Catie managed to squeeze through.

Machine-gun rounds peppered the stationary battlesuit. Andy felt the vibrations shiver through the hardware that warned him the system was coming back online.

The huge hand they stood on jerked spasmodically. The three undamaged fingers closed a little tighter.

"Hold on," Andy ordered as he wrapped his left arm around Catie's waist and pulled her to him. She wrapped her arms around his neck, making it hard to keep his head up. He couldn't walk heavily encumbered, so he chose simply to fall out of the battlesuit's hand.

No sooner had they left the hand than it snapped closed, sounding like a deadly autobus pileup.

Catie screamed as they fell twenty of the thirty feet to the ground. Then Andy tightened his fist inside the jetpack control glove. The jetpack fired and immediately provided them with lift.

Andy rolled his body, getting them aimed in the proper direction, then fired a sustained burst from the jetpack. He ran close to the ground, no more than five or six feet off the ground. *If we crash, we're not going to have to worry about those guys,* he thought.

He flew toward the open head of his battlesuit, cutting power early. He pulled Catie to him more tightly, covering her body with his.

His shoulder hit the upper lip of the access hatch opening, and they ricocheted into the cockpit. He skidded across the steel plate flooring and slammed into the console chair hard enough to drive the wind from his lungs.

"We made it!" Catie shouted in disbelief as she pushed herself up from him.

Andy concentrated on breathing again. Black spots swam in his vision. *Getupgetupgetup!* he shouted at himself mentally because he didn't have the breath to speak. *They're not going to wait for you to get ready!*

13

Dressed in his astronaut-style crashsuit, Mark Gridley jetted through the twisting maze that was the Bessel Mid-Town Hotel's security system. Some of the time-savers he'd implanted in the system earlier had folded when the security system went down.

A small image remained at the bottom of his vision, flatfilm reproduction of the confusion filling the convention hall. He also maintained an open window for any IMs the other Explorers might try to send to him.

He rushed from the latest tunnel, searching for access to whatever security vidcams that might be operational after the latest attack on them. Three directions were open before him.

Pausing for just a moment, Mark shook his right hand twice, accessing one of the search utilities he used to crack and map a computer system's programming. When he opened his hand, three armored butterflies streaked forward, each taking one of the optional directions.

"Passage blocked," the first butterfly search program reported back.

"Passage leads to outside access," the second butterfly informed him. "Data port presently unoccupied."

"Data flowing fine," the remaining butterfly radioed.

Mark kicked in his boot jets again and shot forward, making the hard S-turn to follow the circuitry path. He stretched out his left hand and sprayed a neon orange stripe along the entrance to let himself know he'd been that way. With the collapse of the security system and the virus that raged within it, a number of the circuits cannibalized themselves, creating endless loops as the programs tried to connect.

The system was a total and complete mess. Mark really didn't think he could have done a better job himself, but he hoped he could unravel some of the mess in time to provide them with a few more clues.

"Miss Green."

Maj glanced down at her foilpack and saw Detective Holmes centered in the view. "Where are you?"

"En route," Holmes replied. "I went home and grabbed forty winks, not thinking we'd have trouble so early. Big mistake on my part."

Maj trotted at the heels of the convention-goers who flooded into the Eisenhower Productions booth. Her eyes roved over the beautiful artwork lining the walls. Concept art for the Realms of the Bright Water decorated the interior, and the center of the booth contained a miniature model of the forest they'd seen on holo.

The lack of light and power made the interior of the booth almost creepy. But it didn't slow the convention-goers, who oohed and ahhed over the displays of art, action figures, and clothing. Evidently Eisenhower Productions had kept their marketing staff busy.

"Even if you'd been here," Maj said, "I don't think you'd have managed to affect the situation very much."

"Always loved a vote of confidence." The sound of Holmes's siren screaming echoed over the telecommunications connection. As he glanced over his shoulder, the traffic through his back window was briefly visible. He barked orders over his police wristcom.

Maj gazed through the quasi-twilight that filled the booth. Thankfully, the fans weren't in total riot mode. They weren't tearing things down or open, contenting themselves with investigating what there was available to see.

"I'm also assuming you called for something other than to let me know the bad news."

"Peter Griffen disappeared in the middle of the crisis," May said. "I got the feeling it wasn't planned."

"That's not the impression I got when my sergeant told me about it," Holmes said. "She thinks this was a publicity stunt that got way out of hand."

Maj silently disagreed. She glanced back at the interior of the Eisenhower Productions booth, noticing the security lights hanging above it. All of them were dark. *Something's wrong.*

"My people have orders to pick Peter Griffen up," Holmes went on. "I want to have a little chat with him about some of the civil ordinances he fractured today."

"Do you know what room he's in at the hotel?" Maj forced her way through the crowd, then spotted a door on the right. She crossed toward it.

"Yeah," Holmes said. "I've already had a couple uniforms check it out. He's not there."

Then he's got to be here, Maj told herself. She hopped onto the wraparound booth in front of the door and walked across. Piles of plastic-wrapped shirts lay scattered across the floor. They all held pictures of Sahfrell the dragon. She tried the door at the back and found it open.

Stepping through, she found herself in a small room with an implant chair. "I found the room Peter probably did the holo from." She walked to the implant chair, drawn by the dark stain that covered one side. Even in the darkness the pool of liquid held a crimson gleam. Her stomach turned. "There's fresh blood in this room."

"Hold your position," Holmes ordered. "I'll have a uniformed officer there in just a moment." He broke the connection.

Maj scanned the room. There weren't any other doors, and she really didn't think Peter had enough time to get out of the booth without someone noticing him. *They'd have mobbed him if they'd seen him.* And there was enough blood that she knew he couldn't be in terribly good shape.

She turned her foilpack over, using the scant light from the vidscreen to illuminate the shadows covering the carpeted floor. A trail of blood drops led from the implant chair.

Five feet farther on, they disappeared abruptly.

Maj dropped to her knees and studied the floor, passing the illuminated foilpack vidscreen only inches from the top of the carpet. It took her three tries to spot the seam in the carpet.

She hooked her fingers under the edge and lifted, exposing the square mouth of a utility passage that had probably been set up to allow egress to the various power outlets set into the floor around the convention center floor. Darkness filled the utility tunnel.

Using the light from the foilpack viewscreen, Maj located the ladder set into the side of one wall. At the bottom the tunnel stretched out in two directions, bending immediately in both. Small emergency lights burned with dim wattage, barely illuminating the underground hallways to near-twilight.

Something gleamed on the floor, catching her eye. She knelt and used the foilpack light.

The tiny drop of red blood glistened, and it was only the first of the intermittent trail that led through the access tunnels.

Maj followed, reconfiguring the foilpack to send an IM to Mark.

Winded and hurting, Andy pulled himself to his feet and stumbled into the cockpit command chair. He pulled the jetpack off and tossed it to the side, then thrust his hands and feet into the gloves and boots just as a missile slammed into the battlesuit's side. The big machine rocked and came close to overturning, but the on-board gyros kept it upright.

Sensory feedback from the gloves and boots already had Andy hooked into the battlesuit. He threw one of the battlesuit's big hands out and caught himself, pushing hard to maintain his balance. The head-up-display helmet descended over his head.

"Belt in or log off," Andy advised Catie as he sprang into action.

"I'm staying." Catie spotted the restraining straps on the wall where passengers could tie down. She fit her arms through the loops and pulled the straps tight.

"There's a crash helmet in the locker beside you." Andy moved the battlesuit into a run.

"You're planning on crashing?"

Andy grinned. With the HUD in place, he knew she could

only see his lower face. "You don't plan those things in Space Marines. They just happen."

"Nice game. Those seem to be your friends."

"They like to play rough." A salvo of short-range missiles tore the ground up behind Andy as he ran across the broken terrain. The battlesuit's big feet sank a half-meter into the ground while he mowed down small trees and brush.

"I think I saw Maj's dragon."

"I didn't." Sudden movement on the radar screen drew Andy's attention. The radar tilted, spinning, showing that the most aggressive movement had gone airborne. The battlesuits were also equipped with short-range boot jets that allowed navigation in space and limited flight. "Were you bumped off another game?"

"No. I was in this one when the dragon arrived. Then the armored trolls showed up."

"Space Marines," Andy corrected automatically. He paused and turned, locking his feet down to the ground to brace for the recoil from the short-range cannon.

"We've stopped. Is that good?"

"Going on the attack," Andy replied, tracking the crosshairs onto the flying battlesuit. "These guys aren't as experienced as they act. Man, you don't give up the ground to go flying around. You're not locked down to fire your heavy artillery, and you're nothing but one big . . . fat . . . target." His finger twitched inside his right glove.

Three missiles fired from his shoulder-mounted weapon. They left curving contrails as they rushed toward the airborne battlesuit. All three missiles slammed into the battlesuit's chest area, ripping a huge crater. A moment later the limited-nuke power plant detonated, ripping the battlesuit to shreds.

Andy opened the comm. "Blue Leader, this is designate Blue Thirteen. My advice is to disengage and log off. Playtime's over." He got the battlesuit moving again, flipping up the laser sights and taking out two missiles that streaked for him.

The missiles exploded and rained fragments against his steel hide, but damaged little except the exterior. Blue Leader's response was way less than gentlemanly.

"Guy's going to need his mouth washed out with soap," Andy commented. He moved deeper into the forest and away from

the castle grounds. Mounted men had ridden into the inner
courtyards, but he knew they wouldn't stand a chance against
the heavily armored and armed Space Marines.

He opened a leg hatch and spread an arc of anticavalry mines.
Trees bent and cracked, pulled free of the ground as he thundered through.

Less than a minute later one of the pursuing Space Marines
stepped on the group of mines. "I'm hit! I'm hit!" the pilot
squalled. "My legs are gone!"

"You're a sitting duck, pal," Andy said grimly, tracking the
action in his rearviews. He swiveled the shoulder-mounted cannon and fired. Two missiles hammered the battlesuit's neck
joints, triggering the automatic eject sequence.

The battlesuit's head twisted into position, the chin cutting a
deep furrow into the earth. Then the top of the head fragmented,
releasing the cockpit inside and shooting it skyward.

"Kind of like a skeet trap," Andy said, grinning tightly. He
brought the arm laser online and got target lock. His initial burst
slagged the escape pod before the parachutes ever popped.

Mark paused in his investigation of the circuit paths of the Bessel Mid-Town Hotel's computer paths. He'd ended up tracking
dozens of dead ends and was getting more than a little frustrated.
Data wasn't flowing in any direction, totally stalled out now,
and gave him no reference points at all. But somewhere in there,
he knew, there had to be a virus that allowed whoever had
popped strands on the security system access.

A message flared across the bottom of his vision. MARK, IT'S
MAJ. NEED INFO. IN UNDERGROUND UTILITY TUNNELS UNDER
CONVENTION CENTER. CAN YOU TRACK?

Holding his position in the crashsuit, Mark lifted his arm and
brought up the schematics he'd uncovered for the building, located the service tunnels, and sent them along. Then he added,
DON'T GO ALONE.

Maj ignored Mark's final comment and sent a quick thank-you.
She pulled up the schematics he'd sent and examined them for
just a moment. The blood drips on the tunnel floor had gotten
farther apart, as if the bleeding had slowed or Peter was trav-
eling faster.

After a moment spent orienting herself, Maj took off again.

More confident now, and her vision adjusted to the dim lighting, she stepped up the pace to a trot.

According to the schematic, the tunnel she presently followed opened up in a storage area that was right off the main lobby. From there it was just a short distance to the street in front of the Bessel Mid-Town Hotel.

Gaspar monitored the building through the security sensors he'd rendered accessible only by him. Most of the network was devices Heavener had instructed her people to install. He stood inside the convention center, maintaining the holo as the chaos continued.

When he punched the menu for the utility tunnels beneath the convention center, he was surprised to find an extra presence. He accessed the nearest vid buttoncam Heavener's people had installed along their last-ditch escape route. The vid buttoncam had photo-multiplier capabilities and scanned through the dark easily.

When the girl came into view, Gaspar easily recognized her as Maj Green. *How did she find out about the tunnels?* He didn't let his mind dwell on the questions that filled it. He opened the audlink to Heavener.

"One of the Net Force Explorers is in the tunnels," he told her.

"He will be taken care of."

"She," Gaspar said automatically.

Heavener's only response was to shut down the audlink.

Watching the girl run through the tunnels, Gaspar felt a pang of guilt. She was running to her doom, and he had no way to warn her. But what made him feel really guilty was not knowing if he'd try even if he had a way.

In the Space Marine battlesuit, Andy waded through a stream, marking it instantly as an attack zone. The hillside on the other side of the stream went almost straight up. Even as skilled as he was in the battlesuit, Andy had trouble negotiating the climb. At the top, peering down sixty feet to the stream, he knew he was in a good place.

"We've stopped," Catie said.

"Yeah," Andy said. "These guys are creeps and amateurs, and I don't have time for them. We need to get back to the convention center and figure out what's going on. But we're going on our terms, not theirs."

"It's two against one." Catie huddled against the bulkhead, compacted into a ball.

Andy gave her a grin. "I know. I feel kind of guilty." When the two pursuing Space Marines plunged into the stream, Andy fired his laser at the water, instantly creating huge clouds of steam. "I figure these guys more for line-of-sight operators rather than guys who are used to instrumentation."

The steam clouds rose from the stream, turning the world white, rising to cascade over the hill where Andy stood as well. He shifted over to thermal imaging, the scene suddenly shifting to a patchwork world of reds, oranges, and yellows with a few spots of blue and purple. The battlesuit's interior cooling systems jerked into action, whining and rattling.

"What's that?" Catie asked.

"We're blowing up," Andy teased.

"What?"

"Psych." Andy tracked the two battlesuits stumbling through the streambed. Both of them acted as if they'd lost their way. He readied the short-range missiles and fired a salvo at each.

The missiles struck the two Space Marines and started breaking them down at once. They shivered and shook like tin cans strung together.

Andy opened the comm-channel. "And that's all, Blue Leader. Game over. Thanks for playing."

The battlesuits exploded, showering the nearby terrain with shrapnel.

Andy lifted the HUD helmet and glanced at Catie . . . "We're about done here, I'd say. Ready to see if we can get off-line?"

"Very," Catie said.

"Detective Holmes."

Maj glanced at the vidphone screen on her foilpack and saw that the LAPD detective was getting out of his car. The vid pickup swirled crazily, pulling the man and the alley into conflicting views as Holmes ran. "It's Maj."

"I'm kind of busy here."

"Me, too," she replied tautly. "I'm in an access tunnel under the convention center. The people who've got Peter Griffen are escaping through it."

"How'd you find that tunnel?"

"History," Maj said, her breath coming shorter from the excitement and the exertion. Her feet slapped against the tunnel's stone floor. "We're working on current events."

"Do you know where it lets out?"

"The front lobby. There's a storage area the tunnel accesses around the corner from the main desk. If they get out onto the street—"

"They're gone," Holmes said in agreement. "Got it. Keep this connection open."

Maj ran harder. She leaned into the running, regretting the stale, still air around her because it wasn't what her body needed for sustained effort. Her lungs started to burn.

At the next corner turn Maj folded her arms protectively in front of her, bumped into the wall, then pushed off with her hands to change directions rapidly. Wounded or being carried, she didn't think Peter could move along as quickly as she was. She was certain she was cutting his lead.

The tunnel ended abruptly two turns later. Light glinted off the rungs of the ladder built into the wall. The hatch above was open. She scrambled up the rungs. The air felt cooler in the storage room.

A woman screamed out in the lobby, quickly echoed by other screams and hoarse warning shouts.

Maj opened the door and paused, looking through. The lobby was filled with people from the convention who looked lost and confused. But fear was catching on quick because three men drove a flying wedge through them, knocking bystanders aside with fists, knees, and elbows. Two more men trotted easily behind the wedge, holding Peter in a come-along grip.

None of the men said a word, but the big black pistols in their gloved fists spoke volumes.

"Detective Holmes," Maj said over the foilpack. "They're in the lobby."

"I've got men there," Holmes promised.

At that moment the crowd separated and four uniformed policemen ran toward the group with Peter. "Halt!" one of them ordered in a loud voice.

The three men forming the flying wedge raised their pistols and fired without hesitation. Dulled splats like a hammer driving home a nail echoed in the hallway. The four policemen fell without firing a shot.

Controlling her fear, Maj dashed forward. "Your officers are down, Detective Holmes!"

"How many?"

"All of them." Maj pulled up short and looked at the bodies while the crowd continued to scatter around her. Natural light filtering in through the polarized windows fronting the hotel gave her plenty of illumination. Yellow-feathered tranquilizer darts stood out against the dark colors of the uniforms. The gunmen hadn't fired for the center of their targets, choosing arms, legs, throats, and faces.

"What kind of shape are they in?" Holmes asked. "I can't get radio contact."

"They've been darted." Maj kneeled beside one of the men and put her fingers on his neck. She felt the pulse beating slug-gishly. "They're still alive." She pushed up and ran to the lobby doors, stepping over two more people who'd been darted.

The doorman was dropping at the same time she reached the red carpet under the canopy. The doorman fell limply halfway out into the street. Traffic screeched to a halt in front of him, missing him by inches.

"There's the girl," one of the men said. He aimed his pistol and fired.

Maj ducked back around the door. Glass broke near her right ear, shattering with a double-clap of impact. Pulling away, she spotted the two yellow-feathered darts that had stabbed through the glass pane she'd hidden behind. Hairline cracks spread out from the darts.

Horns honked indignantly out on the street.

Maj watched through the fractured glass as a gleaming, light blue Dodge van barreled down the four-lane street. The driver laid on the horn, pulling out into the oncoming traffic lane, then cutting back in to pull to a rubber-eating stop twenty feet down from the hotel entrance.

The black-suited men, with Peter in tow, rushed toward the Dodge van as the rear door opened. They threw Peter inside, then climbed in. The van took off before they could shut the door. Traffic ground to a halt in both directions, but the van roared down the middle of the street, careening occasionally from the stalled cars with a scream of tortured metal.

Maj dashed after it, trying to spot its license plate. No luck—
it was missing. She lifted the foilpack and gave the best description she could of the vehicle as it sped away. It turned right
at the corner and disappeared.

14

"We lost them," Detective John Holmes announced as he strode into the conference room.

Maj had taken advantage of one of the implant chairs in the room and jumped into her own veeyar. She didn't have access to all the investigation's progress through the LAPD's systems, but the local HoloNet servers were doing a good job.

Logged into her own veeyar and taking advantage of the room's holoprojector systems, she was able to be on hand and access the Net at the same time. She had nine windows opened up to different media servers at present. Several of the stations covering the gaming convention were already doing back-story pieces on Peter Griffen, and she copied those immediately, archiving them as files.

Catie and Megan sat in one corner, engaged in their own conversation. Matt, Mark, and Leif, although actually still in-flight, occupied chairs at the main table with Captain Winters, who was really still back in his office as well. Andy had returned to the game room as the various services came back online.

Holmes glanced at his watch. "Uniforms found the vehicle less than two miles from here. It had been abandoned at a bar."

"What about Peter?" Maj asked.

"He wasn't there."

"He was injured," Maj said.

Holmes shrugged. "The investigating officers reported there was blood in the back of the van, but said it wasn't enough to cause any real concern."

"Other than the fact that Peter was forcibly kidnapped in front of thousands of witnesses."

"We're investigating, Miss Green. But we're also checking into the possibility that this is a publicity stunt."

"They wouldn't have to do that," Catie put in. "Did you see that dragon? That alone would sell millions of copies. And the presentation Peter did had the whole audience wanting more."

"That would seem a little extreme, don't you think?" Winters asked. "If this was a staged event, Eisenhower Productions could be convicted of criminal charges."

"Look, Captain Winters," Holmes said with a trace of fatigue in his voice, "this city is one wild ride after another. We're home to Hollywood, a major portion of the gaming industry, and every vice you can name. With millions of people living here, working here, and visiting, you have to stand out from the crowd if you want to get noticed."

"Peter was already doing that," Maj said.

Holmes was quiet for a moment. "We're following up on a lead that the kidnapping was staged."

"Who has given you that information?" Winters asked.

"Sir," Holmes said, "with all due respect, you're out of your jurisdiction at the moment. The only reason I mention this at all is because your people got caught up in some nasty business last night, and I felt I owed that to you. But for now, we believe that the two events are unrelated."

"I hope you're not forgetting they could be," Winters said dryly.

A nerve twitched at the corner of Holmes's jaw. "No, sir. Not for a minute. But my CO is taking the stance that they're not. I have to follow that line. For now."

"Understood, Detective. I appreciate your honesty."

Holmes turned to Maj. "Look, I know you're worried about this guy. I am, too." He jerked a thumb over his shoulder. "I'm getting subpoenas delivered now to different media branches to access their vid files as well as processing witnesses and accounting for people who were physically here as well as in holoform. That's going to take time."

"I know," Maj replied.

"And if this is some kind of publicity stunt," Holmes said grimly, "Griffen and Eisenhower Productions are going to need a battalion of lawyers to get out of this."

"Even then," Megan said, "fines and court costs are going to be a drop in the bucket against the profits the game makes."

Holmes nodded and glanced around the room. "I don't figure you people are much on listening when someone tells you to keep your nose out of things, but consider this that speech just the same. Because if you step too heavily around this investigation, you're going to find out how downright unfriendly I can be. I hope we're clear on that."

Maj nodded. Even as Net Force Explorers they didn't have any official sanction.

Holmes turned and headed for the door, stopping just short of exiting and looking back at the group. "If you do happen to find out something I should know, make sure I do. You've got the number." He stepped back out into the hallway into a stream of people waiting to be processed through the police cordon.

Maj closed the media feeds and logged off the Net. When she opened her eyes again, she was in the implant chair in the conference room. She sat up and looked at Winters. "Is Net Force going to get involved?"

"Not at this point," Winters told her. "The LAPD is convinced what they're dealing with here is a publicity stunt aimed at increasing game sales. Net Force is in agreement. Personally, I think it wouldn't hurt to take a look and run a few things down. However, there's some political pressure to keep Net Force out. When we get involved, media coverage gets even more pronounced."

"But why keep Net Force out?" Maj asked. "Isn't media exposure a bonus?"

"Except that the gaming community doesn't like the idea of Net Force acting like Big Brother. The gaming world taps into a lot of various conspiracy theories, and throwing Net Force into the mix would only be adding fuel to the fire."

"The other gaming corporations are also talking about suing Peter Griffen and Eisenhower Productions for infringing on their own game advertisements," Leif said. "Apparently that dragon put in an appearance in nearly every game at the convention."

"And you know this how?" Catie asked.

Leif gave a small smile. "I took a peek at my dad's information research agency's reports over what happened out here. Part of the potential profits being set up here involve stock portfolios. Potential liability in the form of civil suits against a corporation are big news in business."

"They may impact profits," Matt said, "but sales of the game are still going to skyrocket, and that will impact profits, too."

Maj knew it was true. Even as the police had closed down the gaming area, there had been hundreds of people lined up, demanding to by the online package that would let them enter Realm of the Bright Waters when it went up on the Net.

"If the profit is big enough," Leif agreed, "lawsuits and litigation are written off as the price of doing business. The kidnapping has sent a tremor through the stock market. Eisenhower shares are presently down, but speculators are snapping them up."

"Is Eisenhower Productions publicly owned?" Winters asked.

Leif closed his eyes for a moment. "Forty-three percent."

"Hold up," Catie said. "Publicly owned doesn't ring any bells for me."

"There are two kinds of stock," Leif explained. "Actually, there are all kinds of stock options, but I'm going to hold it to two for a thumbnail overview. Public stock is shares that are sold to Joe Consumer, anyone who goes online and buys into corporations. Then there's private stock, stock held back from public trading for special investors. Usually other friendly corporations or entrepreneurs."

"Keeping private stock private prevents hostile takeovers," Megan said. "I remember that from the research my dad did on one of his mystery novels."

"True," Leif said, "but you'd be amazed at how many buyouts still happen and no one knows who the players are until the last moment."

"How financially secure is Eisenhower Productions?" Winters asked.

Leif shrugged. "I can look into it."

Winters nodded. "That might be a place to start. It would help to know—*if* they were involved in faking this kidnapping—if they were desperate or just plain greedy."

"Yes, sir."

Winters called the meeting to an end and excused himself, his holoform winking out of existence a heartbeat later. Mark, Matt, and Leif said their good-byes as well.

"We missed lunch," Catie announced, standing up and stretching tiredly. "There's supposed to be a great Chinese place around the corner. Want to find out?"

Maj nodded distractedly. Her mind whirled, trying to make sense of the events that had happened. She didn't doubt for a minute that last night's raid on her hotel room and Peter Griffen's kidnapping were connected. She just didn't know how. But her intuition pinged the connection dead center, and it was something she'd learned to trust over the years.

"—at the Bessel Mid-Town Hotel, where computer game design wizard Peter Griffen was believed kidnapped earlier today. Veronica, what can you tell us?"

Standing at the arrival gate lobby in LAX, Maj watched the HoloNet on units hanging from the ceiling. The view cut from the anchor to the blond reporter she recognized from the news reports that morning. She stood out in front of the Bessel Midtown Hotel in front of a nearby crowd that watched her. Her name, Veronica Rivers, was tagged under the time/date stamp in the lower right corner.

"Things here are still confusing, Frank," Veronica said. "As you can tell from the crowd behind me, there's a lot of interest in the whereabouts of Peter Griffen after today's excitement."

The holo split, picking up the image of the granite-jawed anchor sitting at his desk and placing it beside the street scene of the reporter. "Have police made any headway in the kidnapping investigation?"

"If they have, they aren't letting us know." Veronica waved at the hotel. "In fact, there's a lot of speculation going on now that this kidnapping might not have been a kidnapping at all, but a publicity stunt created by Griffen and his software publishers to generate sales of his new game."

"Those are serious charges," the anchor said.

Maj shook her head. After all the advances in technology, the media still relied on melodrama to capture viewers. She wanted to stop watching, but she found she couldn't.

"Wow," Catie said as she joined her. "They got that out quick."

"No news spreads like bad news," Maj replied. She glanced around the lobby, carefully avoiding the press of dozens of passengers who'd just off-loaded. Megan stood by the gate window, peering up at the sky as they waited for Leif, Matt, and Andy's flight to arrive.

"After the rumors about the faked kidnapping started circulating," Veronica continued on HoloNet, "I asked the lead detective on the case about it."

The view cut away suddenly to a gray-haired man with a hound-dog face and gravelly voice. A tag appeared briefly beneath him: BRUCE TOLLIVER, CAPTAIN OF DETECTIVES, LAPD. "Yes, we're aware of the rumors, and we're looking into them. Since this might be a kidnapping, we have to assume a life may be in jeopardy."

"Have any ransom demands been made yet, Captain Tolliver?" Veronica asked.

"Not yet."

"Isn't that unusual?" the reporter asked.

"Actually, that's not exceptional," Tolliver replied.

"Do you believe there was a kidnapping today?" Veronica asked.

"I can't comment on that."

The scene cut back to the split view of anchor and reporter. "We've had other reactions to today's bizarre events," Veronica went on. A series of sound and vid bytes followed.

"He looked sad," a young woman said. The shot had evidently been taken inside the convention room right after the kidnapping. "Really sad. But I don't think he kidnapped himself. I mean, who would do that? You'd have to be kind of sick, right?"

"This business is all about attention," a guy in his thirties said. A tag under him read, MIKE SIMON, GAME DESIGNER.

"I just want to play that game," a teenage boy said enthusiastically. "It's going to be so cool."

"Now, there's sympathy for you," Catie commented.

Maj nodded.

"We also interviewed Griffen's lawyers," Veronica went on. The scene cut to an older man in an Italian suit.

"The whole idea that Eisenhower Productions or Peter had a hand in engineering something like this is totally ludicrous,"

Brett Harper, attorney-at-law, said. "First off, a fiasco like this is highly irresponsible. The law enforcement agencies involved are not going to be amused, and Peter would never think of potentially alienating his fans in this manner."

The scene cut back to the reporter. "What we have so far, Frank, is a mystery that only Peter Griffen or the people responsible for his disappearance can solve."

"Hey, they're here," Megan called from the gate.

Maj and Catie joined her as the first passengers came through. Surprisingly, Matt, Andy, and Leif were among them.

"First class," Catie teased. "Somebody's moving up in the world."

"It was the only way to get three seats together," Leif said. He looked at Maj with concern as they walked through the terminal. "You look like you could use some rest."

"Thanks. That does my confidence a world of good."

Leif glanced around the lobby. "Okay, it's been awhile since I was in LAX. Where are the baggage claim areas?"

Maj pointed to the signs. As she did, her attention was caught by the HoloNet presentation again. A holo image of Peter from the convention occupied center stage with images of the great dragon hanging high overhead. Her mind flashed on the image of Peter when she'd first seen him, dressed in armor and on Sahfrell's back. Then she noticed the rest of the group was waiting on her.

"Sorry," she apologized. "I'm a little preoccupied."

"Hey," Leif said softly, "it's okay."

Maj shook her head. "I don't think so. According to the police, there hasn't been a ransom demand yet."

"That doesn't necessarily mean anything bad," Megan said. "Kidnappers wait a day or so just to let the family get worried before they make their move."

"That's the way your dad wrote it in his novel," Maj pointed out. One of R. F. O'Malley's best-sellers had involved the kidnapping of an operating room nurse from Walter Reed, and the story got even more complicated from there. "In real life kidnappers have a tendency to kill their victims. No witness equals no crime. More often than not, kidnap victims don't come home to their families."

No one had anything to say about that, and when the holo of

Peter Griffen disappeared from the media broadcast, everything seemed awkward.

Matt walked over and put his arm around Maj's shoulders. "Don't sell us out so early. We're just getting on the ground with this thing. We've always made a difference before."

"We're not above failing, and you know that." Maj remembered Julio Cortez. The Net Force Explorers had tried to help him escape the situation he had been in. They'd gotten his family out, but not Julio.

"We're not going to fail," Matt said, his eyes still showing hurt from that mission. "That's not going to happen."

"It's not about failing, Matt. I'm just afraid we're already too late."

Gaspar Latke sat in the corner of the room that had become his prison and watched Heavener standing in front of one of the blacked-out polarized windows. She talked over an encrypted foilpack in a verbal shorthand he couldn't keep track of. She made things even more complicated by speaking in Russian. It was her habit to change languages on a regular basis.

Heavener was obviously unhappy. The emotion showed in the stiff way she held herself and the clipped tone she used. When she was finished, she snapped the foilpack closed and turned on him with catlike quickness.

She's going to kill me. Gaspar trembled.

Instead, she said, "I'll be back."

"Su-sure." He wrapped his arms around himself, trying to stay warm.

A small smile dusted Heavener's lips, and he knew she was enjoying his fear.

Gaspar peered through the doorway after she left, knowing he'd never open it on his own. It let out into a hallway filled with shadows and blank doors. Heavener faded into the darkness before the door closed.

Feek! Gaspar wanted to shout and vent the frustration and fear that were eating him up. The attention Peter Griffen had gotten at the convention, all that he knew about Realm of the Bright Waters, those guaranteed his death.

He forced himself into motion, dropping into one of the implant chairs and onto the Net. Jumping free of the warehouse location on the Net, knowing he didn't have much time, he boosted himself through a sat-link and headed for Alexandria, Virginia. The reports Heavener had gotten included Madeline Green's home address as well as her Net location.

On the Net, he hovered above her house and quickly sorted through the virtual connections she had to the Net. Most visitors to veeyar never noticed them, but Gaspar had programming that allowed him to make the connections visible. A lot of crackers did.

He blinked, then studied the electronic circuitry that stemmed from Madeline Green's room. All of it was protected behind firewalls that looked like glassy-blue foree fields. Knowing Heavener might return at any moment, he hurried when he should have hesitated. He spun a fiberoptic cable from his chest and shot it toward the system's mail utility link. Since he wasn't breaking in to destroy anything or to try to leave an archived virus bombpack, he knew leaving the message would be easy. But as soon as the fiberoptic cable touched the e-mail utility link, a hand stabbed out of the cable, coated in the same black plastic as the cable. It made a fist around the fiberoptic cable.

"You're not going anywhere," a triumphant voice announced.

15

Gaspar Latke panicked, feeling the incredible pull of the fist wrapped around the fiberoptic cable spinning out of his chest. "No!"

"Yes." Mark Gridley stepped from the e-mail link. Gaspar pulled back, hoping to snap the fiberoptic cable in his chest. The pain when he hit the end of the cable was incredible, almost enough to automatically log him off. He'd extended his pain threshold for Heavener's operations past all usual settings.

"Go ahead and fight," Mark told him. "You're hooked like a fish on a line. Maybe I can't keep you prisoner here, but if you try to log off, the virus I've overlaid into your proxy programming is going to leave a signature I can follow anywhere." He grinned and took one long step across the Net that brought him up to Gaspar hanging above Madeline Green's house.

Gaspar ran a quick systems diagnostic on his proxy and found the embedded virus coding. None of the normal firewalls and detectors he kept as part of the proxy's shielding had even phased it. The kid was good.

"You've got to let me go," Gaspar pleaded. Instinctively he pulled at the fiberoptic cable. "Without following me."

"No, I don't," Mark replied.

"They'll kill me if you trace me."

An uneasy look settled across the young boy's face.

"You didn't think about that, did you?" Gaspar demanded, knowing he had a slight edge. "About them killing me, I mean."

"Who are they?"

Gaspar shook his head. "If I tell you that, they'll kill me."

"What if I don't believe you?" Mark challenged.

"Then you might as well put the pistol to my head and pull the trigger yourself." Despite the overwhelming fight-or-flight reflex filling him, Gaspar made himself relax somewhat. "Have you ever seen anyone die while they were online?"

Even in 2025, with all the safeguards put on the Net, it still happened. A heart patient or terminally ill patient logged on at the time of a massive cardiac arrest was a prime candidate. And no one had found a certain way to predict when a brain aneurysm was going to occur or explode, taking someone's life with it. Gaspar had seen it happen, had seen proxies unravel on the Net. And some nights the dreams still haunted him.

"I don't have much time," Gaspar said quietly. "If they come back and find me online, I won't be given a chance to explain."

Hesitation furrowed Mark's brow. "Who are you?"

"I can't tell you that. I can't tell you anything that will lead directly to me. Or to them."

"What were you doing here?" Mark demanded.

"Leaving your friend a message." Gaspar closed his hand, then opened it, revealing an icon that was a crude parchment with a ribbon tied around it. "This message."

"About what?"

"You're welcome to read it, but I've got to go." Gaspar felt frantic. *How long have I been gone already?* He hadn't even checked the time when he'd logged on, and that was usually one of the first things he did.

"Give me something," Mark said.

"I'm giving you that note," Gaspar replied. "And I shouldn't even be doing that." He pulled at the fiberoptic cable, drawing back. The pain started again, sending crashing pain throbbing between his temples. "Track me back and they'll know and I'll be dead. I slipped through a bolt hole I left in the programming, but there's no way I can get back through it with a trace on me."

"Go." Mark turned the fiberoptic cable loose.

Automatically Gaspar ran a systems check on the proxy and found it clean. He logged off and opened his eyes back in the dark room. Heavener was still gone, but he couldn't quite summon up a true feeling of relief. The clock was already ticking on what was left of his life.

"—and then he was gone."

Maj sat in her hotel room with her friends. Mark Gridley's holo stood at center stage, holding all their attention with his story.

Andy shook his head. He sat on the floor against the wall. "You should have left the trace on."

"If they'd found it, they would have killed him."

Andy spread his hands. "Excuse me for being the cynic here, but you only had his word about that."

Mark looked at them a little uncertainly. "I believed him."

"Don't sweat it," Matt advised. "You did the right thing. The guys who invaded Maj's room last night sure didn't have any problems pulling the trigger."

"Sure, the guy thought he was nailed," Andy persisted. "He was going to tell you any story you'd buy into."

"Sometimes people tell the truth," Megan pointed out.

"A body shows up," Andy said, "you can trace a body."

"That's awfully cold," Catie said.

"I'm just saying."

"And bodies don't always turn up," Leif said. "You'd be surprised how many hostile takeovers among corporations actually turn out *hostile*."

Maj hardened her voice. Andy was a friend, but his cynical streak was definitely a pain sometimes. "How about it, Andy? Think you'd have called it any other way?" She met Andy's gaze fully.

Andy blew his breath out. "No. No, you did the right thing, Squirt. I'm just itching to be doing something instead of sitting around here."

"Something like pulling surveillance in the game room?" Leif suggested. He munched on a banana from the huge fruit bowl he'd had sent up. There was also a selection of cheeses and crackers and bottled water.

Andy's face brightened. "Now there's an idea. If they hadn't shut the game room down, I'd be in heaven." The game room had been sealed by the LAPD while a forensics team scoured the area and processed witnesses. Some off-site gaming centers had been set up that were accessible through the Net, but the experience just wasn't the same.

Maj studied the printout from the letter the mystery guy had left. *Visit the Game Producers' Banquet in the hotel tonight. Look and listen.* The package had also included three unique guest passes that couldn't be duplicated.

"Are you sure it was the same guy you met last night?" Maj asked.

"He had the same proxy," Mark answered. "The same kind of feel to him. I'd say so."

"You know," Matt said, "this could be a setup."

"That crossed my mind," Maj admitted.

"Or it could be contact so they can make the ransom demand," Megan said.

"*That* I hadn't thought of." *And that's a new twist I really didn't want to think about right now,* Maj thought. "But why me?"

"For a messenger," Leif said. "Maybe it's because of your Net Force connections. They've studied your background by now. They'll know who you are."

"They could contact Peter's publishers," Maj said. "That would make more sense."

"Unless you figure maybe they were the geeks who kidnapped Peter in the first place," Andy said. "Or that Peter wanted them to contact you because he helped kidnap himself."

"He wouldn't do that."

Andy snorted. "And you got that from the thumbnail history they've got on HoloNet, right?"

"Back off," Maj said angrily.

"No," Andy said. "Stop and think for a minute, Maj. Somehow Peter Griffen invaded your veeyar here at the hotel while you were showing your sim off to Matt. Guys later invaded your room. Maybe you were supposed to scream 'Police!' last night and get some extra attention. Instead, Detective Holmes and Captain Winters squashed the story."

"You didn't see his face," Maj said. "He was just as surprised to see us there as we were to see him."

"That's right," Matt put in. "And the team who was here last night came prepared to kill anyone who got in their way. That wasn't an act."

"Who knows? Maybe a game will sell better if there's a body count attached."

"Andy," Catie cautioned.

"Actually," Megan said, "Andy does have a point. A somewhat bloodthirsty one, but a point all the same."

"Okay, I'll take that for an answer now," Maj said. "But the question remains about whether we should go to the banquet."

Andy raised an eyebrow and smiled. "It's your call, Cinderella. That's your name on the tickets to the ball."

"And two friends," Maj said. "Want to escort me?"

"To a stuffed shirt convention?" Andy shook his head. "I'd rather have surgery to remove—"

Leif interrupted hastily, "I'd love to go with you, Maj."

"Fine."

"Count me in." Megan looked around the room. "Unless someone else would rather go."

"The three of you should be fine," Matt said. "The convention's going to be heavily guarded, physically as well as virtually, so I don't think you'll have any problems. In the meantime, Catie can hold down the fort here and work as a communications go-between while Mark, Andy, and I knock on a few doors to see what we can turn up."

"What doors?" Maj asked.

"I'll dig into the bio material you've archived on Peter," Matt said. "I thought maybe Mark and Andy could check into some of the online gamesites, places where Peter has been known to hang out."

"Now that," Andy sang out, "is my kind of assignment."

"I'll work up a short list of places to start," Mark said. "I've looked over some of Peter's records. Andy and I will get right on it."

Leif plucked a strawberry from the fruit bowl. "Then I'd say we're adjourned here." He checked the time. "We've got a little over an hour till the banquet." He glanced at the two girls. "I don't suppose you packed anything banquety?"

Megan launched a disgusted sigh. "Nope. I was expecting fun and frolic, and tons of games."

Maj shook her head, thinking frantically.

"Then, if you'll allow me," Leif said, "might I suggest the little shop downstairs."

Maj remembered the cocktail dresses she'd seen in the window of that shop. The price tags were obviously set by NASA. "That's a little out of the budget. Cinderella may have to go as pre-fairy godmother Cinderella."

"I took the liberty while we were talking," Leif said, "of setting up an account for you at the shop. My dad's picking up the tab for this little adventure in return for information I can give him concerning the gaming market. Especially the Peter Griffen situation. He's got people ready to start investing in Eisenhower Productions, provided things don't turn sour."

"Gee," Megan teased, "you don't exactly look like the fairy godmother type. Never even saw the wand."

Leif passed one of his hands over the other, making a rectangular piece of plastic appear. "Universal Credit Card. Don't leave home without it."

"Is this your first time at the game publishers' banquet?"

Startled, Maj turned to face the man who'd suddenly appeared at her side. *Is this the guy Mark saw?* She studied him, looking for a clue.

"I'm sorry. I didn't mean to surprise you." The man was in his early twenties, average height but narrow-shouldered and as compact as a rapier. His black skin glistened in the low light of the banquet room. His head was shaved as smooth as an egg. He wore a black tuxedo.

"It's okay," Maj said, and smiled. "I guess maybe I got a little caught up in playing who's who."

"Derek Sommers." He held out his hand. The blue and white name badge on his jacket read DEREK.

"IPG Games," Maj said, getting a little excited. "You created Banshee's Curse."

Derek smiled and bowed slightly. "That's me."

"I've played your game."

"I kind of figured that. I hope you liked it."

"Are you kidding? The game was a monster hit."

Derek laughed. "Let's hope we can say the same about the sequel."

"You can't miss," Maj said, enjoying the moment. Banshee's Curse was a favorite game. "I mean, the way you just leave the characters at the top of Carrig's Tower, with the first piece of a treasure map they hadn't expected to find, you can't walk away from that."

"Maybe I could get you to write a glowing review for the cover copy," Derek said. "If I knew your name."

"Oh, sorry." Maj introduced herself. "And, yes, this is my first game publisher's banquet."

"Have you got something new coming out that I should be looking for?"

"Actually, I'm here trying to find a publisher for a flight-sim." *And trying to figure out what happened to Peter Griffen.*

"Usually they only let game publishers in."

Maj felt a little embarrassed, but the tickets had checked out good under the scanner the security people were using. If they were fakes, they were definitely top-of-the-line.

"Personally," Derek said, "I'm glad to see somebody who likes my game instead of hearing someone talk about theirs."

Maj grinned, but inside she was still feeling intense. "Well, this year they seem to have added something new. Kidnapping."

Swirling his glass of champagne, Derek shrugged. "If you believe what you see."

"You don't sound like you do." Maj glanced around the room again, taking in the ornate splendor of the huge chandelier hanging from the ceiling, the painted vases, and the way the low walls crammed with plants broke the floor into almost private sections. Trees at the corners of the walls helped carry out the illusion. Still, there were large gathering places near the room's three open bars. A heavily laden banquet table filled the center of the room.

"I guess maybe I've been around too many marketing people," Derek admitted. "They'll use anything they can to hype a product and get it out into the hands of consumers."

"Surely they'd stop at kidnapping."

"Marketing people," Derek said seriously, "don't stop at anything. Trust me."

"I thought that was one of *their* standard lines."

Derek's grin was even broader. "A girl with a sense of humor. I like that, Maj Green."

Maj enjoyed Derek's attention. The shimmering dark red cocktail dress she wore made her feel as elegant as anyone in the room. And Derek's attention didn't come across as flirty, just as fun. "So you think Eisenhower Productions and Peter Griffen are in on the kidnapping together?"

"I can see it happening. In fact, I was even thinking of it as a game hook."

The suggestion caught Maj's attention immediately. "How?"

"You've got Peter Griffen out here introducing what looks a killer game," Derek said. "Only in the middle of everything, he disappears. At least, that's what we're told. I could see marketing coming up with a contest: Enter Realm of the Bright Waters, fight evil wizards, ride flying dragons, and find Peter Griffen to win a million bucks." He raised an eyebrow. "Think that would get the gaming community's attention?"

"Yes." *It's definitely got mine.* Maj ran the scenario through her mind, trusting her instincts. She remembered how sincere Peter had looked as he discussed his game. No way could she imagine him faking his own kidnapping to build up game sales. *Then again, Leif did mention that Eisenhower Productions had been looking for a solid hit for a few years. Maybe they weren't the only ones.*

"Everyone knows," Derek said, "if you get an interested gaming community, you've got an inflated profit. I believe Peter's disappearance has got dollar signs tied to it. Something like this is worth millions in advertising alone. And that's being conservative."

"Do you know anyone at Eisenhower Productions?" Maj asked.

"Acquaintances." Derek glanced around the room. "Nobody I do business with."

Maj had already noticed the table reserved for the Eisenhower Productions crew. Peter Griffen's place card stood at one end.

"Surprise, surprise," Derek said in a low voice, glancing in the direction of a dozen people who'd just been ushered into the banquet room by the maitre d'. "We're being invaded by the media tonight."

Veronica Rivers, the reporter who'd been covering the gaming convention at the hotel, was prominent among the reporters. The maître d' showed them to a table, but the reporters immediately wandered off, staking out interviewing claims.

"That's a vicious little game Eisenhower Productions is playing," Derek said. "If they engineered Peter's disappearance."

"Why?"

"If those entertainment reporters figure out they're getting used, they're going to turn on Eisenhower like a system-wide crash fragmenting a hard drive. With the financial situation they're in, that wouldn't be pretty."

"What financial situation?" Maj asked.

Derek shook his head. "I forgot you weren't in the biz there for a minute. Rumor has it that Eisenhower Productions was about to climb in the old financial coffin before Peter Griffen and Realm of the Bright Waters came along. That's part of the reason he was able to muscle them into agreeing with everything he wanted. However, they ran short on liquid cash. So did Peter, from what I heard."

"I'd heard he was financially stable."

"He wasn't in any danger of starving," Derek admitted, "but it takes a lot of cash to develop a game. Most publishers underwrite development, but in Eisenhower Productions' case, they weren't able to do it. Peter may have gotten more rushed than he wanted. Maybe he and Eisenhower Productions were both desperate."

Maj tried to make that fit with what she had seen of Peter, but it didn't work. Peter had come across too confident, too sure of himself. *But that could have been an act,*

Abruptly a public address system cut on, filling the banquet area with staticky noise. "May I have your attention, please."

The crowd turned to face the speaker's area as the lights dimmed and spotlights ignited one end of the room. A short, heavyset man with a curly beard and glasses stood in the middle of the light. "For those of you who don't know me, I'm Don DeGovia, CEO of Eisenhower Productions."

A slight murmur ran though the crowd.

Maj listened with keen interest, wondering if Peter Griffen had already been found. And if he had been, in what kind of shape he was in.

16

"As you all have doubtless heard," Don DeGovia went on, "an unbelievable crime was committed at the convention today when Peter Griffen, whose Griffen Games imprint, Online and On Target, was getting ready to unleash the new Net experience, Realm of the Bright Waters, was kidnapped and taken from us."

Maj listened intently and glanced around the room, wondering how the other game publishers were reacting. But everyone in the room seemed interested in what was going on.

"Mr. DeGovia," Veronica Rivers spoke up. Evidently her camera and sound equipment were located in her clothing because Maj noticed that the woman wasn't panicking while looking for a cameraman.

"Yes, Ms. Rivers."

"Can you tell us what is being done to locate Peter Griffen?"

DeGovia didn't hesitate. "Everything," he said. "Everything that can be done is now being done. By the police and by the private security guards we maintain. So far, I'm told, there are no leads. We hope to change that." The CEO cleared his throat. "As of tonight, Eisenhower Productions is offering a reward of one million dollars to anyone who can help us find Peter Griffen."

Conversations started up immediately as the crowd reacted to the news.

"And that," Derek said quietly at Maj's side, "is worth more than a million dollars in advertising. By tonight this story is going to be run on every major news service across the planet."

"Do you still think Peter and Eisenhower could be responsible for the kidnapping?" Maj asked.

"Oh, yeah. Legal fees to get out of something like this would be expensive, but not impossible. And the profit we're talking about will more than make up for it." Derek shook his head. "Plus, they still have to get caught at it. If they fake the payoff, they can even give themselves a million-dollar write-off on their taxes."

"You make it sound like it's all about the money."

Derek nodded. "At this level it almost always is."

"My God, DeGovia, do you realize what you've done?" A stout man with short-clipped red hair stepped forward from the crowd. "Making an announcement like this, you've made targets of each and every member of the game design community."

"I'm just trying to help Peter," DeGovia replied. "It's all I know how to do."

"That's Kip Wilson," Derek whispered to Maj. "Creator of Bug Battles."

"It's only been a few hours since Griffen disappeared," Wilson declared. "Give the police a chance to do their job."

"Time is of the essence," DeGovia went on. "I'm doing what I think I need to do."

"Mr. DeGovia," Veronica interrupted, "has there been a ransom demand?"

"No," DeGovia replied. "At present we're all waiting. But we're willing to pay it."

The banquet suddenly turned into a madhouse as everyone started talking at once. Maj looked around her in disbelief. *Is this what I was supposed to see tonight? And if it is, what am I supposed to learn?* She scanned the crowd, wondering if the guy who'd given Mark the message was still waiting to make his move.

"You know," Derek said at her side, "Eisenhower is going to be back in the black profit-wise after tonight. They're going to sell a bazillion games. You can't compete with this kind of attention."

Andy and Mark shot through the telecommunications grid high above Russia, then zipped down to a cyber café in Leningrad.

They'd been steadily backtracking Peter Griffen's trail in the gaming world for the last three hours. Information they'd gotten from the gaming community in Seattle, Washington, led them to Tokyo. Peter had spent a lot of time in different gaming areas learning his craft even after he'd achieved some success.

Andy understood and respected that. Gaming was a way of life, and to really live, you had to spend time at it every day. He could always tell the difference between an occasional gamer and someone who really got into it within just a few seconds of play. He'd never had that kind of attention span to give up weeks and months to a particular kind of game. And most gamers had years of experience on him.

Together, he and Mark walked into the cyber café. It was a small brick building three stories tall, lurched up against an ancient apartment complex three times its size. Implant chairs of all makes and models sat strewn across the black-and-white tiled floor under weak lighting. Techno-rock crashed like thunder in the background. Nearly all of the chairs were filled.

The room blurred as they crossed the threshold and the holoprojectors kicked in with a surge Andy felt along his implants. "Oh, man," he complained, "they need a system upgrade."

"Since we're here asking for a favor," Mark suggested, "maybe it would be wise not to mention that."

Andy gazed around the room. Now that the holoprojector had cut in, the room was cleaner and brighter. The implant chairs were gone and only a few people sat around the tables waiting for someone to game with. They were all in various proxies, some made up, others from various games.

He crossed the room to the cute redhead behind the bar. Bottled water, soft drinks, and bags of chips and candy, all virtual, filled the chillers and the shelves behind her.

"Hi," Andy said.

"Hi," the redhead greeted. "There's a small entrance fee if you're going to stay and play."

Andy shook his head. "Just looking for someone."

The girl shrugged. "If I know them."

"Zenzo Fujikama."

"I know him."

"I was told he was here," Andy said.

"I'll see." The girl touched a com-pad on the bar top. "I've got a couple of newbies looking for Zenzo Fujikama."

Andy looked at the com-screen, but it stayed blank.

"Privacy," the redhead said, meeting his gaze with a little hostility. "A lot of people who game here like that. Maybe it's a new concept where you're from."

On the shelf behind her a winking lens caught Andy's eye. He stared at the button vidcam. "I guess that privacy thing doesn't work both ways, huh?"

"No."

"Send them away," a mechanical voice ordered.

The redhead tapped the com-pad, blanking the function. "I guess they're not interested in meeting new friends."

Mark stretched a finger out. Immediately metallic webbing shot forward, connecting to the com-pad, the vidcam on the shelf, and stabbing through the ceiling. Sparks showered down from the power line overhead. The act caught the attention of everyone in the cyber café. Usually these places were by and large hackproof and left alone by cyber outlaws.

Andy watched in awe as the metallic webbing strand that stretched from Mark's finger to the vidcam suddenly sprouted another strand that wove itself into an eight-inch monitor. The screen cleared after a moment, revealing a view into a small room with four people sitting around a table.

Two of the guys looked European, and the third was an African woman, Andy judged by her dress. Zenzo Fujikama had to be the young Asian guy dressed in the blue and silver Spacehunter leathers.

Spacehunter was a popular anime role-playing game that had come out of Japan. It was violent and filled with exotic creatures and locales. Andy had enjoyed playing the game, but it had been filled with too many diehard fans to make playing it anything other than a short-lived experience.

"Who are you?" one of the European men demanded.

"Andy Moore," Andy said.

The guy had peroxide hair and a long black duster. His canines gleamed when they caught the light. "Doesn't mean anything to me. And if you don't clear out of our café, I'm calling the police."

If you were clean, Andy thought, *that's the first thing you would have done.* This cyber café had a reputation as being a hangout for hackers and had been busted a few times in the past. Mark knew that because he sometimes spent time in places like this one.

"I'm Mark Gridley," Mark said.

"Doesn't mean anything to me, either," the blond guy snarled.

"Wait," Zenzo Fujikama said softly. "The name means something to me." He looked at the screen. "You took on Death-stalker 3000 and wiped it out a couple months ago."

"What's he talking about?" Andy asked.

"A game," Mark replied.

Zenzo shook his head. "Not just a game. At the time it was *the* blackboard game."

Andy understood then. Blackboard games were operated illegally on the Net. They were filled with risky builds that sometimes had uncontrollable implant shock spikes. Some of the damage, although not lethal, had resulted in gamers losing partial link-up ability with the Net. The draw was the risk, but Andy couldn't believe Mark would play those games.

"You played that game?" Andy asked.

Zenzo laughed. "He didn't just play the game. He destroyed it. The guys who built it put nearly a year of development into it. Your buddy destroyed it in seventeen straight hours of some of the best play I've ever seen. When the dust settled, they were out of business. Gridley took out their game, then posted game cheats on every blackboard bulletin server on the Net. After that, Deathstalker 3000 was just a joke."

"Too many people were getting hurt," Mark replied.

"Maybe so, but that's what they were paying to do."

"We're here about Peter Griffen," Mark said. "The word I get is that you guys used to be pretty tight."

Zenzo glanced at the other three people at the table. "Check you later." He stepped forward, and in the next instant he was in the lower floor of the cyber café with Mark and Andy. "Let's take a walk."

Andy stepped in behind Zenzo, flanked by Mark, who dropped the hack he had on the cyber café's vid systems.

"Let me take the lead," Zenzo suggested. "I've got a place I want to take you."

A trickle of nervous fear threaded down Andy's spine. Giving control of his movements on the Net was something he didn't like to do even if he knew the person doing the leading.

"Okay," Mark said without hesitation. Not feeling good about the move at all, Andy did the same.

Zenzo leaped up into the Net, pulling them along after him as he crashed through the telecommunications grid.

Matt floated in his veeyar and chased paper trails. All the files Maj had archived on Peter Griffen had been reduced to a series of icons hanging in the air, grouped by personal history, publishing history, broken down into different game development corporations Peter had worked for.

It seemed like a lot of information, but it really wasn't. Peter Griffen's life was strictly low profile.

A com-link beeped for attention, strobing a pulsing blue wave against the black sky to his left. "Connect," Matt said.

Instantly a vidscreen formed in the center of the blue pulse and framed Catie's face. "Having any luck?"

"Not much," Matt admitted. "I can give you a copy of every tax form Peter's ever filed, every place of residence he's had, the cars he's owned, and so forth, but I can't give you any personal details."

"What about family?"

Matt shook his head. "Peter's had a lot of bad luck. When he was seven, his parents were killed in a car wreck. He survived, but there was no family to take care of him. Or, if there was, they didn't admit to it. He never got adopted and was raised by the state."

"Which state?"

"California. A little town called Patterson that's not far from Sacramento."

"Maybe you could use a break," Catie suggested. "I know I could."

Matt nodded. He closed his eyes and logged off, opening them again in Catie's hotel room.

Catie sat at the hotel desk in front of the communications array Mark had cobbled together to link all the Net Force Explorer teams.

Matt crossed the room and took an apple from the fruit bowl. He glanced over to the corner and saw Andy still logged onto the Net in the extra implant chair they'd asked the hotel to bring up. "Are Mark and Andy having any luck?"

"Mark let me know they found someone named Zenzo."

"Who's he?"

"According to what they found out, Zenzo helped Peter develop some of the computer graphics software used to build Realm of the Bright Waters."

"Maybe Zenzo got to know Peter a little more than most of the people who've written articles about him."

"Have you been able to talk to any of the other gaming companies Peter has worked for?" Catie asked.

Matt nodded. "Most of them have skeleton crews on-site because the majority of the staff is here at the convention. But it doesn't do much good talking to them because they haven't given me anything more than the HoloNet files. Peter was a good guy to work with, very inventive, reliable."

"No hidden neuroses or agendas?"

"If there were," Matt said, "they're still hidden."

"What about the orphanage?"

"The records are sealed, and I couldn't get through to talk to anyone."

"Probably every news service around is calling them."

Matt nodded unhappily. He wasn't used to coming up empty. "The only thing I did turn up was an article about Peter's first few games. He worked with a friend of his from the orphanage. A guy named Oscar Raitt. I've reached his answering service, but so far he hasn't returned my call."

"Where is he?"

"Seattle," Matt answered. "He's working with Steph Games."

Catie leaned her head back into the implant chair. "Let me check the files Mark gave me." She was back in an instant. She smiled. "Steph Games is at the convention. And you'll never guess who one of the representatives is."

"Oscar Raitt," Matt said.

"Bingo. He's staying at the Mohammed Arms. It's just across the street. The Bessel made an arrangement with them to handle some of the overflow. Oscar must have gotten here late."

"Have you got a room number?"

"No. But you should be able to get him through the front desk if he's in his room."

Matt took out his foilpack and punched in the hotel's lobby number. When the call was answered, he asked for Oscar Raitt's room.

"Hi," a deep and pleasant voice said. "You've reached the voice mail of Oscar Raitt. Please leave your name and number, and I'll get back to you. Thanks."

"Oscar," Matt said, "you don't know me, but I'm looking for Peter Griffen. My name is Matt Hunter." He keyed the foilpack to send a copy of his Net Force Explorers ID as well. "I'm staying at the Bessel Midtown Hotel, and I'd like—"

The transmission was interrupted by a booming voice. "Hold on, hold on! I want to talk to you!"

Matt held the foilpack and watched the vidscreen come to life. Oscar Raitt was a big guy. He had curly blond hair, a bullet of a head, and a goatee. Acne-marked pale skin covered his oval face.

"What do you know about Peter's kidnapping?" Oscar asked.

"I was hoping you could help me," Matt said.

Oscar considered that. "Is Net Force involved in this?"

"I'm helping with the initial investigation."

Nodding, Oscar said, "Good. Because Peter disappearing like this isn't right. I've heard a lot of dexters around the convention suggesting that Peter helped himself to his own kidnapping. That's pure DFB, data flowing bad."

"I've got a friend who feels the same way."

"How about you?" The intensity of Oscar's gaze was nuclear.

Matt remembered the men with the pistols the night before, how he'd been fired on before the men knew he was only a holo. "I'm a believer."

"Okay." Oscar nodded. "I've been trying to get people to listen to me that Peter would never do something like this. And there's more going on than what you think."

"What?" Matt's pulse quickened.

"I don't want to talk over a vidphone connection. How soon can you get here?"

"Give me the room number and five minutes," Matt said.

Gaspar Latke sat in the cluttered office of his veeyar, his attention locked on the sixteen different screens he'd opened in front of him. Ten of them were different views of the Bessel Midtown Hotel's banquet room, linked from the buttoncams Heavener's team had put into the room since Peter Griffen's kidnapping. Four more monitored the hotel's main entrances, and two constantly cycled through the various HoloNet news feeds covering Don DeGovia's interview after offering a million dollars for information about Peter Griffen's abduction.

Gaspar's eyes swept the cameras again, watching the people in the banquet room talking. He could remember when a million dollars would have been a big deal to him, too. But since Heavener had taken over his life, he couldn't remember how many millions and billions of dollars he'd helped the corporation steal from others.

Sweat trickled across his face back in the physical world, and his heart rate was slightly elevated with all the stress.

A small, rectangular window suddenly exploded into view above the sixteen monitors. It showed his heart rate, dangerously near the automatic log-off point. But he knew that would never happen. Before she'd left, Heavener had ordered a doctor to insert a hypodermic shunt into the back of Gaspar's right hand. Attached to that was an IV bag containing tranquilizers that would suppress his body's reactions as needed.

They also made it harder for Gaspar to think. He concentrated on his physical self for a moment, blurring the veeyar around the edges, and slowed his breathing, taking deep lungfuls of air.

C'mon. Drop. Just as he was about to give up, knowing his own tension over the medication waiting to be released into his system and maybe take away his last chance at freedom, the indicator level dropped, finally coming to a rest barely within the intermediate safety zone.

He returned his full attention to the veeyar, then swept his gaze over the banquet room again. He spotted Madeline Green talking to a young man in the middle of the crowd.

"Identify," Gaspar ordered, locking a capture window over the young man.

"Derek Sommers," the computer answered. "IPG games. Continue?"

"No." Gaspar couldn't believe he hadn't recognized Derek. It only showed how rattled he was. He stood up suddenly and launched himself through the ceiling, passing through it easily and following one of the buttoncams' telecommunications signal to the hotel through the Net zones. All the security programs and the firewalls had been punched clear by his viruses earlier.

In seconds he was in the banquet room in holoform. Other game design publishers were there in holo as well, not truly trusting circumstances after the kidnapping. And some of them never appeared in public anyway for their own reasons.

The holoprojectors gave Gaspar virtual substance, but even as he started to appear, he triggered a program he had prepared. Instead of looking like himself or his usual proxy, he grafted on the appearance of Matt Hunter. He knew the real Matt was working online, in one of the other girls' rooms. Heavener hadn't bugged the Explorers' rooms, but she had ordered buttoncams placed in the hallways beside their rooms.

Shaking on the inside, hoping the proxy would hold under the scrutiny of the men Heavener had at the banquet, Gaspar approached Madeline Green. "Hey, Madeline." He tried to sound casual, even forced a smile. "Got a minute?"

She turned to Derek and excused herself, then walked toward a small empty area beside one of the walls surrounding the table areas.

Gaspar hadn't realized how pretty she looked in the cocktail dress until that moment. Watching through the monitors back in his veeyar just hadn't been the same.

She turned on him, arms folding across her breasts and her brown eyes stern. "Maybe we need to start with you telling me who you are, because you're sure not anyone I know."

17

Gaspar froze, staring back at Madeline Green, not knowing how he'd lost control of the situation so quickly. "What?"

"All my friends call me Maj," she said. "Ergo, you're not one of them. No matter how much you look like Matt Hunter."

Glancing at the crowd around them, wondering if anyone was paying too much attention, Gaspar pleaded, "Wait! I can explain!"

"Ten seconds," Maj said, "and I'm starting counting now."

Looking at her, Gaspar thought back to what he knew of her. "Peter Griffen's in real trouble. I don't think he knows how deep he's into it."

"Has he been kidnapped?"

"Yes."

"Please lower your voice," Gaspar said. "This room is being monitored by the people I work for."

"Who are they?"

"I can't tell you. Not now."

"I can scream," Maj pointed out. "When security shuts the area down, you might escape, but there's a good chance you'd get tagged with a trace virus."

Gaspar shook his head. "No. They've invaded the system. I can get out as easily as I got in."

"So you say."

"It's true." Angry and frustrated, Gaspar hardened his voice. "Do you want to help Peter Griffen or not? Because if you don't, they're going to kill him."

"How am I supposed to help him?"

"I don't know that yet," Gaspar answered. "I haven't gotten that worked out."

"Do you know where he is?"

Gaspar considered lying for only a moment, thinking he could improve his own worth, then didn't because he was sure she would know that he was lying. "No. I'll try to find out."

"Who are you?"

"Someone who needs your help," Gaspar replied. "I met your friend Mark earlier. I arranged for you to get the invitations tonight so I could meet you."

"You're in charge of surveillance over the banquet?"

"Yes."

"Then shut it down and let's talk."

Gaspar glanced across the room, picking out the two men he knew Heavener had assigned to cover the banquet inside the room. Neither of them paid any attention to him. "I can't. There's someone in charge of me."

"It's going to be hard to help you if I don't know who you are or what's going on."

"I can only hope that it's enough that you know I exist, and that you're right in thinking that Peter Griffen didn't have anything to do with the kidnapping. They set him up, used him, and it's only going to get worse."

Anxious frustration showed on Maj's face. "Where do I start looking?"

Gaspar shook his head. "I don't know. This whole thing is so tangled and I'm so close to the middle of it that anything I say could get Peter and me both killed. We are acceptable losses. There's too much at risk."

"What?"

"I don't know for sure. But I do know these people don't do anything without millions or billions of dollars on the line."

"So it is about money," Maj said.

Gaspar shrugged and felt bad because she sounded so disappointed, which was strange because he was the one who was risking his neck. "Most things are. But this is about a *lot* of money. I just don't know how. Yet." He wanted to say more, but he was afraid to. Anything he said that could lead them back to him was the wrong thing. They need to be led through their own resources to Peter Griffen.

Maj looked at him, studying him. "Where do we—"

Before she could finish her question, Gaspar spotted Heavener approaching the banquet room. The woman wore a deep jade cocktail dress but walked purposefully. Even though the dress clung to the curves, Gaspar knew she could have a dozen deadly weapons concealed on her body.

"What's wrong?" Maj asked.

Heavener checked in through the banquet security easily, using the ID that Gaspar had generated for her. She paused in the doorway and glanced over the crowd. Her lips barely moved as she spoke. Only someone watching her closely would have noticed.

"Latke." Her voice came through the aud-connect Gaspar had set up in his veeyar.

"Yes," he answered, turning to Maj and closing down the aud-send loop so Heavener wouldn't hear him. "I've got to go."

"Is it because of that woman?" Maj clutched at the sleeve of the tuxedo jacket he wore.

Gaspar hesitated, not wanting to leave the safety Maj Green represented but knowing he should log off now.

"Close your net over this room," Heavener ordered. "Execute now. I've got someone in here with a mask program passing himself off as Matt Hunter."

Cold hard fear filled Gaspar, and he couldn't help looking at Heavener across the room. *How did she know?*

"Latke, close the net."

Automatically Gaspar closed the net, securing holo traces in a minefield over the immediate area. That had been only one of the safeguards Heavener had insisted on. Now if he tried to leave the room along the Net, he'd be tagged with a trace virus, and Heavener would know he'd made contact with Maj Green.

And he didn't even know where to tell Maj to find his own body.

Heavener circled the room, talking to the two men inside the room over the audlink running through Gaspar's veeyar system.

"I've got to get out of here," Gaspar said to Maj, taking her by the arm and pulling her. He scanned the room. There were three other exits. He glanced over his shoulder. Heavener and the two men had spread out, going slowly and steadily through the crowd, closing in like pincers. They easily covered three of the exits. The exit on the other side of the room was his only hope.

"What's wrong?" Maj asked, resisting his urge to move.

"They're on to me."

"The woman?" Maj still wasn't moving, and Heavener was getting closer.

"Yes. But she doesn't know it's me. She sees your friend Matt, the same as you do."

Maj got into motion, following at his side. "What happens if she finds out it's you?"

"Then I'm dead, and your friend Peter is probably dead, too." Gaspar struggled not to run for the exit. They were ahead, but it was going to be close.

"Latke," Heavener called over the audlink. "Do you see him? The guy with Madeline Green?"

Gaspar had to restrain himself from correcting Heavener and telling her it was Maj, not Madeline. "I see him. Are you sure that isn't Matt Hunter?"

"Matt Hunter left the room where he was a few minutes ago," Heavener responded. "He's another problem I'm having to take care of at the moment."

"I missed that," Gaspar said. Panic flooded his senses, and he knew his heart rate was accelerating beyond control again. He tried to control it, knowing the tranquilizers would definitely affect his ability to do everything he needed to do.

"We'll talk about it when I see you again," Heavener said.

Gaspar felt like an animal with a leg in the iron jaws of a bear trap. He hurried toward the glass doors of the exit. "I need you to open the door," he told Maj. "It's not programmed for holo interaction. There are holoprojectors out in the hall for the hotel guests, so I won't be immediately tossed out of the hotel, but if I just walk through the door, Heavener's going to know I'm a holo instead of a person in a mask program."

"Heavener's the woman?"

"Forget you heard that name." Gaspar couldn't believe he'd let it slip. "The door. Get the door." He held her arm, the sensation almost feeling normal thanks to the holoprojector feed-backs.

Maj hit the door release lever, and they walked briskly out into the hallway. Gaspar trotted alongside her, listening to his heart thunder back in his physical body. He expected to feel the hot burn of the tranquilizers rushing through his system at any second.

"Stop!" Heavener's voice barked behind them.

Maj broke into a run, yanking Gaspar after her. He stumbled and almost fell, prey to the realistic approach of the holoprojec-tors. The hallways were safe, he knew from his research on the hotel, and so were most of the rooms. He glanced over his shoulder, watched in escalating terror as Heavener started clos-ing the distance. Maybe Maj would have been able to outrun her on her own, but he couldn't keep the pace.

"She's catching up," he gasped.

Abruptly Maj turn and shoved him ahead. "Keep going!"

Gaspar hesitated just a moment, watching as Heavener pounded down the hallway. The two men followed behind her. "Matt's in danger. That's how they knew I was here. Don't forget." Then he ran, wishing there were someone else in the hallways to help Maj, wishing he didn't think he was such a coward for running.

But he ran as hard as he could, taking the first corner to the left that he came to. Releasing the holo form, he jumped back to his veeyar.

"Peter's a brilliant guy," Oscar Raitt said. "He's always got a head full of ideas. Twists on programming no one else has ever even thought of. If there was ever anyone born to work in the gaming world, it was Pete."

Matt sat at the small desk in the hotel room where Oscar was staying. "You don't think Peter disappeared on his own?"

"No way." Oscar was adamant. He was at least six feet eight or six feet nine, with the broad shoulders of a woodcutter or a linebacker. He sat on the bed, obviously more at home there than in one of the hotel's regular-sized chairs. He wore a tank top and shorts, his massive feet clad in Roman sandals. A choc-olate mint was stacked on top of the pillow behind him. "That production number Pete had up front? That was his show, man. In his book, this would be an all-time low."

"Had you been in touch with him much?"

"Sure. We talked a lot." Oscar grinned. "We saw each other at least once a month. He was the reason I got to know Paris so well."

"Paris?"

Oscar nodded. "Yeah. You know. Paris, France. Eiffel Tower. Arch of Triumph. Napoleon."

"Got it. What was Peter doing in France?"

"Developing Realm of the Bright Waters. That's where Eisenhower put him up to do the design work."

"I didn't know Eisenhower Productions had a Paris office." Leif had mentioned that Eisenhower was based in Seattle.

Oscar lifted his broad shoulders and dropped them. "Beats me. But that's where Pete worked on the game. He didn't take much time off, but when he did, he usually called me, and we spent some time prowling the city. Art museums because any video graphics designer is going to tell you that you just can't see enough stuff. And we spent some downtime at the cyber cafés. A true game junky just can't get away from it."

"What did you talk about?" Matt asked.

"The usual. What he was working on, what I was working on. What we thought of some of the games that were out there."

"Peter didn't mention any problems with Eisenhower Productions? How they wanted to market the game?"

"No. Peter didn't concern himself with that. Realm of the Bright Waters was strictly his baby. They couldn't make move one without his okay."

"Isn't that unusual in the gaming industry?"

"Like finding a frog with wings. In the real world."

"Don't the publishers underwrite a lot of a developer's expenses?"

"Most deals," Oscar said, "they underwrite entirely. Financial freedom doesn't come without a price, though. They usually control the milestones and deadlines more than you do, and they can make you release a game that you know isn't right. It's hard to blame them, though. They've got investors and accountants crawling over them with microscopes."

"You two worked together on some games in the past, didn't you?"

Oscar nodded. "Peter said he thought he might need me on this game at the end. He had some problems with the game engine. He built it from scratch, you know, to maximize play possibilities."

"I don't understand," Matt admitted.

"One of the chief gripes of the CRPG players," Oscar said, "is the whole campaign structure. Take a game like Sarxos. It's interactive, with a constantly varying number of players online, all with their own agendas. They raise armies, battle each other for regions, cities, rights to water, whatever. But you can't introduce new elements into the game without playing havoc with a lot of ongoing campaigns."

"Give me an example."

"Okay, say you and your group have been in Sarxos. Maybe building up a carnival complete with goods and jousting tournaments. Something to draw the populace and line your own pockets with gold. Another bunch of players decides the game has gotten too dull in that area, and they go attack goblin or bandit camps. They get all the goblins or bandits stirred up. Next thing you know, the goblins or bandits come tearing out of the hills and totally raze the carnival. The second group got the excitement they wanted, but the first group loses all their investment time. On one hand you got guys saying you've got a great game. But on the other, you've got a lot of unhappy campers."

Matt nodded. He'd seen it happen more than once.

"Different people like to play the game at different speeds," Oscar said. "The hack and slashers want action and a Monte Hall dungeon. But the builders want a game they can basically build another existence in; a place where they can chill out from a stressful world. That was one of the major draws Pete had with the new game engine. It was designed to offer the option to integrate with any ongoing campaign."

"So each adventure could be individual and at a pace the particular gamer wanted."

"Yes."

Matt thought about the concept. "That's almost like building a million different games at one time."

Oscar grinned. "You're getting it now. Individually tailored for the individual player."

"The programming must have been intense."

"I saw some of the coding Pete wrote for it. Groundbreaking stuff. And that game, when it hits the market, is going to go huge. Pete's already got story arcs mapped out for the game."

"What kind of story arcs?"

"Plagues. Invasions. In one of them a magic spell tilts the whole planet on its axis, causes a year-long winter to fall over the world. Can you imagine that?"

Matt shook his head. He couldn't, but the whole idea sounded fascinating.

"This world is going to be more interactive than Sarxos for the gamer," Oscar said. "The people who put Sarxos online have kind of had to maintain the status quo. No coloring outside the lines. No huge story or environment changes. With Pete's world he could introduce anything he wanted to. The players could play it then, later, or not at all."

The idea was staggering. Matt wasn't as informed and as excited about Net games as Mark and Andy were, but he liked them on occasion. Realm of the Bright Waters sounded nothing short of awesome. "You said Peter thought he might need your help."

"Yes. He had some game engine problems. See, I taught Pete everything he ever learned about game engines. We started tinkering with them at the orphanage. Pete and I were both state raised."

Matt nodded.

"I think that's why he's so good at building worlds," Oscar said. "He was always a quiet kid. Polite. Didn't ever raise a big stink about things. He stayed to himself a lot. I didn't know what to think of him. But when the home got online and brought in implant chairs, that's when I saw Pete really come alive. It turned out that I had some skill at programming. Pete wanted to learn. That's how we met. I could write programming and teach it to Pete, but he's the one with the ideas. I can do a little world-building, setting up environments, and pulling a cohesive storyline together, but I can't keep up with him. Nobody could."

"Why did he go off on his own instead of signing a deal with a major publisher?"

"Because he wanted the control. Publishers have their own ideas about things. Too many hands in the pot. And, basically, I think Pete was building his own world that he could share with others. It's supposed to be a place where he can stay and control things. No car wrecks. No losing his parents. Total control."

"And he wouldn't want to give that up."

"No. No way."

"How did he get along with Eisenhower Productions?"

"Everything with them was hurry. They'd have had the game out six months ago if they could have."

"Peter held them up?"

"Yeah. They didn't like it, but they didn't have a choice. Part of it was their fault. When he asked me to help with the game engine, they told me I couldn't. They maintained that much control."

"Did they say why?"

Oscar shrugged. "They didn't want anything about the game getting out was what they told him. I think it was a petty vengeance thing. He told them wait on the game; they told him he couldn't use me."

"Did he ask anyone else?"

"No. Pete wouldn't have."

"So he worked through the game engine problems himself?" Matt asked.

"Yes."

"Did he say what they were?"

"We talked about it a little. What he was having was a bleed-over problem."

"Bleed-over?"

"Sure. You have more than one player in a multi-user game, you have to build in boundaries so one player doesn't affect the other player's gameplay. What Pete was trying to do was isolate whole worlds, yet at the same time have them all remain accessible. So the concrete facts remain concrete. If he wanted to introduce a new creature or a new spell, he needed to be able to integrate as a sys/ops change, not have to write new programming for each offshoot a player had made. Understand?"

"Separate but equal," Matt said.

"Kind of lame," Oscar said, "but that's the general idea."

Matt remembered last night, when Peter Griffen and the dragon had invaded Maj's veeyar. "Is it possible that the bleed-over you're talking about could affect other games?"

"You mean the way they did at the convention today?" Oscar asked.

"Yes. I was in one of those games. I saw that dragon."

Oscar grinned. "Yeah. A lot of people did. I'll bet they never forget it, either. I never saw the bleed-over that Pete was talking about, but from his description that was exactly how it was. I was going to go over to him and talk to him about it. You could see the surprise on his face. He had no clue."

"He thought he had the bleed-over fixed?"

"Pete had to have thought he had it fixed," Oscar said. "Otherwise that game would never have seen the light of day."

"He'd stop the release on Saturday?"

"In a heartbeat."

That, Matt figured, *might be a good reason for Eisenhower to get Peter out of the way. Maybe Peter figured the overlap into Maj's veeyar was just a fluke, a small hiccup in the programming the night before.* But there was no way to mistake what had happened at the convention.

"Pete didn't know the bleed-over bug was still there," Oscar said. "I'd bet my life on it."

"Do you have any notes Peter sent you regarding the game engine bleed-over?"

"He called me last night," Oscar said. "I wasn't here because I was out wining and dining some game developers who are interested in some ideas I have. I think the message is still on my veeyar at home. Maybe I've got a few other e-mails still lingering around. A lot of Pete's e-mail had jokes and stories in them that I like to read over occasionally."

"Can you get whatever you have?"

"Sure. I talked to Pete last night after I got in. He thought he had it under control again then. We were going to get together after his presentation today. But that didn't happen." Oscar paused. "Do you think Pete's okay?"

"So far," Matt said, "there's not any reason to think otherwise."

Oscar nodded, but he didn't look convinced.

Matt's foilpack rang unexpectedly. He excused himself and opened it.

Megan's face filled the vidscreen. "Trouble," she said breathlessly. "Maj just ran out of the banquet room with a couple guys that looked as if they match the descriptions of the men who invaded her room last night. Leif went after them, too."

"I'm on my way." Matt stood up and headed for the door at a trot.

"Something wrong?" Oscar asked.

"A friend needs me." Matt opened the door. "Download a

copy of Peter's e-mails and get it to me over at the Bessel Midtown front counter. I'll meet you there."

"If it will help find Pete, I'll be there with bells on."

"I think it will." Then Matt was through the door, running for the stairwell that would take him down to the third floor where the above-street enclosed walkway was. He ran to the other hotel, not really noticing the shadows at the other end till one of them stepped out at him. Instinctively he tried to turn to defend himself.

Something crashed into the side of his face, detonating what felt like a small nuclear device on his right temple. His legs turned to jelly, and he went down. Falling over onto his back, he glanced up with double vision and saw the hard-lined shadow lean down over him.

"Stay out of this, kid," a raspy voice advised. "You're in way over your head." The shadow raised its arm again, the blackjack showing this time.

When it landed, Matt lost consciousness, and he knew he wasn't going to be able to help Maj.

18

"Go away, little girl, before you get hurt."

Doubling her fists, Maj stared at the woman in front of her.

A cruel grin curved the woman's mouth. Anticipation danced in the predatory amber eyes. "You're making a mistake, Madeline Green."

Maj knew the woman was using her name to try to shake her up. "Where's Peter Griffen?"

Heavener, if that was the woman's name, took a step forward, keeping her weight balanced and giving a clear indication of familiarity with martial arts. "Is that what he told you? That I know someone named Peter Griffen?"

"You're at a game convention and you're not going to know?" Maj countered. "Especially after today?" She glanced past Heavener to the two men in the hallway behind her. Farther back, Leif was just getting through the door, followed by three men who looked like hotel security officers in tuxedos.

The woman launched a front snap-kick without warning and a stiletto heel punched toward Maj's face. There wasn't any time to block the kick, so Maj slipped to one side, acutely aware that she was handicapped by heels and a cocktail dress herself.

Still in motion, Maj dropped down to the floor on her side and attempted a leg sweep, intending to knock the woman's feet from under her. Instead, the woman performed a full somersault in the air. When she landed on her feet, managing to keep the high heels intact, her grin was even wider.

"You know how to play," Heavener said, lifting her own hands and curling them into fists.

"Company," one of the men called behind her.

"Cancel it," Heavener snarled.

Both men flanking her pulled out oversized pistols and fired almost pointblank at Leif and the three security men. The glass door shattered as Leif and the security team went down.

The shrill scream of a security alarm knifed through the hotel lobby.

Holding her position, Heavener tilted her head and regarded Maj. "Your friends, no doubt. You are beginning to get annoying."

"Wait till you really get to know us," Maj said, wishing her voice hadn't cracked so much when she'd said it.

"I guess we'll forego this little pleasure." Heavener dropped her fists and waved to the two men. One of them pointed his weapon at Maj.

Maj stepped back, knowing the guy who'd talked to her in the banquet room was gone. Heavener wouldn't be able to catch him.

"Another time," Heavener said. She strode purposefully down the hall, putting a hand to one ear as if she was listening. The two men followed.

Another minute and they were gone around the corner. On the ground floor the way they were, Maj knew Heavener and her people would have a choice of escapes. And there was nothing she could do about it.

Maj ran back to the doors where Leif was getting to his feet. "Are you okay?" she asked.

"Missed me," Leif said in surprise, running his hands over his body in disbelief.

Megan stepped through the shattered door, her foilpack in her hand. "I called the front desk and notified them, but they say the security cams aren't picking up anything. They set the alarm off manually." She stared at the fallen guards. "I also called Matt. He's on his way."

Two of the guards were unconscious from the effects of the tranquilizer darts that had hit them. The other man was delirious from the drug.

Running footsteps caught Maj's attention. She turned around just as a young, slim man in a bronze turtleneck and khaki slacks sprinted up with a 9mm Beretta naked in his fist. Wheat-colored hair stuck up in spikes and wraparound dark sunglasses hid his eyes. He swept the hallway with his gaze as hotel security guards in regular suits fell in behind him.

"Madeline Green?" the man asked in a polite voice.

"Yes."

"I'm Special Agent Jon Roarke," the man said, flipping open an ID case. "Net Force. Captain Winters sent me."

Maj faced him and took out her foilpack. "You don't mind if I check on that, do you?"

"No. But maybe you want to bring me up to speed really quick."

"You're looking for a blond woman," Maj said to Agent Roarke as well as the security team behind him, then gave a quick description of Heavener. The men moved out at once, but Maj knew they weren't going to find her.

"Can you penetrate the masking utility he wore?"

Gaspar Latke sat in his cluttered workspace and replayed the vid captures of his meeting with Maj Green. He hadn't planned on becoming one of the star interests in Heavener's investigation, but then Matt Hunter was supposed to have been a safe bet. Heavener's people hadn't been able to put buttoncams in the Net Force Explorers' room because Mark Gridley had beefed up security. With Matt logged on to the Net, it made sense that he might have visited Maj briefly.

"Not without more time," he answered. The masking utility he used was proof against anything D'Arnot Industries had on-site at the moment. He'd designed it himself.

"We don't have more time," Heavener called over the com-link connection. Irritation reached an all-time high in her voice. "The time is now."

"All we have to do is get through Friday and we're home free."

"No, we're not," she said coldly. "That got blown out of the water when Peter Griffen's game bled over into that girl's veeyar."

"I told you that the revision he had wasn't stable," Gaspar said desperately. "The game engine is too huge and complex. And if I plugged up too much of the coding, it wouldn't have performed." It wasn't his fault. But he knew that didn't matter. If Heavener wanted to blame him for it, she could. And she would. "Peter's not a fool. That's why he opened one of the release packs at the booth instead of using the rev he'd been playing with. All of those should have been the modified rev he's been working with the last couple months."

"Shut up," Heavener ordered.

Gaspar fell silent. He hoped what he'd given Maj Green would keep her active and on Peter Griffen's trail.

"We have another problem," Heavener said. "Matt Hunter found Oscar Raitt. I'm sending a team over to his hotel now. I want you to make sure they get in and out without being seen or heard."

So they'd found Raitt. Excitement flared through Gaspar as he realized the Explorer team was closer to the truth than he'd thought. Then the feeling quickly dimmed when he realized he was being ordered to take that lead away. He hesitated only a moment, knowing he had no choice.

"All right," he said, and prepared to hack into the Mohammed Arms, hoping he was too late.

Something stank. Matt Hunter shook his head, trying to get away from the stench, but it was impossible. Every time he tried, the stench returned, stronger than ever. *Smelling salts,* he realized. He shook his head and opened his eyes. Bright lights painfully filled his vision.

"Easy," a woman said gently. A strong hand clasped Matt around his upper left arm, steadying him. "You're probably going to feel woozy for a bit. You took a couple nasty raps on the head."

Matt glanced around the small room. It had shelves of medicines and bandaging supplies, a small sink, and the hospital bed he was lying on. "Where am I?"

"The hotel first-aid station. Can you tell me what hotel?" The speaker was a small woman in her forties with graying red hair and a pinched face. She threw away bloody swabs and sanitized the medical tray she'd used. The instruments went into a specially marked biohazard holder.

"Bessel Midtown." Matt found that speaking caused his jaw to hurt.

"Can you tell me what happened? It's for the official report."

"I was attacked."

"By a mugger?"

Matt felt in his back pocket, finding his wallet and his foil-pack. "A mugger would have robbed me. This was someone else."

"Do you know who?"

"No."

The woman continued putting things away. "Do you feel up to answering some questions?"

"I thought I already had been."

"From the police. There's an LAPD detective outside. Your friends are out there, too." The woman returned with a small hand mirror. "I had to put a couple stitches in your temple. Whatever hit you split the skin. You may have a slight concussion. Do you know what to look for?"

Matt nodded and regretted it instantly. His head pounded unmercifully. "Double vision. Nausea. Dizziness. Headaches."

"Oh, you're going to have a headache, no doubt about that. I'll give you some analgesics." She handed him a small plastic vial. "As soon as you can, you need to get to bed. Are you staying here at the hotel with anyone?"

"A couple friends."

"Have them keep an eye on you." She looked at him carefully. "Personally, I think the authorities should ship you to the nearest ER and maybe even schedule you for a CAT scan. Whoever hit you knew what they were doing."

"Why am I here, rather than getting that CAT scan?"

"I was told the hospital might be too dangerous for you. I'd feel better if you'd go see a doctor the first chance you get. The hotel set up the triage station here for the convention. Things get crazy here when the gamers are in town. I've worked here during for the past three years, but I've never seen anything like the day we've had today."

Matt stood carefully, feeling light-headed. "Do I owe you anything?"

"No. The hotel takes care of my bills."

"So I can go?"

"If you think you're ready."

Matt thanked her, then showed himself to the door. Maj, Megan, and Leif waited out in the hall, looking worse for the wear themselves. Matt checked the time and discovered he'd lost nearly an hour while he'd been out. Then he noticed the guy leaning against the wall to the right talking to a Hispanic woman in a plain gray business suit.

"How are you feeling?" Maj asked, looking concerned.

"Like I got hit by an autobus," Matt admitted. "Someone's supposed to be waiting at the front counter for me. We'll talk on the way."

"Hold on there," the man leaning against the wall said crisply.

Matt froze at the tone of authority in the man's voice. "Who are you?"

"Jon Roarke," Maj said as the agent brought out his ID. "Net Force. And that's Detective Becerra. Both of them have questions."

"We've got to find Oscar Raitt," Matt said. "He's been in contact with Peter Griffen."

"Since the kidnapping?" Detective Becerra asked.

Matt started to shake his head, then immediately thought better of it. "No. I'll explain on the way."

"So where is he?" Agent Roarke clearly didn't look convinced or happy.

Matt gazed around the huge lobby. More people than usual lounged in the chairs and sofas, talking up business in the pit groups. He didn't know how many of them were really there and how many were there in holo form, but there was one thing he was sure of. "Oscar Raitt's not here."

"Maybe he got tired of waiting on you," Megan suggested. "He could have gone back to his hotel."

Matt flipped his foilpack open and punched in the hotel number for Oscar Raitt's room.

"I'm sorry, sir," the desk clerk said, "but there's no one in that room."

"Maybe he's coming back," Matt said. "Can I leave a message?"

"Sir, our files show no one in that room. Perhaps you have the wrong room. What is the name of the guest?"

"Oscar Raitt." Matt waited, wondering if the blows to his head had altered his memory of the room number.

"Sir," the clerk responded, "no one by that name is checked into the hotel. And no one has been in that room for two days. May I help you with anything else?"

"No, thanks." Matt closed the foilpack, thinking furiously in spite of the pain in his head. "They say Oscar never checked in."

"Maybe you got the wrong hotel, kid," Roarke suggested. "You got your egg scrambled pretty good."

"Maybe," Matt said. "But I didn't make up Oscar Raitt."

"This is highly irregular," the desk clerk complained.

"Maybe you want to whisper," Roarke suggested in a low voice. "You've got guests sleeping, and we're getting pretty close to the room. If someone is hiding inside, I'd hate to see them blow your face off just because you were talking."

Matt watched the agent in awe. Roarke wasn't exactly the buttoned-down type that made up most of Net Force's ranks. He looked at Maj, who walked down the Mohammed Arms hallway with him.

"He's got a rep as a wild man. I talked to Captain Winters about him," Maj whispered. "He transferred out of the Navy SEALS to get into Net Force."

Roarke moved like a force of nature. The young clerk watching the desk at the Mohammed Arms had caved immediately when the agent had flashed his credentials. It helped that Detective Becerra had added her weight, pointing out that the LAPD would appreciate the assistance.

"Where's he usually assigned?" Matt asked. "A war zone?" His head throbbed but he scanned the hallway, remembering details from his earlier visit.

"I didn't have time to ask."

The night clerk halted a few steps from the door, hesitating. Then he handed Roarke the swipe card master. "Maybe I should let you handle this."

"Good idea," Roarke said, snapping the swipe card from the man's hand. He glanced back at Matt, Maj, Megan, and Lisa. "You guys stand back. Winters's orders were that you guys were supposed to stay out of the line of fire."

Matt chafed but knew better than to ignore the man. Winters wouldn't tolerate it. "Yes, sir."

"Sir?" Roarke appeared surprised, but he quickly turned his attention back to the door. Detective Becerra stepped up beside him. He glanced at the woman. "Done this lately?"

Becerra gave him a tight nod. "I've been through a few doors. I'll take low." She took a Sig-Sauer 9mm from a holster at her back. The safety snapped off, and she ran her forefinger along the trigger guard.

Roarke grinned tightly. "We do it on three." He crept to one side of the door and pulled his weapon from beneath his sweater. Holding the swipe card near the lock, he counted in a low voice. As soon as he hit three, he swiped the card through the lock and grabbed the handle.

The click of the lock releasing sounded like a cannonshot in the hallway. The agent twisted the handle and shoved the door open, holding it back with his free hand. The laser sight mounted on his pistol strobed the darkness in the room. "Got it?"

Becerra held her own weapon while in a kneeling position. "Go."

Striding into the room, Roarke disappeared from Matt's view. Then a moment later, the agent called, "Clear." The lights came on inside the room. "No joy."

Becerra followed him in, staying alert.

Matt was at her heels, swinging into the room an instant after the detective. He scanned the room quickly, taking in the neatly made bed, the clean room, and the total absence of Oscar Raitt.

19

"Peter wasn't one for the rough stuff," Zenzo Fujikama was saying as he guided Mark and Andy through the Net. "But he showed up pretty often to learn. Hacker hangouts are some of the best places to go to learn cutting-edge programming. *And* who's doing it." In freefall over the huge metropolitan area below, he glanced back over his shoulder at Mark. "But you already knew that, didn't you?"

Mark didn't reply.

Andy studied the city below as they fell through the fog toward it. The coastline and the bright lights looked familiar. When he saw the Space Needle, the unique saucer design flattened out below him, he knew where they were. "Seattle?"

"I've got some friends I want you to meet." Fujikama stretched out his arms.

Andy's vision went away for a moment. When it returned, he was standing inside a small warehouse that looked condemned. Smashed crates, broken boards, and debris covered the scarred concrete floor. The blacked out windows allowed no outside light in. Illumination came from a small room at the back. "What's this place?"

"Spy headquarters," Zenzo said, grinning. He started forward and lifted his voice. "Yo, Tommy T!"

Mark kept his voice low. "Don't get fooled by this place, Andy. It might not look like much, but there are lots of layers we're not seeing."

Andy nodded, understanding. "Spy headquarters?" he asked Zenzo.

Zenzo nodded. "Sure. Every year a group of us stake out the gaming convention. We hack into communications feeds, media feeds, the hotel security systems. Whatever we can find."

"That's illegal," Mark said.

"Maybe," Zenzo admitted. "But it's the only chance some of us have got."

"Got for what?" Andy asked, intrigued. The warehouse smelled rank, and he kept curling his nose up, breathing shallowly. He knew they were down near the docks leading out into Puget Sound. The way some of the shadows shifted and moved led him to believe they were rats.

"To break into the biz," Zenzo said. "If you're a true gamer, that's like the quest for the Holy Grail. You game?"

"When I get the chance."

A door at the other end of the warehouse opened, letting more light into the warehouse and the thundering crash of techno-pop rock. A heavy guy in jeans and a black T-shirt with an imprint of Arachno-Boy in full battle mode stepped out. "Zenzo?"

"Yeah, Tommy," Zenzo said. "It's me. Want to shut off the security so we can come in?"

Tommy lifted a hand and pointed. A green button formed in the air, and he pressed it.

Andy saw dozens of light beams suddenly strobe to life, bouncing from one corner of the warehouse to the other, running from side to side and from top to bottom. The only neutral ground inside the warehouse was the spot Zenzo had brought them to.

"Oscar Raitt's records have been purged from the gaming convention database."

Matt looked at Catie's face on his foilpack's vidscreen. "What about the off-site location?" He'd asked her to check the records, looking for some kind of proof that Oscar had existed.

They'd already checked the phone records from his vidphone

link, but they had been erased from the phone company. The phone company remained a prime target for hackers, and with all the access they had to promote in their business, they were still easier to penetrate than most corporations.

"I checked there, too," Catie confirmed. "Nothing there."

"Thanks. I'll be in touch." Matt closed the foilpack, wishing his head didn't hurt so badly.

"Hey, kid," Roarke said. The Net Force agent stood near the hotel room windows overlooking the enclosed passageway leading back to the Bessel. A helo with police markings buzzed through the sky. "Don't get so down."

"Kind of hard not to," Matt said. "If I didn't know better, *I'd* say I was imagining things, too."

Roarke shook his head. "These people, whoever they are, can try to cover up this stuff as much as they want, but it's already gotten through the seams. When it gets this messy, more than likely we're going to figure it out."

"More than likely?" Maj echoed.

Roarke gave her a grin. "Better than fifty-fifty odds." He leaned against the wall. "The trick is to figure it all out in time. These things tend to have a perishable date on them."

Matt couldn't help thinking of Peter Griffen. *Is he still being held hostage somewhere, or has that date already run through?* He glanced up at Maj and saw the dark look on her face, knowing she was wondering the same thing.

"Agent Roarke?"

They looked at the door to the hotel room and saw the three men in green overalls standing there with equipment cases in their hands.

"You forensics?" Roarke asked.

"Yes, sir."

"You know what you're doing?"

"Yes, sir."

"Well, if you're waiting on me, don't."

"Yes, sir." The three men moved into the room and opened their cases, removing aerosol applicators. "Where do you want the luminol, sir?"

"Let's start with the floor," Roarke ordered. "Blood tends to follow the laws of gravity. If we find anything, we'll broaden the search."

Matt swallowed dryly as he watched the men work.

• • •

Standing in the huge warehouse, Andy watched the security systems wink out around them.

"We make it hard for anyone to find us," Zenzo said. "And if they do, we make sure we have plenty of time to log off and run." He started forward. "Anyway, getting back to the games. As I was saying, any true gamer's dream is to design games other people will play. A lot of guys build games and put them on the Net for free."

"I've got some friends who do that," Andy said.

"I could have figured that. Maybe you're not hardcore, but I bet you know the guys who are. There's a lot of natural talent out there, and there are also a lot of guys who really aren't as good as they think they are. However, that doesn't stop them."

Andy followed Zenzo into the small room at the end of the warehouse. It was filled to capacity with five workspaces and the three guys and two young women who occupied them. Computer hardware lined the walls, and Andy didn't doubt that over half of it was designed for security.

"We design games," Zenzo said, "but it's tough getting the attention of publishers. They've got their own people. They're not looking for guys like us, total independents who've taught themselves."

"They usually recruit people from video game design colleges," Mark said.

"Yeah, and they make money off those colleges, too." Zenzo said with obvious cynicism. "They make profits off the guys they choose who become successes, and they make money off the dreamers, too. And *that* is truly bogus."

Andy scanned the monitors around the workspaces. A few of them showed lobby and restaurant scenes.

"We don't just stake out the Bessel," Zenzo said. "We wire up local restaurants and clubs the publishers like to visit." He smiled. "We know all."

"So you spy on these people," Andy said in disgust, "and try to leverage your way in to them to sell your games?"

"No." Zenzo looked offended. "We're doing market research here. We take a good look at all the publishers, try to figure out who's looking for what, who might be more interested in what we have to offer. Then we disburse the information to other game designers. Despite all the colleges the publishers create, despite all these wonder programmers they produce, they still need people like us."

"And like Peter Griffen," Mark said quietly.

Andy studied the other monitors. Two of the people worked on backgrounds while two more worked on character design. Tommy T appeared to be testing gameplay.

"Peter's one of us," Zenzo said. "He didn't go to their schools. He sent in samples of his work they couldn't ignore. Blistered them with stuff they'd never seen before and made them come looking for him. Then, when he could have named his own ticket with any publisher out there, Peter pulls a fade for a year and announces he's putting together his own imprint, subsidized by Eisenhower Productions. That takes brass."

"You respect him," Andy said.

Zenzo grinned. "No, man, I want to *be* Peter Griffen when I grow up. He's an example to every self-taught gamer who dreams of making it big. That's why I want him found. Eisenhower Productions isn't going to just bury him and take his game away from him if I can do anything about it."

"What do you mean?"

"It's in the contract," Zenzo said. "If anything happens to Peter Griffen, all rights to Realm of the Bright Waters revert to Eisenhower. All rights, and every last nickel and dime in profit."

"Why would he sign something like that?" Mark asked.

"Peter doesn't have any family," Zenzo said. "He grew up in an orphanage. That's why he didn't have a problem signing the agreement with Eisenhower. Who was he going to leave it to?"

"You think Eisenhower had something to do with his disappearance," Andy said.

Zenzo nodded. "Without a doubt. They were the ones who chose the floor space over that underground tunnel. That seems kind of suspect to me."

"Why would they abduct Peter?" Mark asked.

"After that thing today, when the dragon appeared in all those games, Peter was going to pull the game. We overheard two of the Eisenhower execs talking about it in the lobby right after it happened." Zenzo turned to the heavyset guy in the Arachno-Boy T-shirt. "Tommy T, roll that vid."

Images came to life on the monitor in front of Tommy T.

Andy watched as a young man burst through the doors of the Bessel convention center into the hallway.

"The feek's hit the fan in there," the man said to another man in his mid-thirties. "Peter must have used one of the game packs instead of the rev he had."

"Why?" the older man asked.

"I don't know, but something's going to have to be done. He's demanding to pull the game. He's getting ready to step back out and announce that the game is flawed."

Without another word, the older man shouldered the younger one aside and sprinted back into the gaming convention center. The vid ended abruptly.

"Unfortunately," Tommy T said, "all our cams and audlinks inside the center were down due to the bleed-over."

"So you don't know what happened inside the Eisenhower booth for sure?" Mark asked.

"I don't think you have to be a rocket scientist to figure it out," Zenzo erupted. "Peter Griffen would have pulled that game. That effect, that rollover into all the other games, that wasn't an advertising stunt the way some people think. That was a glitch that he wasn't going to allow."

"You think they kidnapped him?"

"To keep him from pulling the game? To keep him quiet?" Zenzo nodded. "Oh, yeah. Eisenhower Productions had every reason in the world to do that." He studied Andy and Mark. "I'm giving you this so you can do something with it. We could pass it on to a HoloNet server, but they're not going to take it. Not from guys like us. They'll say we created it ourselves, to get attention. In the meantime, Peter Griffen's going to be rotting wherever they left him."

Looking at Mark, Andy said, "I'm in. Zenzo may not have sold me everything, but I want a closer look."

Mark nodded and shifted his attention back to Zenzo. "What else can you give us?"

Zenzo grinned hugely and swept a hand around the computer hardware–packed room. "Access. And there's nothing in the world you can't do when you have access. Peter's out there somewhere. Let us help you save him."

"Do you know what luminol is used for?"

Maj nodded, not wanting to look at Roarke. The Net Force

agent was too dispassionate in her opinion. They watched from the hallway as the forensics techs finished spraying down the room with the chemical. "It makes blood patterns show up. Even if an area has been scrubbed, trace evidence remains that the luminol can detect."

"Right." Roarke leaned against the wall, seeming to watch in the idle speculation, like the whole investigation was just a text-book exercise.

"Agent Roarke," the lead forensics man called out. "I believe we're ready."

"Light it up," Roarke commanded.

The men placed the ultraviolet projectors in the room to play over the treated carpet areas. They turned them on and switched out the room's lights.

Immediately a soft blue glow shimmered into being on the carpet. Most of it was gathered in a single area, but there were splatter patterns leading off from it. Maj knew the blue glow represented the amount of blood that had been spilled there re-cently. *God, that's a lot.*

"He was a big guy," Matt whispered as he came up beside her and put a reassuring hand on her shoulder. "And maybe that's not all from him."

Roarke pushed off the wall and pulled his foilpack out. "Do the entire room. Every scrap, every fiber. I want it all yesterday, and I want it done right." He glanced at Maj. "Think you and your friends can cover the hospitals? Call and see if someone was admitted to an ER tonight that fits Oscar Raitt's descrip-tions? I'm going to see what kind of help Captain Winters can scrounge up for us."

Maj nodded and took out her own foilpack. Her mind whirled with the possibilities, but it felt good to have something to do. She just didn't know if Roarke knew that or was just handing off a job he didn't believe in and didn't want to do himself.

Back in her room Maj looked over the notes she'd made during the phone calls to all the city's emergency rooms. It was a short list. Thankfully Oscar Raitt wasn't just an average person. She'd been surprised how many people had been admitted during the two-hour time frame in question.

Out of all those, only two had any potential for being Oscar Raitt. One of them was in Orange County lockup for attacking a sheriff's deputy, but Maj didn't want to overlook any possibilities. She doubted Oscar'd had time to attack a sheriff's deputy, but maybe he'd gotten spooked. Or maybe the charges were ersatz. Either way, it had to be checked out.

The other possibility was a young man of towering proportions who'd checked into the ER long enough to have a scalp laceration tended to, then walked out when the nurses and doctors weren't looking.

Maj glanced at the time/date stamp on the muted holo in one corner of the room. It was a handful of minutes past seven A.M. Friday morning. Her eyes burned and she felt worn down to the bone.

Andy was crashed out on the floor in front of the holo, his hands folded behind his head. He snored gently. He and Mark had been out late and had been a little mysterious about what they'd been doing, but Mark had assured her that what they were bringing in would help. Mark was either at home or on the Net.

Catie and Megan had given up only a little while ago, returning to their rooms to grab a shower and a few hours' sleep. Matt slept facedown on her bed, totally beat. The right side of his face had purpled up dramatically overnight. He'd refused to leave last night, insisting on staying there to guard her.

Some bodyguard. Even though she'd only thought it in jest, Maj felt guilty. It was a further sign of how tired she was because she knew she had nothing to feel guilty about.

Leif Anderson had wandered off, presumably to bed.

And the mysterious Agent Jon Roarke hadn't bothered to reappear after last night's disappearance.

Maj underlined the two ER incidents she'd isolated from all the lists they'd generated. She answered the vidphone automatically, punching the connect button.

Captain Winters's face appeared on the screen. A heavy five o'clock shadow tanned his cheeks, but the knot in his tie looked fresh. "Good morning, Maj. I took a chance that I'd find you still up."

"I'm not sure how good it is," Maj replied.

"I don't know if I'm going to make it any better. Do you mind if I stop by? A holo transmission through the Net will be much easier to encrypt than the phone."

Maj nodded.

A moment later Captain Winters stepped into her room. He

gazed around at Andy and Matt. "Attrition in the ranks?"

"More like exhaustion."

Winters nodded. "I won't take up much time. You need to get some sleep as soon as we finish here."

Maj recognized his words as an order, not a suggestion. "Yes, sir."

"Intelligence turned up a file on Heavener," Winters said. "If it's the same person." He gestured and another holo formed beside him. This one was of a slender brunette.

At first Maj didn't key in on the similarities between the brunette and the blonde she'd encountered last night. The shape of her chin and jawline had been altered. And the blonde's lips were more full. But there was something about the eyes—even though they were blue on the holo instead of the tiger's-eye amber—which made the identification unmistakable.

"She looks a lot different now," Maj said, "but it's her."

Winters waved a hand through the holo, and it shattered into millions of pixels and disappeared. "Heavener is only one of the aliases she uses. She's a very dangerous woman."

"I gathered that from last night."

"I've got a full report I'll send," Winters said, "but I'll give you the highlights now. Her real name—our intelligence division believes—is Katrina Mahler. She's in her late twenties. She's worked for the German terrorists, became a specialist in demolitions and close-in assassinations."

Remembering the cold lights in the woman's eyes, Maj believed it.

"When the German counterterrorist organization, GSG9, turned up the heat on Heavener, she fled to the Balkan countries and set up shop there for a while. Three years ago she apparently gave up political terrorism for the corporate world. There's no real proof of that, but that's been the speculation of the GSG9 people."

"Do they have any idea of who she's working for?" Maj asked.

"I'm checking around," Winters replied. "So far the answer is no."

"Her working for Eisenhower Productions seems unlikely— a gaming company and some kind of industrial espionage or security work?"

"Our profilers agree," Winters said. "Heavener is addicted to danger. Her assignments in the past have always been a step over the edge. Whoever she's working for, it's someone big. Someone with a huge agenda."

"But it must tie into the gaming world."

"She's here," Winters agreed. "We have to acknowledge that. Figuring out who she's working for would be a big help, but I want you and the other Net Force Explorers to stay away from her. She won't think twice about harming any of you."

"Yes, sir," Maj replied, dreading hearing Winters order them off the firing line. But she didn't want to wait. "Are we going to stay involved in this?"

Winters hesitated. "At this point I don't have enough authority to get a team from Net Force down there. And if I did, Jay Gridley and I feel showing up in force prematurely would make Heavener and her employers shut down. Whatever they've got planned, it's been underway for a long time. There's no guarantee that if they backed away from the operation here that we'd have nullified it. And whatever they're planning may even be in play now."

"Yes, sir." *Enthusiasm at this point,* Maj told herself, *would be sooo out of place.* She restrained herself.

"The convention lasts another three days," Winters went on. "For now, I want you and the rest of your team to keep your eyes and ears open and to stay away from Heavener and her group."

Maj nodded.

"And keep me apprised of any changes in the situation immediately."

"Of course. Could I ask a question?"

"Certainly."

"I need to know about Agent Roarke." Maj felt guilty for bringing it up. Winters stood firmly behind anyone he put into the field.

"Jon Roarke," Winters said, "has a lot of abrasive qualities, but he's a good man. Before he got this assignment, he was on administrative leave."

Uh-oh, Maj thought. *Read that as bucking the chain of command.*

"He achieves his assignments," Winters said, "but his manner of achieving them has sometimes left muddied waters. Even so, I feel lucky to get him."

"Thank you," Maj said. "That's what I needed to know."

Winters said good-bye and faded from the room.

Maj peered out the hotel windows at the early morning sunshine breaking over downtown Los Angeles's skyline. Despite the promise of sunlight, a cold feeling of dread seeped into her.

20

"Look what the cat dragged in," Andy Moore said, jerking a thumb at Leif Anderson.

"I protest," Leif said, dropping into a cross-legged position on the carpet in Maj's hotel room. "There was no dragging of cats or other creatures in any of the gaiety I involved myself in."

"It's eleven o'clock in the morning," Andy said, pointing to the tuxedo Leif wore. "Isn't it premature to go out partying again?"

"Again?" Leif squared up the wilted carnation in the jacket's boutonniere. "Actually, anyone who wimped out after the banquet last night missed the real parties where business was done. I was scouting the terrain." He glanced up at the huge breakfast cart room service had brought up at Maj's request. "Are those muffins?"

Maj scooped a muffin up from the tray. "Blueberry."

"My favorite." Leif took the small saucer with the muffin Maj passed to him. He sighed contentedly.

"You've been out partying till now?" Catie asked in disbelief.

"Yes." Leif broke the muffin into halves and munched, then

swallowed. "I had a few glasses of champagne and lots of coffee, but nothing to eat. Crumbs on a tux are just too tacky, especially when you're trying to impress corporate execs who don't admit to human frailties."

Maj sat in one of the room's chairs, her knees pulled up beneath her chin and her feet resting on the chair seat. All of the Net Force Explorers were gathered in her room, getting ready to descend on the convention center. "Were any of the meetings productive?"

"Most of them, no. However, I did get some information on Eisenhower Productions that was very interesting." Leif took another bite.

"Okay, consider the time limit on the dramatic pause over," Matt advised. He sat in the floor as well, the right side of his face a mask of purple bruising.

"If you'd looked at the business history of Eisenhower Productions two years ago," Leif said, "you'd have felt certain the corporation was about to go under. They hadn't had a solid hit title in four years. With the inflated cost of doing business after having a few profitable years, they'd cut designers and programmers from the payroll."

"That's stupid," Andy snorted. "If you can't make anything, how are you supposed to sell anything?"

"They tried to make it by just publishing games independent designers came up with. That didn't work out too well. The guys at the top of the corporation were coasting, getting by on residuals from earlier games that still sold. Frankly, they were on a slow boat to bankruptcy."

"But two years ago," Maj said, "something happened."

"Peter Griffen approached them and started negotiating the release of Realm of the Bright Waters. He'd put together concept art, computer graphics, the story line, and some gameplay. They knew they had a winner on their hands. The only sticking point was that Peter would be the one to set the actual release date. However, at that time Eisenhower was two months away from insolvency."

"They didn't tell Peter that," Maj said.

Leif shook his head. "It would have been suicidal on their part. Peter was even picking up the tab for most of the development so he could maintain control over the game. They didn't try to buy out any more of the interest than Peter was willing to sell."

"Because they didn't have the money," Megan said.

"Bingo. However, they weren't going to survive. They were desperate, so they started trying to find someone else to pick up their tab while they waited on Peter."

"Why should anyone touch them?" Matt asked. "All they'd have to do was wait them out, let their contract and deal go south, then go to Peter."

"Right," Leif agreed. "And I'll bet the CEOs and production managers handling the deal were on the verge of total melt-downs. Here was a goose that laid golden eggs, and they couldn't even wait around for the first one to drop."

"Why did Peter pick Eisenhower Productions?" Maj asked. "There were probably other corporations just as approachable."

"There were," Leif agreed. "It was just luck of the draw. However, the funding they got is like a national secret. Two years ago somebody poured a mountain of liquid cash into Ei-senhower's coffers. That's how they were able to do all the marketing for the game today, and how they were able to shore up Peter when his money ran dry."

"It's a wonder Eisenhower didn't try to strong-arm Peter when he was down," Andy said.

"The way I hear it," Leif replied, "they did. Only Peter stood his ground, offering to shut the game down till he did other work to pay for it, or take a loan out for the necessary funding from them. They gave him the funding and at a decent interest rate."

"Where did the other cash come from?" Maj asked.

Leif shrugged. "No one knows. But that's what they're telling me happened."

"Someone believed in Peter's game," Catie commented. "That's the only thing that would have made them invest."

"But why do it secretly?" Megan asked. "Why not just step forward, buy Eisenhower Productions out if the game was that good, and restructure the deal with Peter? This other corporation could have put pressure on Peter, put him in court with no money, and taken what they wanted."

Andy shook his head. "Sheesh, you're beginning to sound like a financial adviser."

"Profit Channel on HoloNet," Megan replied. "As the daughter of a writer, you'd be surprised how much extraneous information you pick up."

"Because whoever invested wanted Peter handling the game," Leif said.

"Yet Eisenhower wouldn't let Peter bring Oscar Raitt in when there were game engine design problems. Oscar told me that cost another two months of time to straighten out."

"It meant one less person they'd have to control," Leif pointed out. "And evidently this mystery fund-raiser has money to burn."

"Delaying a return on an investment isn't good business," Maj said.

"It is if the business isn't ready but you know it will be good."

Maj turned the possibilities over in her mind, trying to fit the pieces together. "They had more at stake than just the money."

"What?" Matt asked.

She shook her head. "I don't know. But I think if we find out, all of this is going to make sense."

"Well," Matt said, "you can understand why the Eisenhower execs would start panicking when Peter mentioned pulling the game. They were about to see their reprieve yanked away from them."

"Can you trace the money Eisenhower got?" Maj asked Leif.

"I'm trying now. Dad even let me borrow the resources of a couple of his key people who are really good at this kind of thing. If it's there, they'll find it. But I'm betting there's no trail. They're good, these people."

"And they're probably the people Heavener is working for." Maj had filled the group in on the woman at the beginning of the meeting. "If we can find one trail, we're going to find them all." She glanced up at the HoloNet display in the corner.

"But you've got to ask yourself," Matt said, "what the tie is between a freelance industrial spy and an online game."

No one had an answer, but Maj was deep in thought, thinking about the bleed-over that had occurred. She watched the holo with interest. The holo's sound was muted, but the picture was clear. Thousands of fans were already in the convention center downstairs, buying the Realm of the Bright Waters game launch on the Net the next morning. *The Guinness Book of World Records* was already on hand to watch history in the making as the game sold in the convention, in stores across the country, and over the Net.

"How is it going?" Catie nodded at the marketing representative currently testing Maj's flight-sim. The man sat in an implant chair provided by the convention at a demonstration booth she'd rented for two hours.

Maj shrugged and willed herself not to pace. It was hard because, as tense as she was, her body craved movement. "Okay. I guess." She paused. "I don't know. This waiting is killing me."

"Lighten up." Catie smiled. "You knew this was going to be the hard part. This isn't like showing the sim to Matt."

Maj exhaled. "I know. I told myself that, but it's different actually living it."

"So who is this guy?"

Maj looked at the card the man had given her. "Harold J. Dawkins, Fortress Games. He's a producer."

"Meaning he can license your sim for the company."

Maj nodded.

"Fortress is a big name. I didn't know you had them on your list."

"I didn't," Maj replied. "He just walked over a few minutes ago and asked me if I had the time to let him run through it. Two other reps didn't show up, so it was no problem."

Catie crossed her fingers and showed them to Maj, smiling.

Maj tried to ignore the butterflies beating their little brains out in her stomach. "Has Leif found out anything about Eisenhower's mystery investor?"

"No. Roarke and Matt are busy trying to trace Oscar Raitt's movements. They found his plane ticket reservation from Sea-Tac, and they've located the shuttle driver who brought Raitt into the hotel. However, the hotel's stance is that if a guest isn't registered in their computers, that person was never a guest. Holmes has put a detective on the investigation as well, but Matt doesn't think they're going to find anything."

Disappeared, or dead? Maj wondered, feeling very cold inside. *The guy who met me at the banquet last night was plenty scared.*

Harold J. Dawkins sat up in the implant chair. He was in his mid-twenties, with clipped peroxide-blond hair and a boyish grin. He wore athletic clothing but didn't look like he owned a club membership anywhere. "Hey, great sim. It's like you're really there." He planed his hand through the air in front of him and made jet engine noises.

Maj smiled, relieved. "Thanks. I put a lot of time into that build."

"Trust me," Dawkins said. "It shows. I'm glad I came over here." He took a PDA pad from his pocket and switched it on. "I think we just might be able to work something out. If you're ready to license the property."

Catie looked at Maj with rounded eyes that Dawkins couldn't see and mouthed, *Wow!*

"Sure," Maj said. "I mean, are you sure?"

Dawkins laughed. "I've been licensing games for a while. I think I know a good one when I see it. If you could, I'd like to talk to you about the potential arrangements. If you have the time. And that's assuming you don't have any other offers you'd like to consider."

Maj was stunned. "Uh, no, there aren't any other offers."

Catie frowned at her, then turned to Dawkins with a sweet smile. "Of course, there are still a few other companies who are going to demo the sim later today and tomorrow."

"I understand, but I'm prepared to go to contract over this," Dawkins said. "Right now."

"Just like that?" Maj asked.

Dawkins shrugged. "It's a yes-or-no proposition. My company puts me out here to buy games, that's what I do. If I see something I like, I'll know it, and then I license it. I guess you could make this harder than what it is, but I never have."

Everything in Maj wanted to say yes. It was a confirmation of her talents and instincts. But a feeling persisted in her that suddenly everything wasn't quite right. The offer just didn't *feel* right.

"Can I get back to you on that?" Maj asked.

Consternation and irritation showed on Dawkins's face. "I'd really like to talk to you about this now."

"I know," Maj said. "But my dad wants me to talk to him first if anyone is interested in the game." It wasn't a lie. Her dad took an interest in everything she did, and he probably would want to talk to her first. "Can I give you a call after I've talked to him?"

"I'm really used to getting what I want out of a deal," Dawkins said.

"I'm not saying you won't," Maj replied.

Dawkins hesitated for a moment, as if struggling for something to say. Finally he smiled and left.

Maj watched the rep go, suspicion darkening her thoughts.

"She didn't go for it," Heavener said.

Seated behind the cluttered desk in the comfortable disarray of his personal workspace veeyar, Gaspar smiled despite the fear that thrummed steadily in him. Maj Green was proving to be quite resourceful. All the Net Explorers were. He watched Heavener through a buttoncam.

Heavener talked on the encrypted comm-line, and he was only able to hear her side of the conversation. "Maybe Dawkins overplayed his hand," she said, "but it was within the parameters of his assignment." She paused. "No, I don't think the girl is overly suspicious of him."

Gaspar glanced at the other monitors open to him on the desk, surveying the convention. Heavener's tech teams had been very quick to reestablish the spylines. As yet, she hadn't given him any concrete assignments other than to monitor the situation and keep the confusion going on concerning Oscar Raitt.

He'd felt good about the Raitt connection Matt Hunter had turned up. That had been perhaps the only link to Peter that Heavener hadn't accounted for. The woman had her flaws—other than being a deadly killer and psychotic.

"Stronger measures are called for," Heavener said. "After ten o'clock Eastern Standard Time tomorrow, it will be too late to stop it."

Gaspar listened intently. Ten EST was when Realm of the Bright Waters was due to launch. He'd known Peter's game was the centerpiece of their plans, but he didn't know D'Arnot Industries was only waiting on the launch. He still wasn't completely sure what the corporation was going to do with the game's disruptive programming.

"We kill her," Heavener said.

Gaspar's blood turned to ice in his veins.

"Captain Winters will get involved in finding out who executed her," Heavener continued. "By the time they cordon off the convention and get the investigation set up, they won't be thinking about the game."

On the monitor screen Heavener listened for a short time, then she smiled coldly.

"I have a very simple plan in mind," Heavener said. "Oscar Raitt, the game designer we kidnapped last night, can be used to take the fall. I will set it up so it looks as if Raitt killed Green and Griffen out of jealousy over his friend's successes. We'll make it look as if Griffen faked his own disappearance to enhance the marketing of his game. Eisenhower officials will back us up, saying Peter was zealous in making the game a hit. After he murders Green and Griffen, Raitt will be shot dead by one of the hotel guards we've bought off."

Gaspar listened to the silence that followed Heavener's words. He felt short of breath, liked he'd been running hard.

"Tomorrow morning shortly before the game's release on-line," Heavener agreed, then tapped the touchscreen to break the connection. She turned and walked to Gaspar's body lying in the implant chair. A knife magically appeared in her hand.

She knows I've been listening. The realization hit Gaspar like a depth charge.

"Listen, little bug," Heavener said in a cold, sandpapery voice, "I know you've been spying on me." She tucked the knife blade up under Gaspar's physical body. "I let you live so you'd know how futile anything you might try is."

Gaspar couldn't breathe, couldn't speak. The connection he had with his physical body was dimmed because of the neural interface with the Net, but he still felt the chill of the knife edge at his throat.

"What happens if I slice across the carotid artery here?" Heavener placed the blade's point against his neck. "You bleed to death, of course. But do you choose to watch your own death from there? Or do you return to your body and die here?"

Gaspar couldn't answer.

"And if you watch from there," Heavener went on, "when you die here, do you simply wink out of existence there? Like the last spark in a broken lightbulb?"

Shivering fear ran all through Gaspar. The stress overload indicators flashed a warning in the air beside him. If his reactions didn't stay under control, the Net would kick him out and put him back in that chair. He struggled to stay calm.

Abruptly Heavener pulled the blade away. "Don't fail me. There are worse things in life than dying. I know them all." She stepped toward the buttoncam mounted on the wall and slammed the butt of the knife into it, smashing it.

Inside the veeyar workspace, the monitor changed to a cold, flat empty gray.

21

In her hotel room Maj lay back in the implant chair and leaped onto the Net. She opened her personal workspace and placed a call to Leif's foilpack.

On the third ring Leif answered, his head appearing in a monitor. "Yes."

"I was just offered a licensing agreement for my flight-sim," Maj said without preamble.

Leif looked near-exhaustion, but he smiled. "Congratulations."

"I don't think so," Maj replied. "I think it was a setup. This guy didn't want to take no for an answer and seemed a little put out when I didn't want to start talking negotiations immediately.

"Nobody does business like that," Leif said.

"He says he does."

"And what do you think?"

"That someone sent him my way as a distraction," Maj answered honestly.

"Because of Peter Griffen's disappearance?"

"It's bigger than that," Maj said. "And I think it's more than just the money involved."

"Maj, when you're talking about corporations, money's always the bottom line."

"Actually, there's two things," Maj replied. "You're used to looking at business somewhat altruistically. Wealth is like politics and is usually about two things."

"Money"—Leif nodded, understanding—"and power. So if it's not about the money, where does the power come in?"

"I don't know. I thought maybe you could look into Fortress Games. They're a major player in the software entertainment business, but maybe they've got partners."

"I'll take a look," Leif promised, "and let you know."

Maj thanked him and broke the connection. Then she placed a call to Mark, catching him on the Net as she'd expected. A vidscreen opened up in her workspace, showing Mark dressed in his crashsuit.

"Andy and I are taking a close look at the Realm of the Bright Waters online gaming package," Mark said. "Want to come up?"

"Find anything interesting?"

"Maybe," Mark admitted. "But it's nothing really glaring. Come take a peek." He extended a hand through the vidscreen.

Maj took his hand and let him pull her through the Net telecommunications system. The Net blurred around her. In the next instant she stood on a high cliff overlooking a tree-strewn valley. Bright river water reflected the sun as it rushed through the valley's heart.

"Is there any reason we're wearing these?" Maj waved at the crashsuit she wore that was similar to Mark's.

"The game pack has a tendency to want to react with any kind of programming in it," Andy said. He sat hunkered down at the cliff's edge, dressed in a crashsuit as well. "Really user-friendly."

"Is that unusual?" Maj asked.

"Not so much," Mark admitted. "A lot of game packs tend to be automatically engaging. They present the world and the possibilities, and hope to catch someone's eye long enough to sign them up for the online services."

Maj peered into the valley. Brightly colored birds sped

through the trees, winged heartbeats of red, orange, emerald green, and shimmering dark blue.

"I wanted us here without triggering all the interactive programming," Mark said. "When we first got here, we were attacked by a primitive culture."

"Real Stone Age throwbacks," Andy agreed, with a grin. "But I had my sword, and Mark had a couple spells tucked away. He set his hair on fire at one point. You should have seen them run."

"Sounds like fun," Maj said.

"Like I said," Mark went on, "the interactive feature is pretty standard. It entices the gamer to want to see the rest of the world. Good stuff. Well designed and well thought out. However—"

"This," Maj said, "is the part I was waiting for."

"I checked for the anomaly you and Matt ran into in your veeyar. I ran some diagnostics against what's being offered in the game pack against what you experienced. The anomaly isn't here."

Maj considered that, trying to make it fit with what she was thinking. "It should have been."

"It's not. But I checked over the game pack programming and discovered other interesting details. A lot of the normal programming from an online interface is missing."

"The game pack is defective?" Maj asked.

"No. When a user logs on and downloads the outline programming from the game server, the missing files will automatically be patched in."

"So why leave them out?"

"I don't know," Mark told her.

"The first thought," Andy put in, "would be to conserve space on the game pack datascript. But that's not an issue because the files are archived and fit easily in the space that's provided."

"And there's the possibility that Eisenhower shaved production time off the game backs by not including all programming that downloads automatically from the Net."

"But they could have simply issued a download site on the Net," Maj said.

"Yeah," Andy agreed. "But there's nothing like putting a brightly colored box into a gamer's hand. That's total euphoria, and that's why game companies haven't gone totally online with releases."

"Massive downloads can still be a problem online," Mark said. "A corporation can stumble and fall and fail to provide for all the immediate demand by consumers."

"All the more reason to produce a complete game pack and keep downloads short," Maj said. A dragon drifted lazily across the sky above them, but it wasn't Peter's dragon. A thought struck her and she looked at Mark. "Did you try adding in the programming that the Net automatically adds?"

Mark nodded. "First thing. But there wasn't any change in performance. No bleed-over anomaly."

"Then how did it happen at the convention yesterday?" Maj asked.

Mark shook his head. "The only thing I can think of is that Eisenhower is going to upload some other files beyond the normal Net load."

"They could blend that programming in with the Net upload, couldn't they?" Maj asked.

"Sure, but the Net checks for viruses."

The thought felt right and Maj stayed with it. "I don't think we're looking for a virus or a Trojan Horse, or a worm. What if it's just part of the game programming?"

"Veeyars will accept it and won't think twice."

"Yeah," Andy said, "but if the bleed-over effect can be canceled, why didn't they?"

"Because maybe it's not so easily canceled once the whole program runs," Maj answered. "But I think it's because Eisenhower and whoever is behind them want the bleed-over in there."

"Why?" Andy asked.

"That," Maj replied, "remains the big question."

A knock at the hotel door woke Maj. Her head felt as if it had been packed with sawdust, and her eyes were too heavy to lift. She stumbled up from bed and pulled a robe on, then looked through the vid security plate. Leif stood out in the hallway. She let him in.

"Catch you sleeping?" he asked in a voice that was simply too cheerful to stand.

"It's after midnight," Maj said.

"So?" Leif was dressed in a fresh tux and carefully groomed, but his eyes looked glassy.

"You haven't been to sleep yet?" Maj asked in disbelief.

"Things to do." Leif dropped into a chair. "And I thought you'd want to be the first to know."

"Know what?"

Leif grinned. "Who Eisenhower's mysterious benefactor is."

"Tell me."

"Allow me my moment of drama," Leif said. "After you gave me Fortress Games, I had my dad's people start checking on them, find out who'd invested in them. There are generally a few players in any corporation. He turned up a string of shell companies that led back to a source. However, that started me thinking. The way my dad's guy was able to find out who was behind Fortress Games was through the money manipulations. They crossed a dozen borders, nearly three dozen banks, and sixteen different governments."

"Sounds complicated," Maj said.

"Very complicated," Leif agreed. "My dad hires some very good people, though, and Hendricks is one of the best. Anyway, I asked Hendricks to look back through other funds that had been funneled along the same routes, marking the dates as around the time Eisenhower got their healthy boost of vitamin cash."

"Same source?"

Leif nodded. "Oh, yeah. Ever heard of D'Arnot Industries?"

"D'Arnot Industries," Captain Winters said, "is a France-based corporation heavily invested in the production of munitions." His holo stood in the center of the hotel conference room. A Net Force team had secured the premises, encrypting telecommunications that passed between all interested parties. The captain's image blurred and his words sounded hollow occasionally because those telecommunications were being cached and sent as bursts, making them even harder to access over the Net.

Maj listened intently. During the hour it had taken Winters to arrange the meeting place, she'd done some research on D'Arnot Industries herself. The other Explorers and Roarke occupied chairs around the room.

"The corporation got its start back during the Cold War in the 1960s," Winters went on. Slides and vid projected in the air as he spoke. "They produced small arms through most of the 1970s and 1980s. By the 1990s, when all the unrest started in the Russian satellite countries, they started producing tanks and attack helicopters as well."

"It was a major corporation after 2002," Leif said. "They made a bigger profit every year after that. They also invested heavily in software development."

Winters nodded. "War makes for good business. It always has. However, D'Arnot traded freely with whomever they wanted, using shell companies to sell some of the goods they produced. There were times during the crises then that D'Arnot or their affiliates supplied both sides of a conflict."

"You said they're based in France," Matt said. "That's where Oscar said Peter Griffen stayed while he built his game."

"After D'Arnot arranged the financial deal with Eisenhower," Leif said. "We took a peek at Griffen's passport. The dates all match up."

"Then why aren't we busting D'Arnot?" Andy asked.

"Because it's not a crime to invest in another corporation," Leif answered.

"They hid the money," Andy protested.

"That's suspect," Winters replied, "but not criminal. So far, we've yet to uncover any malfeasance on D'Arnot Industries' part."

"What about Heavener?" Maj asked.

"We can't prove that she works for D'Arnot."

"What about her passport?" Catie asked. "Has she been in France lately?"

"It depends," Winters said, "on which passport you're looking at, under which name, or which intelligence report on her movements you want to believe. The woman is a ghost."

"Even if we had anything against her, kid," Roarke said, "we'd have to find her. I've got a feeling that's not going to be easy."

"As many people as she's had on the scene here," Winters said, "she's got a local base of operations. I've got security teams going through records on this area and the surrounding counties. If they can be found that way, we'll have them."

"What about a Net Force team?" Roarke asked.

"I've got one in-bound," Winters said.

"There are local guys," Roarke pointed out.

"And they're all tied up, Agent Roarke," Winters said with the steel in his voice that Maj had seldom heard before. "I need a team here who has worked together before, not one cobbled together on a moment's notice."

"I'm just saying maybe we should get these kids out of the way."

"I don't think these young women and men are in any danger here, and to enforce that belief I want you to stay with them."

Maj could tell by the look on the agent's face that the assignment didn't sit well.

"They also serve who baby-sit," Roarke grumped.

"Agent Roarke," Winters said, "at another time, you and I will discuss that point of view regarding my people. At length."

"Yes, sir."

Winters turned his gaze back to the Explorers. "Pulling you people out of the convention after Heavener knows who you are might be safe, but it could also tip our hand. It would be better if they thought this meeting was over the ongoing investigation regarding Peter Griffen's disappearance. If you vanish, they're not going to believe that."

All the Explorers agreed.

"However, if any of you want to leave, you're free to do so." No one took Winters up on the offer.

"I think we're safe here, sir," Maj said. "Besides, you may have a Net Force team on-site, but they can't move until you prove a crime has been committed by D'Arnot Industries."

"Heavener has a record under two other aliases," Roarke said. "D'Arnot must not have known that."

"Or they chose to ignore it," Winters agreed. "A female agent is overlooked a lot in this field." The captain paused for a moment. "She is their weak link. We've got six hours and thirty-seven minutes till Eisenhower Productions goes online with Realm of the Bright Waters."

"If we find Heavener before that time," Roarke said, "we can bring her in, sweat her, and see if she'll give anything up to make a deal. No one's going to look after her interests, and she knows it."

Maj looked at the neutral expression on Roarke's face and knew the man was talking from personal experience.

"Agreed," Winters replied. "Net Force Explorers, make the most of these remaining hours. Keep your eyes and ears open, and stay in contact with each other. If the slightest thing feels off, get out and call me at once."

Gaspar Latke sat in his veeyar workspace, for the first time in his life feeling crowded in by everything around him. He watched the monitors.

The central monitor showed the hallway outside Maj Green's hotel room. The image was broadcast by a buttoncam worn by one of the three men Heavener had with her.

"Shut down the alarms," Heavener ordered over the comm-line.

Gaspar's breath was tight in his chest, and the back of his throat felt raw. He knew those were physical sensations seeping over from the flesh-and-blood world. He drew a circle in the air with his forefinger, and a blue knob appeared, linking him with the virus he had in place to circumvent the hotel's security system. He pressed it, sending it on its way. For the next twenty-two minutes and nineteen seconds, the hotel wouldn't know the room existed.

"Done," he hissed, feeling like a traitor. *Forgive me. I thought maybe we could help each other.* Only he'd put her in danger by meeting with her.

One of Heavener's people moved forward and took a short crowbar from his jacket sleeve. They all wore street clothes and wouldn't draw a second glance from the gamers still wandering the halls. The man fit the crowbar into place and popped the lock, shouldering the door open.

Heavener and the next man stepped through the doorway. Gaspar's main monitor view was now through Heavener's sights. Ruby laser beams tracked through the darkness filling the room.

For a moment Gaspar thought Maj was in bed. But as Heavener got closer, he saw that it was only the twisted bedclothes.

"She's not here," Heavener said irritably. "Find her. Find her *now!*" She waved the men from the room and closed the door behind her.

Gaspar's relief drained from him as he started to scan the hotel vidcams he'd hacked into. "Searching."

"In twenty minutes and thirty-four seconds," Heavener said, "that little mojo you've used on this room is going to elapse and the alarm will sound. If we haven't found that girl by then, she's going to run, and Net Force may take a big interest too soon."

"Give me a minute." Gaspar searched through the hallways and banquet areas, using a computer search engine working with Maj's image as well. The convention center was open, and he thought she might be there.

"Very soon," Heavener went on, "the game goes online. I don't have time to wait."

An alarm buzzed.

Gaspar looked up, panicking.

"Eisenhower's online site just registered a hacker," Heavener said.

"I'll check it out," Gaspar said. Hackers trying to get into the system weren't anything new. Ever since the gamepacks for Realm of the Bright Waters had been released, gamers had been trying to break into Eisenhower's site. None of them had succeeded, but they'd kept him busy. Eisenhower's regular security staff was good, but not as good as people Gaspar ran with, diehard hackers who lived for the crack.

Gaspar leaped onto the Net and sped to Eisenhower's site. The building stood tall and prestigious against the cybernetic background. He passed into the secure files where the game programming was kept. The room representing the archived files was huge, filled with library stacks representing the various programs.

Gargoyles sat by the stacks, myth-shapen monsters with bat wings, long talons, and horrid faces. They'd dealt with intruders skilled enough to avoid the regular security system, casting them out of the Net nastily.

Suddenly one of the gargoyles turned to look at him. "Is it you?" it asked in a creaking voice.

Suspicion filled Gaspar and he almost lifted off-site. "Who are you?"

The gargoyle shimmered as it stepped off its pedestal. By the time its foot touched the carpet, it was Mark Gridley.

"You became part of the security network?" Gaspar asked. No one had ever done that before.

Mark shrugged. "It took hours, so don't be too overwhelmed. I've been trying to get into the stacks, but they're all encrypted. At least, the ones that I've been able to access are."

Gaspar took a step back. "You tripped the alarm on purpose."

"Yeah. I hoped you'd be the one to answer it."

"Why?"

Mark waved at the stacks. "Because we're running out of time. We know about Griffen's game and the bleed-overs."

"How much do you know?" Gaspar asked.

"Pretty much all of it," Mark replied. "We know about D'Arnot Industries, too."

"They'll kill me."

"When Maj told us she'd been contacted by someone wearing Matt's proxy last night," Mark said, "I guessed it was you. And the only reason you'd do that is if you wanted out."

"I do."

Mark nodded, his young face serious. "Then you're going to have to play ball with us. I could break into this system given enough time—I'm that good—but I'm all out of time. Realm of the Bright Waters is going online, and by then it will be too late."

"Get me away from them," Gaspar said. "If you don't, they're going to kill me."

"You think they're going to kill you," Mark said. "That's why you contacted Maj."

Gaspar didn't say anything, feeling all his leverage drain away. "I need help."

"And I need an access code," Mark said.

"You can't leave me to them," Gaspar pleaded. "It would be the same as killing me yourself."

Mark didn't appear convinced. "Where are Peter Griffen and Oscar Raitt?"

"Heavener has them."

"Where?"

"At the hotel. She's going to kill them, set it up so it looks like Raitt killed Griffen after faking his own kidnapping."

"When?"

Gaspar lied desperately. "I don't know."

Mark glanced around the room, but he never looked desperate. "It's your call. Give me a code so I can get into the system and let me trace your signal back."

"How can I trust you?"

Mark returned his gaze full measure. "How can you not? There's a Net Force team in the city that's ready to move. They just need a location."

"I don't know where I am."

"We'll find you."

Heavener buzzed for attention, using the comm-channel Gaspar had left open for her and her team. Gaspar felt torn, knowing he was gambling everything when there was nothing left to lose, but feeling scared anyway. He closed his fist and downloaded the access code, creating a simple icon in the form of a red agate marble. "Find me quick," he said. "Or you'll find me dead."

"Trust me," Mark said. "I won't let you down."

Gaspar tossed the marble across. Mark caught it, then tossed a glowing blue pyramid back. "The trace utility?" Gaspar asked.

"Yes." Mark reached forward and a control panel appeared in the air before him. He punched a button and the alarm shut off. "Get moving before they get suspicious."

Gaspar tried to think of something to say but couldn't. He leaped back onto the Net and returned to his workspace.

"What was it?" Heavener demanded.

"One of the gamers," Gaspar replied. "He got deep into the system, but it rejected him." *Please let Gridley be as good as I've heard he is.*

"Where's the girl?"

Gaspar searched the screens. Suddenly crosshairs flared into crimson life on one of the convention monitors. They bracketed Maj Green as she passed through the early morning convention crowd waiting for Realm of the Bright Waters to go online.

Hesitation locked Gaspar up. *How long will it take for Net Force to find me? How long before Gridley breaks into the mainframe supporting the online game?* If he didn't tell Heavener where Maj was, she'd know something was up. And he'd die. It was that simple. "She's in the convention center," he said. "I've got her onscreen."

The buttoncam view on Heavener's screen shifted abruptly as the woman and her team changed directions. As they raced through the hotel hallways, other cameras picked them up.

Gaspar tracked the collision course as if hypnotized. "God help us," he whispered.

22

Maj looked around the packed convention center. A lot of the people around her hadn't left the room at all, but most of them had returned over an hour ago. The Realm of the Bright Waters game was due to go online in less than twenty-four minutes. Excitement was building.

"Man, if I'd known this was going to be this big," one of the guys next to her grumbled, "I'd have reserved a room with an implant chair. I've called every cyber café in the city and they're booked."

"I know," the guy next to him said. "If you don't have access to your own system, you're not going to get on for a little while. At least we're not alone, and we'll get to see what it's like."

"Yeah, but it's not the same as being there."

Maj listened and felt edgy. Too much stress and not enough sleep was a bad combination. But there was no way around it. Sleep was out of the question. Even knowing the Net Force team lurked in the shadows wasn't as helpful as it might have been for the her stress levels. Once the game was launched, Eisenhower Productions and D'Arnot Industries didn't need Peter Griffen alive. That realization left her feeling cold.

Her foilpack buzzed, and she answered it.

Matt's bruised face appeared on the small screen. "Mark's inside the system. He made contact with your guy. A Net Force team is already en route to his location. If anything's going to happen, it's going to happen quickly."

"I know. I'll stay in touch." Maj closed the foilpack. Matt and Catie were handling the comm-loop for their end of the operation, patching the Net Force teams in through the pass-through communications ports Mark had created in the Net. Leif and Megan were on the move through the hotel, watching for Heavener.

Maj walked through the game booths, listening to the excited chatter of the gamers. She felt all wound up inside. It didn't make sense for Heavener to be in the hotel, even though the woman didn't know she'd been identified. But Maj knew she couldn't have just gone to her room and waited.

Her foilpack vibrated in her pocket again. "Yes."

Matt's worried face filled the vidscreen. "I just got a patch in from Andy. He's hacked into Heavener's cyberguy's systems. They're tracking you on the hotel cameras. Get out of there. Go somewhere safe"

Anxiety filled Maj. *Why is Heavener tracking me?*

"Get moving," Matt said. "I'm on my way."

Struggling to keep from glancing around, Maj headed for the nearest door. *Maybe they'll think I'm meeting someone for breakfast.*

She kept her steps unhurried but purposeful, weaving through the crowd. She didn't look at the ceiling where the cameras were. But when she opened the door leading out of the convention center into the main hallway, she came face to face with Heavener.

The woman smiled cruelly, not a blond hair out of place. "Hello, Madeline," she said. Three men stood behind her, blocking any chance of escape.

Seated in her veeyar workspace in her hotel room, Catie opened the comm-patch to Agent Roarke, Matt, Leif, and Megan, who were converging on the convention center.

"Heavener found Maj," Catie said. She stared at the screen and tried to remain calm.

"Where?" Matt asked.

"At the main entrance on the north side," Catie replied.

"I'm on my way," Roarke snapped. "You kids stay back."

Hooked into the hotel security system through the spycams from the gamers Andy and Mark had met, Catie watched as her friends ignored the agent's orders. She knew they weren't going to let one of their own down. *But why would Heavener be after Maj? The woman's profile doesn't read like she's into grudge matches.* Catie sat and watched, feeding information to Captain Winters.

Andy monitored Mark's progress through the Eisenhower Productions systems, marveling again at how his friend slipped through security like a greased eel. No one equaled the Squirt when it came to evading intruder programming.

Then Catie's message about Maj's situation came in. He opened a com-link to Catie. "Use Catie's foilpack vibrator to send a message in Morse code. They can't intercept that." The programming wasn't normally on most foilpacks, but Mark had recently added the option to theirs after a Net Force mission debrief. "Send the words *Hocus Pocus.*"

"Mark's spoof program?" Catie asked. "Will it work with holoprojectors?"

"We're going to find out," Andy said, then relayed a message to Mark to let him know he was going to be gone for a moment. He reached up into the Net and launched himself at the Bessel Mid-Town Hotel. He stepped into the virtual world only a short distance behind Heavener and the three men with her. "Catie?"

"I sent the message."

"Then here comes trouble," Andy said. He accessed the programming that gave him holoform in the real world.

"Net Force knows about you, Heavener," Maj said.

The woman's smile only turned frostier. "Do they?"

"They know about the bleed-over effect in Peter's game, too. They know you're going to use the bleed-overs to access the computers of anyone who downloads the game."

Heavener shrugged. "It seems a little late to stop that now. You even had your own little part to play in this. If your own veeyar hadn't inadvertently picked up Griffen's game, we wouldn't have had to kidnap him."

Maj felt relieved. *Kidnapped* was a long way from *dead.*

"And if we hadn't kidnapped him, we would never have gotten the media coverage we did. Maybe I should have planned for that all along."

"Don't you mean D'Arnot Industries should have?" Maj asked.

The announcement took some of the smile from Heavener's face.

"With kids and adults downloading the game onto computers owned by the government," Maj continued, "the private business sector, and military installations, they could have used the bleed-over effect to hack into almost anything they wanted. Someone would have gotten suspicious, but even a few hours free access could have meant potential billions in earnings for D'Arnot Industries. They could have seized secrets, research and development, and military emplacement information to sell to terrorists across the world."

"Bright kid," Heavener rasped. "Too bad you're a dead kid." She took a small 9mm pistol from her pocket.

"I'm only telling you this," Maj went on, "to let you know the game's over. You lose."

"Oh," Heavener said, "there's still time to take a few pieces off the board." She raised the pistol.

Clad in his crashsuit, Mark eyed the heart of the Eisenhower Productions game engine. On the Net, linked through his perceptions and programming, it took on the form of a man-shaped mechanical dreadnought easily fifty times as large as he was.

The blank, featureless face turned toward him. Yellow lights glimmered where the eyes should have been. "Your access code, please."

Mark offered the code he'd been given.

"Access denied," the ponderous giant replied. It stretched out a hand, launching rockets immediately.

Closing his hand, Mark activated the crashsuit's boostjets, throwing him from the path of the rockets. Another switch on his palm brought down the HUD system, giving him a 360-degree view around him. After thousands of hours logged into the crashsuit as well as the games he played, it all felt entirely natural.

Onscreen, he watched the five rockets pinwheel around and lock on to him again. His left glove contained the suit controls for the boostjets that fired from his boots, back, chest, and the top of his helmet. His right hand controlled the weapons array he had in the form of attack and defense programs he used in hacking.

Laser beams lanced from Mark's fingers, swiftly targeting the rockets closing in on him. The rockets evaporated in a rush, shimmering, then gone. He spun around and launched himself at the game engine's near-AI. He knew the systems alarms had to be ringing back in the real world and that he wouldn't be alone with the game engine for long.

Only six minutes remained till Realm of the Bright Waters went online.

Andy stepped toward Heavener and her group, waving at Maj.

Maj's eyes widened as she saw him.

"Hocus Pocus," Andy mouthed slowly. He accessed another program from his own veeyar workspace and created a holo of an MP5 submachine gun from one of his training programs.

Maj gave a brief nod.

The movement alerted Heavener, who spun instantly and brought up the small pistol from her pocket. She grabbed Maj's arm.

"Catch you international terrorists and industrial spies at a bad time?" Andy asked, raising the MP5. He squeezed the trigger and the ripsaw of autofire filled the hallway.

Heavener and her group dropped to the floor. Maj swept a hand across Heavener's in a martial arts move that tore the woman's grip from her arm.

Andy kept firing even when the ruby sights lit him up. Bullets hammered through his chest. He smiled. "Good shooting."

"He's a holo!" Heavener snarled, pushing herself up from the floor. "After the girl!"

Smiling, Andy accessed the spoof program Mark had written that they'd used in various games and hacking runs on the programs they'd been asked to test for flaws. He slammed it into the hotel's holoprojector system, targeting Maj as she ran back inside the convention center.

Instantly, instead of one Maj fleeing through the crowd in the convention center, there were over a dozen. All of the holos were dressed exactly alike, and they ran in different directions, scattering through the crowd, crisscrossing each other's tracks.

In a heartbeat even Andy didn't know which one was real.

Andy dropped back onto the Net, knowing Mark had begun the final attack on the game engine. He scanned the screens that appeared in front of him, noting the arrival of eight security personnel in space-bound fast-attack craft.

He opened the comm-link to Mark. "Are you ready to rock and roll, buddy?"

Maj ran through the convention crowd, bumping into people and throwing apologies over her shoulder. She streaked for the other side of the center, knowing Matt, Roarke, Leif, and Megan were on their way.

A young man stepped around one of the booths too late for her to stop. She slammed into him, taking them both to the ground. Her martial arts reflexes made her roll instinctively. She got to her feet as the guy stayed there and groaned.

Other convention attendees opened a path before her, shouting out warnings.

Glancing to the side, Maj spotted one of her holo-induced doppelgangers running *through* people. Their reactions were a little delayed, and they stepped aside after the doppelganger had burst through.

Heavener and her men charged through the convention center, roughly shoving aside anyone who got in their way.

Maj opened her foilpack and punched a quick dial number. "Catie, where are Holmes's police teams?"

"Investigating a break-in alarm at your hotel room," Catie replied. "I'm trying to get through to Holmes now to call them off."

Maj ran toward the nearest door. Before she reached it, a man burst through with a pistol leveled at her chest.

With Andy at his back, Mark turned his attention to the search engine, jetting straight for it. The HUD relayed the information about the eight security programmers streaking toward him, overtaking him quickly because this was their home ground. The home team always had the advantage because their programming interfaced more directly and more quickly than someone breaking in.

"Andy," Mark called calmly.

"I've got your back, buddy."

In the next instant Mark's HUD picked up Andy's arrival. Since he didn't have to worry about stealth anymore, and he could use Mark's signal from inside the program to transport to, Andy arrived in a spacetank copied from a Space Marines game. The spacetank was an armored nightmare, fully stocked with weapons. Lasers cut through the virtual world as it locked on to targets and fired.

Three of the attacking security personnel vaporized immediately, thrown off-line by the savage attack.

"Boo-yeeaahh!" Andy cheered. "And we're rolling up a score."

Less than two minutes remained until game launch. Even if Captain Winters overrode the Net and had a warning issued by Net Force, a lot of gamers would ignore the warning and download the files anyway, thinking it was a prank by jealous gamers who didn't have the game pack, or an attack by rival gaming companies. It had happened in the past.

He initiated a systems diagnostic using the access code he'd been given, hoping to find a weak link that would allow him into the gargantuan game engine before him. Lasers flashed from the thing's eyes as it sought to protect itself.

Mark evaded the lasers as Andy blasted another security man out of the loop, checking over the program's codes. Surely there was a feed coming in from somewhere. He fired two disruptive virus programs in the form of thermal nukes, but they glanced off the search engine's armored body like a flat stone on water.

The diagnostics flashed on the HUD, stripping away the mechanical body the search engine inhabited. *C'mon, c'mon. There's gotta be something to work with.*

"I'm hit," Andy called out.

The system defenders were down to three, but Andy's spacetank hadn't gone unscathed. Internal gyro problems had developed, a visual interpretation of the defense coding attacking his intrusion into the system.

A bright green blip flared into life on Mark's HUD. It dawned at the tip of one of the search engine dreadnought's fingers. Mark tapped out a search-and-identify program. "I've got the weak point," he told Andy. "There's a satellite feed coming in from the Balkans that Net Force broke into a couple weeks ago for black-market software trafficking that hasn't been changed.

The story never made HoloNet, so D'Arnot Industries wouldn't know about it. I can get in through there."

"Go," Andy called. "I'm on a full-fledged crash-and-burn here." His spacetank remained barely viable, breaking down even as Mark spotted it on the HUD.

Mark left the Net, knowing his pursuers would think he'd logged off. He streaked through the upper atmosphere and into the telecommunications array. In seconds he flashed through England, France, Australia, South Africa, Brazil, Israel, then into the Balkans, disguising himself every step of the way. When he hit the satellite feeding the Balkans connection, he insinuated himself into the satellite feed D'Arnot Industries was using to coordinate the world launch of Realm of the Bright Waters.

He returned to the Eisenhower Productions site just as Andy's spacetank was reduced to cybernetic ash. Powering the crash-suit's jets to the max, Mark streaked into the dreadnought's finger, following the hollow tube of the arm toward the brain.

"Stop! Police!"

Maj experienced a momentary burst of relief as the man in front of her shifted and pointed his weapon at Heavener. But the moment was short-lived. Two shots rang out, one hammer blow on top of another, and the plainclothes policeman flew backward into the door behind him.

Instant pandemonium spread throughout the convention center. Andy's earlier gunfire might have been mistaken for gameplay, but the man smashing up against the door with blood on his jacket was too real. Gamers screamed and tried to get away, knocking each other down in their haste.

Knowing that she'd be the next target if she stopped to help the policeman, Maj shouldered her way through the door, smashing through, hitting the floor and rolling. She caught herself against the far wall of the hallway, feeling the vibration of bullets smacking the tiles to pieces only inches from her.

"Over here!"

Instinctively Maj crawled toward the voice, recognizing it as Roarke's only a second later. The Net Force agent stood in a Weaver's stance, his pistol resting lightly in both hands.

Heavener burst through the door first, dropping into a flat slide on her stomach across the tiled floor. Her pistol spat flame as Roarke's first shot split the air above her head. The agent's next two rounds caught both men who hurtled through the door after Heavener, punching into them.

As Maj got to her feet and ran past Roarke, she saw the agent stumble backward, blood spraying from his left shoulder. Even as he went down, Roarke fired again. Then he was hit once more, sprawling backward.

Horrified, Maj ran on, knowing the Net Force team in the area had to be closing in. The rapid slap of shoes against the tile floor came up behind her. Then an arm went around her waist and a shoulder hit her back. Off-balance, she went down hard, Heavener on top of her.

"You're dead, Latke!"

Heavener's promise rang in Gaspar's ears as he stared at the screen showing the hallway where the woman had captured Maj Green. Heavener grabbed a handful of Maj's hair and held her pistol to the girl's head.

"Get up," Heavener ordered, yanking Maj to her feet. "You're my ticket out of here."

Gaspar logged off the Net. There was no doubt that Heavener had commed instructions to the men where he was being held to kill him. He pushed his way out of the implant chair, his heart thudding in his chest. Weakly, exhausted by lack of sleep and stress, he staggered for the door. He twisted the knob, but it was locked.

Then the knob turned in his hand. He stepped back, hoping.

When the door opened, it revealed one of the hard-faced men he'd seen with Heavener. The man raised the pistol in his hand without a word.

Gaspar closed his eyes when he heard the shot ring out, waiting to feel the bullet smash through his chest. But he didn't feel anything. *Maybe that's how it feels.* He was surprised when he opened his eyes.

The man in front of him fell, revealing a black-clad warrior with an MP5. "Net Force agent," the man said. "Down on the floor. On your face. Move it."

Gaspar dropped instantly, grateful for the feel of the plastic cuffs pulling tight around his wrists. Bursts of gunfire echoed in other parts of the building. There weren't any prolonged gunfights.

"If you're who I think you are," the Net Force agent promised, "we'll get you out of here."

"I know," Gaspar said, tears running down his face. "I know." But he felt guilty as well as relieved. He should have warned Maj.

Mark sped through the dreadnought's interior. Defensive programs inside the game engine tried to overload the crashsuit's parameters as well. He fired a phalanx of rockets ahead, clearing the tunnel of the machine guns and lasers that lined the way.

He wasn't sure how much time remained before the game launched.

In the next instant he was through the shoulder and up into the dreadnought's neck. The central core of the game engine opened to him. It looked like a huge orange gem, twirling madly, showing him countless reflections of the crashsuit.

Mark raised his hand and strafed the game engine with every nasty bit of programming at his disposal. Fractures ran through the jewel at once, then it went to pieces in a silent, explosive rush.

"Game over," Mark said.

"Get on your feet," Heavener ordered.

Pain shot through Maj's head as the woman yanked her to her feet by the hair. Black spots danced in front of her eyes.

"Move." Heavener shoved her down the hallway, keeping the pistol muzzle buried between Maj's shoulder blades. She shifted her grip from Maj's hair to one of her wrists, using the hold to pin her arm behind her back.

"You're not going to get out of here," Maj promised. "Net Force has this hotel surrounded."

"They won't hurt one of their own." Heavener pushed her from behind, almost at a run.

A group ahead spread across the hallway, freezing in place.

"Net Force won't let you get away," Maj said.

"Out of the way!" Heavener ordered. When the group didn't move fast enough, she pointed the pistol and shot one of the men at the front of the group. The rest of the group fled.

Before Heavener could place her weapon back between Maj's shoulder blades, Maj dropped to the floor and swept her leg back, knocking her captor's legs from under her. Heavener tried to maintain her grip on Maj's wrist, but Maj twisted her wrist toward Heavener's thumb as she'd been taught. Her hand came free immediately.

Heavener tried to bring her pistol to bear.

Maj kicked out, connecting with the woman's wrist and sending the pistol flying. She tried to get up, but Heavener backhanded her across the face. As Heavener pushed herself up and toward the fallen pistol, Maj grabbed her ankle and tripped her.

Heavener came down hard, snarling curses. She kicked her foot free of Maj's hand, then drove it at Maj's face. Maj caught the kick on her arm, blocking it to the side. She rolled to her feet as Heavener did, placing herself between the woman and the pistol.

"You can't take me," Heavener said, raising her arms.

"I don't have to," Maj replied. "All I have to do is delay you."

Heavener attacked without warning, launching a kick at Maj's head. Maj ducked, then curled an arm up around the ankle. She halted the foot, but slammed her other hand behind Heavener's knee, breaking the woman's stance. Heavener leaped, rolling in the air and bringing her other foot around to smash into Maj's cheek.

Pain flared in Maj's head and she released her hold. Concentrating was difficult, but she focused on finding the pistol as Heavener got to her feet. Maj ran across the hallway, dropping to her knees and sliding on them to reach the pistol. She picked it up and pointed it at Heavener, using both hands and keeping her finger out of the trigger guard the way she'd been taught.

Heavener's smile curved as sharply as a shark's. "Are you really going to use that on me, little girl?" She took a step forward.

Maj's hands shook. "D—d—don't move!" *Please don't move!* She couldn't imagine actually pulling the trigger. But maybe Heavener was the only person who could tell them where Peter Griffen was.

Heavener's smile stayed in place. "If you want me to believe that you'll shoot, you're going to have to do better than that." Blood trickled from the corner of her mouth. She kept coming.

Maj watched the woman helplessly.

"How about this, little girl?" Heavener popped the sleeve of her jacket and a short, wide-bladed knife dropped into her hand.

"Think this can inspire you?" Light twinkled from the hard metal.

Maj's finger curled over the trigger. *I can't do it, I can't do it!*

"You can't do it, little girl," Heavener said. "You're just a child playing at spy. And you're going to die unless you can take my life first."

Maj stared through tear-blurred vision as the woman approached. She had no doubt that Heavener would do exactly what she said.

"Come on, little girl, shoot me."

Suddenly a dozen ruby lights lit up across Heavener's chest.

"She doesn't have to," a cold voice said. "Take another step and we will."

Heavener froze, pulling her arms up at her sides.

Maj glanced over her shoulder, spotting the Net Force team that had taken up positions in the hallway. Captain Winters stood at their side in holoform.

One of the agents came forward and plucked the pistol from Maj's hands. Other agents rushed forward, pushing Heavener facedown on the carpet and handcuffing her.

Maj stood on trembling legs.

Winters approached her, his face grim and concerned. "Are you all right?"

"Now," Maj whispered. "I'm all right now."

EPILOGUE

"Most of the D'Arnot Industries executives were arrested over the weekend," Captain Winters said. "We'll sort through who was and wasn't actually involved, but it won't be hard with the information we're getting. Those people are looking to make a deal to avoid serious prison time."

Maj nodded. She was in Captain Winters's office in holoform the following Monday. The other Explorers had chosen her to debrief them once Winters debriefed her. "What about Peter's game?" She hated thinking that the young designer would lose the world he'd so painstakingly developed.

"Once we're sure all the bleed-over programming is corrected in the game, it can be released. Mark Gridley is helping out with that. I don't think it'll be more than a month late."

"A month is a long time in the gaming industry," Maj said defensively.

Winters smiled. "Maybe for most games, but I don't think the public's going to forget this one."

Maj knew that was true. Public outcry against the game being pulled was tremendous. The Net was full of supporters wanting it to be released. Peter Griffen stood on the threshold of a fortune. "What about Roarke?"

"It was touch and go," Winters admitted. "But Jon's always been one of the tough guys. Another week or two and he'll be talking about rehab and getting back out into the field. With the recommendation I'm giving him, he'll probably get there."

"He's a good agent," Maj said. "Maybe a little Neanderthal."

"Yep, but we still need men like him. And Jon Roarke is one of the best."

"And Heavener?"

Winters's face clouded. "She's going to get her day in court. It's going to be a crapshoot to see who actually throws her in prison first."

"That leaves Gaspar Latke."

"Mr. Latke has proven to be an interesting young man," Winters admitted. "He's been involved in a few operations Net Force didn't quite get to the bottom of. I think his future may hold a few surprises. But I'm guessing he'll be okay."

After the debriefing was finished and her report filed, Maj returned to the airflight taking her back home. Leif's dad had paid for first-class seats. She glanced around the cabin. Everyone was asleep, except for Andy, who was online gaming. Somewhere.

Her foilpack buzzed and she answered it, finding Peter Griffen's smiling face in the vidscreen.

"Hey," he said. "I hope I'm not interrupting."

"No," Maj replied, smiling a little herself.

"I heard I wasn't the only one who had an interesting weekend," Peter said.

Maj shook her head. "No."

"Nobody at Net Force wanted to give me your foilpack number," Peter said. "I had to do a little digging."

"It seems you found it."

"I'm good at what I do."

"So what can I do for you?" Maj asked.

"I think you've done enough," he replied. "I just wanted to thank you for your part in my rescue. And in Oscar's."

"My pleasure."

Peter seemed kind of stuck for words. "Thanks, doesn't seem like enough. If it's okay, I'd like to ask you something."

"Sure," Maj said.

"Net Force shut down the online launch of Realm of the Bright Water, but your friend Mark Gridley has already debugged a copy I have. They want to experiment with the game for a while, make sure that the fully interfacing game engine I designed doesn't bleed over anymore, but I have access to this one. I though maybe if you weren't busy—" He hesitated.

"You're asking me if I can come out and play?" Maj laughed.

"Well, I wasn't going to put it that way," Peter responded. "But, yeah. I've got a whole world out there, Maj. I'm ready to share it with someone. I've been waiting for a long time."

"Where can I find you?" After Peter gave her the Net coordinates, Maj leaned back in the implant chair. When she opened her eyes again, she stood on a blue-silver cloud overlooking the world. Peter stood in front of her, clad in his beautiful armor.

"In the game," Peter said, "you won't be able to stand on the clouds. Not unless you know the secrets. But I wanted you to be properly impressed."

"I am. I'm looking forward to seeing what else your world holds."

Peter held out his hand. "Then join me."

Maj took the offered hand. In the next minute the cloud swirled beneath them, quickly becoming the plum-colored dragon, Sahfrell, she'd gotten so acquainted with over the weekend. She felt the dragon's muscles bunch beneath her as it flew through the sky. "I take it clouds don't usually become dragons, either," she said. She took her place in the front of a dual saddle.

"Not unless I want them to," Peter told her. "What would you like to do?"

The wind streamed through Maj's hair, and she stared at all the beauty beneath her. "I just want to see everything I can."

"As you wish," Peter said, and the dragon dived toward the world waiting below.